DECEPTION ISLAND

JANICE BOEKHOFF

Lost Canyon
PRESS

Lost Canyon Press
P.O. Box 624
Bettendorf, IA 52722

Trade Paperback ISBN 978-1-948003-08-7

E-book ISBN 978-1-948003-07-0

Cover by Kim Mesman (mesmandesignco.com)

For Arnold and Deloris
You welcomed me into your heart even before I married
your son. I have been so blessed by your encouragement.
Thank you for accepting and loving this crazy girl who
dreams of petting dinosaurs.

In a world where genetic manipulation is the newest superpower, dinosaurs are brought back from extinction and released on the American population. After several gruesome fatalities, the military hunts down each specimen and transfers it to a sanctuary—the newly formed island of Costa Rica. Contained by an expanded Panama Canal to the south and the freshly dug Nicaraguan canal to the north, the dinosaurs flourish in the tropical climate.

However, the costs required to purchase the land, evacuate the residents to nearby countries, and construct the sanctuary leave the United States saddled with enormous debt. This cost, coupled with an overworked prison system—a result of a decline in the moral fabric of the country—leads to the signing of a new death penalty bill, dubbed by the media as *Jurassic Judgment.*

After four months of accelerated appeals, death row

inmates are given a choice: immediate execution or ... exile to Extinction Island.

Wrongly convicted of her best friend's murder, reptile expert Oakley Laveau chooses the island and survives for two terrifying weeks among genetically modified dinosaurs and ruthless convicts. In that time, she's discovered her own genetic modification and the identity of who framed her. But her hunt for the truth is just beginning.

CHAPTER ONE

THE CRACKED mirror hanging on the bathroom wall of the cave reflected a distorted image. Oakley Laveau peered closely. There was a shifting darkness hiding behind her bright blue eyes. The darkness ran deep within her, infusing her cells and clinging to her soul like a smoky mist.

This darkness wasn't primitive—like the slaughter inflicted by the dangerous dinosaurs outside—it was more devious. Something that had changed her on a cellular level.

Leaning over the vanity, she clasped the sink with both hands and pinched her eyes closed. She couldn't get rid of the darkness, but she could push it down with all her strength ... at least until she found out who had modified her DNA and what it all meant.

As if called forth by her closed eyelids, the dream from last night resurfaced.

Mama faced her while walking backward along a tight corridor. Mama's mouth was moving as she gestured with her hands down the hallway, but the words were muted and unrecognizable. She opened a thick, gray, metal door and stepped through.

When Oakley followed, a warm, humid breeze blew through her hair, whipping it around like a dark curtain. She stood on a catwalk across from Mama. The metal grate hovered over the ocean, far enough out to sea that no land was visible on the horizon.

Mama's voice broke through the silence like the sudden tuning of a radio. "We made you here. Come home."

Before she could ask how, Mama shoved her with both hands, sending her tumbling over the low railing. With a silent scream, she twisted and flipped as she fell. The ocean rushed closer and closer, its foaming waves waiting to suck her under.

"Are you ready?" Cane LeBlanc's smooth voice came from outside the bathroom curtain.

Oakley's eyes flew open. She sucked in a deep breath. The prickle of her electrical power surged in her core like a storm cloud crackling, but she kept it in check. Despite her racing heart, she was safe in the cave with Cane and the others.

What had he asked? Oh, yeah, whether she was ready. "I'll be a minute."

She submerged a cloth into the basin that was half full of rainwater and ran it over her face and neck.

The curtain didn't afford much privacy, but they had

a working toilet, sort of. The toilet consisted of a wooden base over a hole in the floor of the cave—Cane had called it a natural joint in the rock—that ran down and emptied far below her feet into the chasm outside the cave's entrance. Liquid waste went straight out. Solid waste required flushing a bucket of water down. Needless to say, everyone knew which business had been completed and how often.

The cave was a far cry from the luxury, eco-friendly resort she'd stayed in when she'd first arrived on Extinction Island. Right off the prison transport boat, the Cazador gang had kidnapped her and taken her to their compound. A place of terror for the first few hours, but then it became a refuge. Not because of the better accommodations, but because of her kidnapper.

Kaleo Palani had protected her, charmed her, and drawn her in with his unexpected bursts of sarcasm. She'd opened up to him more than anyone, even her dad. If only she could have stayed at the resort with him.

When she came out of the bathroom, Cane was eating a bowl of meat, probably from the *Oviraptor* they'd killed yesterday. Flank shots from Cane's arrows had driven the animal over a small cliff where it had broken its neck. The gruesome act of cutting up the meat hadn't stopped her from eating her fill last night. Today, though, she couldn't stomach it. She sat on a stool and picked up a bowl of fruit.

"In my personal opinion," Cane said around a mouthful of meat, "leaving is a bad idea."

What was she supposed to do instead? Live the rest of her days on Extinction Island, forever wondering who made her and what she was? Perhaps he had a point about not following the dream urgings of the woman who had tried to kill her as a child, but her dream mother wasn't her real mother. More likely, it was her own subconscious pushing her to find answers.

Rather than respond, she slowly bit into a strawberry. She wasn't going to debate the merits of leaving the island again. Cody, her pet *Coelophysis*, nuzzled her hand. She stroked his downy head a few times before dropping him a strawberry.

"What else do you need that you don't have here? Friends, dinosaur meat,"—he winked at her while pointing to the bow and arrow set in the corner—"and weapons. We even have a safe room in the back if anything were to happen in here."

"You do?"

"It's for the women. Most of the men couldn't fit through the small vertical opening." He spun his fork around one finger. "The point is I can keep you safe here."

She could hardly blame him for being concerned. Her plan was risky, even with her own enhanced protective defenses, but the dream had convinced her. Somewhere in the floating lab lay the answer to what was programmed into her cells. She needed to know the truth behind her strange abilities.

Cane had accepted his abilities as gifts from God and saw no reason to investigate further. Why God would have allowed someone to give him killing chemicals that came from between his fingers seemed inexplicable. But Cane's logic frequently escaped her. She, however, needed a little more explanation. "How can I know who I am if I don't know where I came from?"

With her government tracker currently disabled, this would be her only chance to leave the island undetected. Her only chance to find out exactly what had been done to her, and also to Cane.

He got up, put his bowl in the sink, and let out a resigned sigh.

She finished the berries before speaking again. "I need to tell Kaleo I'm going."

"I know."

She looked sideways at him. "You're always the voice of reason, which means you never agree with me."

He chuckled and the musical note in his laugh calmed her frayed nerves. "I've learned when to pick my battles."

She gave him a grateful smile. Somehow, he understood that she would go without him, and yet he refused to let her do this alone. Maybe such grace and kindness came with the job of being a pastor. Was loving God the only reason this kind man in his twenties with no criminal record had come to the largest, most dangerous prison on the planet? So far, he hadn't confided much about his past.

"It will take us about a day to get to the boat," he said. "Last time I checked on it was a year ago. I'm praying the motor still works."

He hefted one of the packs they'd stuffed full of food

and supplies onto his back, then helped her with hers. She slung a bow and quiver over one shoulder, and he did the same. They both moved to the front of the cave where a steady wind blew in from the open cave entrance. An ocean of verdant trees stretched out in the valley below.

Cane strapped into the zip-line harness that would take him across the deep chasm to the jungle cliff beyond. With a wave, he jumped and raced across.

On the other side, he removed the harness and gave it a shove. She pulled it back using the guide rope. Once she secured it around her legs and chest, she gave Cody a quick pat, then stepped off the ledge.

As she sped toward the cliff on the other side, the view down the canyon took her breath away. A wondrous expanse of emerald trees and dark rocks curved into the distance. Beneath her feet yawned a three-hundred-foot drop to the jungle floor. Dizziness swamped her, and the dream surfaced in stark reality again.

Falling toward the ocean. Flailing as rushing wind flew past her face.

She shook her head and thrust the images away. This was the jungle, not the middle of the ocean. The zip line was perfectly safe, or at least safer than most places on this island.

She landed next to Cane on unsteady feet. He helped her slip from the harness. Normally, they left it hooked to a nearby tree so they could use it to return. But they wouldn't be returning for a while, so she shoved it back along the wire. Someone from the cave, probably Neve Torres, would pull it in later.

A flash of guilt pulsed through her heart. She was taking Cane away from the people he wanted to protect. But Neve, with her healing skills and calm presence, would take care of them in his absence. She was a native Costa Rican who had chosen not to evacuate when Extinction Island was created, and she knew her way around the jungle better than most of them.

Cane pushed into the trees and Oakley followed, practicing the stealthy tactics both he and Kaleo had taught her: Watch for footprints to avoid traveling on game trails. Pay attention to the wildlife because animals go quiet when predators are near. Listen for rustling in the undergrowth. Trust your instincts.

She kept her gaze focused at eye level. Although the sight of an immense *T. rex* would be terrifying, the smaller dinosaurs were her gravest concern. At barely over five feet tall, she wouldn't even be a snack for a *Tyrannosaurus*.

Of course, that hadn't stopped Camocroc, a twenty-foot-long camouflaged *Saurosuchus*, from coming after her during her first week on the island. Some of the dinosaurs seemed to have an uncanny penchant for finding her. Perhaps they were attracted to her scent. Or maybe they could sense the darkness lurking within her.

The leaves surrounding them blew gently in the wind, and her nerves pulled taut. Were there other dinosaurs tracking her right now? Slow, even breaths helped her muscles to relax as they descended a steep hill. She was with Cane. His instincts were second only to Kaleo's.

They crossed a small creek and headed up the slope on the other side. Just before they reached the crest of the hill, a hush came over the forest. Cane heard it too, because his steps slowed.

She fingered the string of her bow. For the last couple of days, Cane had been giving her archery lessons. According to him, she was a natural with quick reflexes.

He gave her a subtle nod. In barely a second, she swung the bow out, swiped an arrow from the quiver, and nocked it. With no clear target, she swiveled in a semi-circle with the bow drawn.

The jungle closed in like a leafy cocoon, broken only by small sight lines between the trees. Tiny shafts of light streaked through the canopy above, creating dancing shadows in the breeze.

She turned her head back and forth to angle her ears in each direction. No sounds, not even the twittering of birds.

She caught his gaze and shook her head. His answering look meant he hadn't heard anything either.

Her arms relaxed, then went rigid again as pounding thumps stomped about twenty yards away. Whatever it was, it was large and coming right at them.

Cane also drew his bow and nocked an arrow. He spun around, putting his back to hers in a defensive stance, and guided her toward the cover of a huge kapok tree trunk. She kept her arrow trained sideways toward the noises.

Thump. Thump. Thump.

The running animal drew closer, shaking the ground beneath her feet, but not enough for something like a *T. rex.* This dinosaur was smaller.

The pounding noises came faster, overlapping. Another animal was pursuing the first. A creature with thundering footsteps as powerful as the fleeing animal, maybe more so.

Between small gaps in the foliage, she caught glimpses of something long and blue racing toward them. Cane pressed her against the back side of the tree trunk. She lowered her bow and arrow as he moved in front of her.

She craned her neck to look around his shoulder. An adult *Parasaurolophus* broke through the undergrowth and smashed into the front side of their tree. Its swooping blue head crest shaved off thick branches near the middle and sent wood crashing down on their heads.

Cane dove on top of her and covered her as the weight of the branches pinned them to the ground.

The *Parasaurolophus* thrashed against the tree and stomped, shaking the ground. It boomed out a deep honk. More branches cracked and continued to rain down.

The pounding thumps of its pursuer drew closer. The predator had to be almost on top of them as well.

Whoosh!

Heat rolled over them like the first flush of propane in a gas fireplace. Cane grunted and pressed tighter into her back. Even with him as a buffer, the heat smothered her head and arms. Sweat erupted on her entire body.

The para must have righted itself because branches stopped falling. Its heavy footsteps thumped away. Apparently, it had escaped the predator just in time.

Wood smoke filled her nostrils. Something had caught fire. Cane rolled to the side and began shoving the branches off.

She grabbed his arm. "Wait," she whispered.

A sharp twinge tightened deep in her gut. The predator hadn't moved on yet.

Tense moments passed. The only sounds came from the crackle of burning wood and the distant thump of the para's feet. The air became a misty haze. She covered her mouth and nose with her sleeve to filter out the ash.

Cane shifted to the side. She squinted at him through the smoke. His eyes were closed. One hand was stuck out at an angle through the branches. Clearly, he was using his ability to release hydrogen cyanide in order to deter the predator. Several minutes passed where she continued to breathe through her sleeve.

The heat died down. The crackling eased to a dull smolder.

Just as the faint smell of almonds started to come through her makeshift mask, heavy thumps shook the ground near their tree. The creature circled once, then moved off in the direction in which the para had fled.

They waited another full minute before crawling out from under the charred branches. By that time, her head swam from lack of oxygen. She sucked in deep breaths as she dragged her bow and quiver away from the smoldering embers.

"Are you okay?" Cane asked.

"I should be asking you that question. You took the brunt of it."

"I'm fine."

She looked him over. His neck appeared to have a slight burn, but his clothes had protected the rest of his body. Satisfied he truly was fine, she moved around to the front of the tree.

Half of the trunk had turned to charcoal. Bits of bark flaked off in dark slivers. The fallen branches on this side had been reduced to smoldering piles of ash.

What kind of genetic monster could create damage like that? Cane appeared as surprised as her. Had this dinosaur moved in from another area?

She touched the flaking charcoal on the trunk. It crumbled off, leaving a dark stain on her fingers. Her heart gave a quick jump. Could new dinosaurs be coming to the island? She'd have to ask Kaleo if he'd seen anything like this.

An hour later, she and Cane stood on the opposite side of the wide chasm across from the Cazador gang's resort compound. A shiver of apprehension snaked through her belly that had nothing to do with strange predatory dinosaurs. What would Kaleo think of her plan to leave the island?

Cane drew his bow, nocked an arrow, and let it fly. It

bridged the chasm and buried itself in a wooden pot on Kaleo's balcony—the signal announcing their arrival. If he was in his room, he'd hear it.

The two of them retreated to the designated meeting place at the head of the neighboring canyon, the same place Kaleo had left her after faking her death almost a week ago. So much had happened, it seemed as if she'd been on Extinction Island for months instead of a mere two weeks.

Within fifteen minutes, Kaleo's tanned face appeared from around the side of a tree trunk. The dark intensity of his eyes kickstarted her heart. Powerful, bordering on arrogant, and fiercely protective, Kaleo's presence couldn't be ignored.

Despite his size, he moved toward her on feet that didn't make a sound. When he stood inches from her, he stopped, reached up with the back of his hand, and traced the curve of her cheek. Warm tingles flooded down her spine. He hadn't forgotten about her yet.

Beside them, Cane fidgeted with the string on his bow. The nervous action was so uncharacteristic that she had to squelch the urge to ask him what was wrong. Asking would only make this moment more awkward.

Kaleo shifted his gaze to her lips. Bittersweet memories of their two stolen kisses bubbled up inside her like champagne fizz. She bit her lower lip. What she wouldn't give for one more kiss.

Cane took several steps away to give them privacy.

She cleared her throat. "How are things at the compound?"

"Fine." Kaleo folded his arms across his chest. "Wyatt is still our main guard. Orion has taken up Chubs's old position as keeper of the compound."

The mention of Chubs turned her stomach. Hard to believe a baby-faced boy would murder his teacher, but behind his innocent face lurked a lustful, controlling manipulator. For a taste of more power within the gang, Chubs had been ready to present Oakley as a plaything for Daric, a serial killer. Kaleo had kicked him out for the betrayal. Barely eighteen years old, Chubs was on his own in this deadly jungle. Maybe he was dead already.

"How's Misty?" In her sixties, Misty was a woman from the compound with long gray hair and subtle wrinkles around her eyes. Her crime was poisoning several husbands. The convicts usually left her alone, thanks to Kaleo and her dangerous background.

"As reclusive as ever. And still in charge of maintaining the poisonous traps in the jungle." He dropped his arms and cut the distance between them in half. He leaned down to whisper in her ear. "You smell like the ginger lilies they keep at the cave."

Heat crawled up her neck. Small talk was safer than being so close to him. He grabbed her arm and guided her farther from Cane.

Then, he bent his neck and brushed his scruffy cheek against hers. The rough sensation thrilled her. With a tilt of his head, he gently kissed her earlobe and along her jawline. By the time he reached her lips, she responded eagerly. He drew her into a deep, dizzying kiss.

When he pulled away, she swallowed hard and fought to slow her heavy breathing. She'd let him distract her, very nice, but she needed to get back on task. She took a step away and put a hand on his arm. "I have something to tell you."

He flinched as if he knew what was coming, though he couldn't possibly.

She bit her lip before pressing on. "I had a dream about Asperten." It sounded silly, almost irresponsible, to take action on a dream, but even now the memory of it was as real as being here with Kaleo.

Mama's sharp voice saying, "We made you here. Come home."

"Your dad's company?" he asked.

"Yes. My mother worked there too. In the dream, my mother was at that lab. I think I can find answers there."

What she wouldn't tell him—what she hadn't told anyone—was that she now remembered putting her mother into a coma as a child. At only seven years old, she'd acted in self-defense and then repressed the memory to block out the trauma. The dream had to be connected somehow.

Kaleo wrinkled his forehead.

He opened his mouth to speak, but she cut him off. "I'm leaving today. Cane has agreed to come with me."

His forehead didn't relax. His gaze darted to Cane

and then back to her. His mind was churning, trying to find a way to talk her out of this. "Does Raptor know?"

Her former boss, Ogden "Raptor" Greene, did *not* know of her decision, and she was going to keep it that way. "I can't tell him."

Raptor, a reptile expert like her, traveled to Extinction Island every month to check on the dinosaurs and the ecological systems. His salary was funded in part by Asperten International and in part by the federal government. If the government found out she'd left the island and Raptor knew about it, he'd be arrested. She couldn't let him take the risk.

Kaleo moved closer again. He towered over her, his broad chest filling her vision. She looked up into his chestnut eyes, hidden in the shadows from his thick hair.

He trapped her chin with his thumb and forefinger. "What if you find something you don't like?"

His husky voice speaking her fear aloud almost prompted her to abort her plan. *Almost.* She pushed down the visceral effect he had on her. "This is my only chance to find the truth."

Her government-issued tracker had shorted out after she'd used her electrifying ability on a *Velociraptor*. Until the government found her to reinstall her tracker, she could leave Extinction Island of her own free will, the same as Cane, who had never been convicted of a crime.

Kaleo grasped her gently by the forearms. "Even though you're at the cave and I'm at the resort, I've started to think of this island as beautiful because I know you're here somewhere." He took a deep breath. "But if you go," a sad smile crept over his expression, hardened by the firm line between his brows, "I need you to promise me something."

"What is it?" she asked in a quiet tone.

He tightened his grip. "Don't come back."

CHAPTER TWO

DON'T COME BACK. The words echoed through Oakley's mind. No doubt Kaleo meant to protect her, but those words penetrated deep into her heart. He could have insisted she stay or gotten jealous that she was leaving with Cane—something more to show he cared. Instead, he was liberating her, giving her the freedom to escape. And it was infuriating. He stood stoic, his face a mask of granite as she walked away from him.

She trailed behind Cane as he led them north into the dense jungle. This trip had been her idea, but every footfall was a struggle, almost like her feet didn't agree with her intentions.

For the first time since she'd been arrested for her best friend's murder, she could disappear anywhere in the world. Melt into the populations of either Nicaragua, north of the deep trench, or Panama, south of the canal.

As long as she didn't return to the United States, she'd have a chance to elude the FBI.

Although the scenario was tempting, she couldn't do it. A life on the run meant never seeing her dad or little brother, Eric, again. Not to mention the long-term trouble she'd cause for Raptor. Not telling him about her plans would protect him for a time, but if she didn't come back, the government would send FBI trackers to find her. If they found no evidence of her at all, they'd assume she escaped and that Raptor helped her because she used to work for him.

"Where are we going, exactly?" she asked Cane. His hidden boat was supposed to be in a cove somewhere.

He shot her a teasing glance. "If that's your version of 'Are we there yet?' the answer is no."

"Actually, I just wanted a little more information." She hit him lightly on the shoulder.

"Fine," he said with a laugh. "The prison ships dock near what used to be Puerto Limón, several hours walk from the cloud forest. My boat is waiting about twenty miles up the coast in a canal near Tortuguero."

Her steps faltered. "Twenty miles?" A sigh escaped. "So, we're not getting there today."

He shook his head in mock exasperation. "This is your trip, princess."

From anyone else, the nickname would have been offensive, but Cane had a gentle way of delivering his critique. And she *was* acting like a princess. Time to shut her mouth and let her legs take over.

They traveled northeast for many hours in silence. Based on the increased humidity, they were growing closer to the beach with every step. They stopped once to gather berries and relieve themselves. Other than a few small dinosaurs, which were easily discouraged by the point of an arrow, their journey had been uneventful.

As the shadows around them lengthened, she reached up to run a finger along the bow string stretched across her chest. Arrows wouldn't do much against most of the huge predators lurking in the twilight. They should find a place to stop for the night. She tapped him on the shoulder to get his attention. He flinched under her fingers, but he didn't look at her. He was staring at the trees to their left. His steps slowed, then stopped.

The hairs on the back of her neck stood on end. A rustling noise spiked her adrenaline.

Her fingers brushed the taut bow string again. A craggy growl rumbled.

From behind a tree, a gigantic dinosaur stuck a ridged nose through the branches. She sucked in a shaky breath.

The predator broke free of the jungle. An *Allosaurus* with a long, muscled body stretching out more than thirty feet. Its dripping jowls and piercing eyes signaled it was ready for a small snack.

It lifted one leg and stomped, causing tremors in the ground beneath her feet. If she ran up and grabbed its leg, could she use her power to disable it? She'd never tried to electrocute something so large.

Its head shifted quickly from side to side, giving the

impression of a bug-eyed lizard. Why did it keep doing that?

She peered at its face. Behind the ridges, this dinosaur had deep-set eyes attached to the sides of its head, not forward facing like the *T. rex.* This configuration was found mostly in prey animals like deer, but also in crocodiles, so they could watch for danger from all sides.

An idea formed. She moved a few feet to the left to test her theory.

The *Allosaurus* swiveled its head to track her.

She moved back to her original position.

It shifted its head again.

This could work. "Get behind me," she whispered to Cane.

To his credit, he obeyed her instantly. Probably in respect for her herpetology skills, which had helped them evade other predators.

She pulled her bow around, selected an arrow from the quiver, and nocked it. "Stay as close to my back as you can."

Slowly, she moved forward, fighting all her instincts to run away, until she stood staring at the middle of the dinosaur's bowed head.

When it raised its head to roar, she darted under the gaping maw of the beast. Cane still clung to her with his hands resting on the top of her shoulders.

She looked up at the underside of the *Allosaurus's* neck. It lowered its head, and the snout hung suspended above them. She couldn't see its eyes, which meant it couldn't see them.

As expected, the *Allosaurus* turned its head to find them. She quickly moved in the opposite direction, keeping their position in line with the huge dinner-plate-sized nostrils above them. Cane wrapped an arm around her so their steps would remain in sync.

The key to her plan was staying out of sight. If the dinosaur realized they were right below its mouth, it could chomp both of them in one bite. As if dancing a crazy tango in a ballroom, she swept back the other way as the dinosaur swung its head again. Cane followed in tandem.

The creature couldn't get a good look at them. It let out a hissing screech and turned its head faster.

She darted from side to side, panting from exertion. They couldn't keep up this pace.

On their next swing, she bent backward and let the arrow loose, aiming for the creature's left eye.

An angry roar tore through the air. The creature whipped its head back, but its feet held position.

She'd grazed the eyelid, not injuring it. Only making it angry.

The affected eye locked on to her. They had to get back in the *Allosaurus's* blind spot.

"We need to—"

Her words were cut off when Cane tightened the arm around her waist and swung her off balance. The dinosaur's head came crashing down right next to her.

As soon as Cane set her down, she nocked a second arrow. She might not get another try.

The dinosaur pulled its head back in confusion, leaving behind a six-inch depression in the ground.

"Let's do that again," she said.

Cane gave her a devilish smile as if she'd asked him to keep his arms around her for romantic reasons. Of all the times for his playful side to come out, but it was a good look on him.

She shifted their position until the *Allosaurus* could barely see the top of her head. It tried to get a better look at them, unsuccessfully swiveling its head as they danced out of sight.

Frustration set in, and the creature lunged forward.

Cane pulled her away quicker this time, her body momentarily suspended against gravity. She shot the arrow while weightlessness held her somewhat suspended.

She missed, but her first arrow had made the dinosaur gun shy. It ducked out of the way.

As Cane set her down, she quickly nocked another, took careful aim, and let it fly.

The creature blinked, its eyelid coming open a fraction of a second before the arrow struck. The point sank deep into its soft eyeball.

A roar of pain shook the air around them. The eyelid closed over the shaft, snapping the wood in half and leaving the metal tip firmly embedded.

Rearing back, the creature stomped on the ground. It

rubbed its injured eye in the dirt, throwing up clouds of dust.

She and Cane darted between the dinosaur's legs, racing for the jungle beyond. As the trees closed over her, she glanced back one last time. The dinosaur rubbed its eye along the bark of a tree. Poor thing. It was just an animal. But she wouldn't let it eat her simply to fulfill its animal instincts.

Fifty yards away, the strained moaning subsided. They stopped running. She breathed a little easier.

Cane turned around and winked at her. "I think we make a good team."

He was right. They communicated with surprisingly little effort, probably thanks to the chemical signals from the pheromones programmed into their DNA. It had to be the pheromones, right? But if it was just chemical cues that kept them in sync, why did admitting it make her feel so guilty?

MIST HUNG HEAVY over the tree canopy as Leo Coleman—Chubs to everyone on the island—trudged wearily through thick branches and vines. Under his breath, he cursed Kaleo, who had not only kicked him out of the gang's compound, but late this afternoon, evicted him from the tree house sanctuary.

Of course, as leader of the Cazador gang, Kaleo could have decided to kill him at any time, so banishment was better. Except Chubs didn't know where to go.

He kicked a thick, fallen branch out of his way, then picked it up and snapped it in half just because he could. It might be time to dump the name Chubs. When he had first arrived at the age of seventeen, the men had given him that nickname because he still had baby fat on his cheeks. He pounded a fist on his hard chest, then on his lean abs. No more baby fat. As the youngest person sentenced to Extinction Island, he should have earned some respect in the gang. The rest of the world saw him as a remorseless killer. But in this place, he was young, naïve Chubs. Even so, he couldn't easily shake the name off. Probably because Leo no longer fit either. Leo was the kid who'd been in love with his teacher, Teresa Walton. That kid had died, along with Teresa.

The crinkle of rustling leaves snapped him out of his thoughts. Was it the stir of a breeze? Or something else?

His gaze jumped from leaf to leaf and twig to twig. Nothing moved. But the tension hardening his gut only grew. What would he do if a dinosaur attacked? For the last year, he'd been safe inside the gang's resort compound, handling menial tasks while guys like Kaleo did the hunting. He hadn't traveled alone any farther than the garbage pile twenty feet from the front door.

Twilight dimmed the jungle around him. This was the worst time for Kaleo to kick him out, right before the night predators began hunting. Never mind that Kaleo had good reason after he'd sided with the newcomer,

Daric, and tried to take Kaleo down. But this punishment was over the top. Hard labor, kitchen duty, or even a beating would have been fine. Out here, Chubs would die.

The worst part was that Kaleo hadn't done it out of vengeance or anger. It was a calculated move.

To protect Oakley's secret.

If the rest of the gang knew she was alive, they would kill her *and* Kaleo. Except now that Chubs was banished, they wouldn't take his word for it. He'd have to find Oakley and bring her back to the compound to prove it. Not an easy task.

A faint rustling came from the bushes in front of him. He took several steps to the side, away from the bushes, until he came to a fallen tree. He scrambled over. As he straightened, something above him caught his eye. A bare wooden platform rested about fifteen feet up, between the branches of a sturdy tree.

He circled the trunk. Sure enough, there were wooden footholds nailed into the bark all the way up one side. Some sort of hunting blind.

A stick cracked behind him. He spun around, his heart hammering in his throat.

Nothing. At least nothing visible through the thick foliage. Leaves floated on moving branches, concealing everything beyond arm's reach. He edged closer to the tree.

A low growl came from the jungle to his left.

He picked up a large stick and pressed his back

against the trunk. Should he climb? Or wait to see if the creature moved on?

A blur of red and green broke from the surrounding leaves and barreled toward him.

He sidestepped and spun, a move that had once brought him cheers on the football field, but now caused him to drop the stick. Not that it would have done him much good anyway. A red crest with feathers slashed through the top of the dinosaur's head—this was Red Grizzly, the largest *Utahraptor* on the island. It had killed two people he knew, leaving the last one so mutilated she could only be identified by the tattoo on her ankle.

Red Grizzly slammed into the tree but quickly recovered.

Chubs dodged, keeping the trunk between him and his attacker.

The raptor swung its head around and snapped at him. Its serrated teeth sliced off chunks of bark.

He spun again. The next bite grazed his elbow. No time to worry about the injury. One more spin and he'd make it all the way around the tree to where the footholds were.

He spun, then leaped at the wooden pegs, catching his feet on the second tier.

Not high enough. He scrambled against the rough bark as Red Grizzly regrouped.

The raptor jumped again with its claws extended.

He grabbed at a higher peg. A tug on his tennis shoe pulled him back down. His right foot floated free.

The creature landed hard with only a shoe as its prize. An enraged rumble came from deep in its throat.

Chubs swung his leg back to the tree and clung to the pegs. Below him, RG tensed its legs to jump again. He needed to get higher.

He pulled himself up as the raptor slammed into the trunk inches below his feet. It tried to hold fast, as Chubs had done, but its claws wouldn't dig into the bark. It slipped back to the ground, scratching all the way down.

Chubs kept climbing until he reached the hunting blind, well out of jumping range. He looked down. RG was sniffing and scratching at his tennis shoe. Let it gnaw on a mouthful of rubber and canvas. Maybe it would choke.

He expelled a weary breath. If things had gone differently last week, Daric Perkins would have taken over the compound, and Chubs would be sharing in the spoils of the coup. Daric had promised Oakley to him. He should be living in luxury with her fulfilling his every whim. Instead, Daric was dead, and he was trapped like a cat up a tree. But this wasn't the end. He would find a way to turn it around.

CHAPTER THREE

HUMIDITY AND SALT infused the air as Cane and Oakley drew closer to the coast. The sound of crashing surf filled her ears, although the water wasn't visible yet. The trees formed an ever-thinning envelope surrounding them.

They'd spent last night in an empty shack. Sleeping together on a blanket was both platonic and awkward. She'd awakened later than normal to find him staring at her, his hand poised as if ready to brush the hair from her cheek. Or perhaps he'd already done it and had woken her. The forlorn tenderness in his eyes had moved her. But what did it mean?

Better not to know. Things were complicated enough already.

Cane pushed ahead, his steps becoming faster. She watched his tall, strong form as he weaved around obstacles and cut through tangles of vines. Often, he held branches out of the way for her until she could pass through. With his machete in one hand and the bow and quiver on his back, he looked the part of a modern-day Robin Hood. And in a way, he was that—bringing his worthy gifts and talents to the poor inhabitants of the island.

They'd been walking most of the day with few water breaks. It was her own fault for sleeping well past dawn. Cane should have woken her earlier.

With a final push through the trees, they came out into the open air on top of a cliff. No boat in sight. She held back her sarcastic comments about his sense of direction and instead waited silently for his next move.

Without pausing, he continued to trek through the grass.

She followed him for several paces until she couldn't hold it in any longer. "Um, Captain Ahab, are we searching for an actual boat?"

While keeping stride, he glanced back and raised his eyebrows at her. No witty retort. No scathing comment. In fact, she couldn't remember any of her remarks ever getting under his skin. Maybe she didn't need to be cautious with him after all. And yet, it seemed odd to express her sarcastic side to a pastor, albeit a young, good-looking one.

As they walked along the top of the cliff, she peered over the edge to where the sea curled into the rocky wall and splashed up the sides of a small cove. She bit her bottom lip. If the boat was down there, it might have been smashed to pieces by now.

Cane led her over the cove below, then he turned and descended a grassy slope toward the rocks. She would have never come this way since the moderate slope appeared to drop off to the ocean in a steep cliff, but he cut sideways across the ground.

He approached the end of the grass with confidence. At the edge, he stepped out into thin air. She almost cried out when he pitched forward, but then his body stabilized. Something unseen held him up.

She crept closer.

A small ledge of rock, about three feet down, supported Cane with just enough space for his large feet. The ledge meandered along the face of the cliff, not held together like a sidewalk, but interspersed with gaps and missing sections. It led downward diagonally to a barely visible black circle. Probably a cave carved out of the rock by the waves.

He helped her down, rolling his ankles to place her feet between his before moving to the next foothold. She copied his slow progress, sometimes stretching to the full length of her legs to make it across.

As they neared the dark circle, the dimensions of the cave became clear. It was definitely big enough to hide a boat.

Ten feet above the opening, the ledge abruptly broke

off. Either it had never continued all the way down or it had fallen into the sea long ago.

"Now what?" she asked.

He gently grabbed her hand. "Now, we climb."

After giving her hand a slight squeeze, he bent down, placed his palms on the gritty ledge, and lowered his feet. For several seconds, he searched with his boots for a foothold.

Finally, he found one and regained his balance. "The rocks are far apart. I'll have to help you." He took another searching step down before reaching up to her. "Lean over the edge. I'll guide your feet."

She hesitated. The rock he teetered on sat well past the length of her body. What was easy for him would mean blindly sliding down the rough rock for her.

"Don't you trust me?" His words were tinged with disappointment.

It wasn't about trust. She trusted him without question, quite uncommon for her. This was about moving forward without being able to see ahead. But there was no way around it. She grabbed the rock ledge and spun around to face the cliff, then stepped off.

Her body slid until she was stretched out with only her hands gripping the sharp ledge. Below her, the turbulent sea thrashed, spraying up in slender tendrils, as if the long fingers of the ocean were reaching for her.

She pinched her eyes shut.

With strong hands, Cane grabbed her ankles and guided her feet to the left. "Okay, let go."

"*What?*" Allowing herself to dangle over the cliff side was hard enough, but prying her fingers off the ledge might be impossible.

"It's okay, Oakley." The timbre of his tone rose over the rush of the sea. "Just let go."

With a cold wave of dread, she obeyed. Gravity yanked at her body. She gasped. The free fall lasted less than a second before her toes hit a large rock. Cane's stabilizing force anchored her feet to the outcrop. She leaned into the cliff and smiled down at him, likely more of a grimace. "Not gruesome, at least."

"Good attitude. Three more to go."

She rolled her eyes skyward and bit her lip. "Not four? Please, can we do four?"

He was already moving down, too focused to acknowledge her remark.

When he directed her, she demonstrated her trust again and slipped off the ledge. By the time they reached the cave, her limbs shook from adrenaline and fatigue. Trust exercises were not her thing, but she'd made it through.

Her triumph evaporated at the sight of the boat before her. It was a twelve-foot-long shell of scratched and dented fiberglass. The stiff roof, previously held on by four poles, now tilted to starboard, thanks to a missing pole. The jagged rocks and shifting tides had inflicted a lot of damage.

Was this the condition Cane had expected to find it

in? He made no sound as he climbed aboard. She stayed on the rock ledge, not willing to risk sinking the boat until it proved capable of holding the weight of one person.

He leaned down, then came up holding a long white cylinder. "I found the support pole."

After waiting several minutes while he struggled to insert it, she sighed impatiently. "Can't we rip the roof off?"

"Not unless you want to be stranded in the middle of the ocean. Those wide panels on top are solar panels that power the electric motor."

"They've been inside a cave for a year. The cells will be dead. Are you expecting us to float aimlessly until they're charged?"

He gave a throaty chuckle. "That's one option. However, I suggest we use the gas-powered motor until the solar panels have stored up enough charge."

She smirked at his uncharacteristic snark. One thing about Cane, he was full of surprises.

He helped her climb onboard, then began checking the instruments. "Please tell me you know where to go from here."

"Generally northeast?" She gave a sheepish grin. "If we hit the mainland, we've gone too far."

He raked his hands through his reddish-blond waves. "I'm going to need a little more than that."

"I know it's about a hundred miles off the coast of Louisiana because my dad flies out to it."

"That's a big area, but you're in luck. Since I came from that way, I've got nautical maps of the Gulf of Mexico. We can dig them out once we're underway." He placed his fingers on the key start. "Let's pray this works."

Pray. Back home in Louisiana, saying you would pray for someone or something didn't mean you would talk to God, it just meant you cared. But no doubt Cane was actually praying right now. At this point, she'd take all the assistance they could get.

The gas-powered engine took three tries before it engaged. He said something about the gas being stale. Whatever. At least it hadn't completely expired.

Cane took his spot behind the wheel and whisked them out of the cave, through the cove, and to the open ocean. She took a deep breath of salty air. The engine rumbled beneath the fiberglass floor. Wind whipped through her hair and rushed past her cheeks. She was leaving her island prison behind. No one was looking for her. No one besides Kaleo knew she was gone. For the first time in months, she felt free.

***

LUMAS VERRET, director of Asperten International, crawled from his bed with a pounding headache reminiscent of a hangover. Not from alcohol, but from lack of sleep. Tension had kept him awake all night. Perhaps he needed to send for another woman from his dating service. These days, it was easier to pay for companionship. His secluded life at the research laboratory in the middle of the Gulf of Mexico had destroyed every relationship he'd started since Penna Gallardo left him fifteen years earlier.

Penna was the creator and architect of the Biological Termination DNA program. She'd been his partner in every sense. But he'd wrecked their relationship by keeping too many secrets from her. No regrets though. He'd do it all again. She wouldn't have stayed voluntarily if she'd known his true objective for the program.

No woman since her could fulfill him. Especially not in the lab. Penna's genetic genius was unsurpassed. His mood lifted. He had reason to believe she was still alive. One day soon, he'd find her and convince her to come back.

He slipped into starched pants and a button-down shirt, then made his way to the control office of the building.

Glen Rekow, his technological expert, already sat at his desk, ready to report.

"Any progress?" Lumas asked.

Glen nodded, his dark ponytail swishing along his shoulders. "Oakley and the other male subject have boarded a boat. I'm convinced she's following the dream we induced."

"Good. She found a way." He clapped Glen on the shoulder. "For now, she's acting on faith. So, how are we going to get her to our exact coordinates?"

They had talked this through over and over without a

good solution. The eye implant—installed into Oakley's right eye before she'd left for the island—had been invaluable for surveillance, but the technology had limitations. They could observe without listening, and even induce impressions during sleep, but the mind was a complicated organ. Trying to send exact coordinates would probably end up a jumbled mess because of the neural cleanup known to happen during sleep. If they displayed them during broad daylight, a set of numbers appearing before her eyes would either convince her she was schizophrenic or alert her to the presence of a strange device in her head.

Glen tapped the screen, which showed a map marked with a red dot representing Oakley. He pointed to the ocean stretching before her. "We've already given her the impression of northeast. What if we signaled her when she gets close?"

"What do you mean, signal her?"

A half smile tipped Glen's mouth. "I can bump up the strength of our aircraft warning lights and turn them green so they will stand out."

"Make it so." Lumas chuckled at his own *Star Trek* reference. The last frontier certainly could be interpreted as space, if one meant the space between specific nucleotides in the DNA sequence. Biomedical research had already changed the world far more than the last twenty space missions combined.

He indulged in a self-satisfied smile. Oakley was coming home. Though she had never known this place as home, she'd been created here, literally stitched together on the molecular level in the laboratory one floor below. Her mother, Lillian Hebert, had worked side by side with Penna to generate phase after phase of embryonic trials until they'd succeeded in modifying the human genome.

With Lillian dead and Penna gone, the research had suffered until Auburn, Oakley's twin, took up the mantle. Problem was, Auburn continued to stumble through the modification process because she was working solely from Penna's notes. If only Penna were here to guide her. The two of them could create fantastic modifications.

He had to find Penna. For years, he'd accepted that she must be dead, until the genetically modified dinosaurs on the island started having their tracking chips removed. No one else would know how to do it. The sabotage had to be Penna's doing. She was on Extinction Island somewhere.

Auburn strode into the room. Her long, dark hair was pulled back into a tight braid, and her eyes were rimmed with dark circles, the result of a long night waiting for Adler Calais to return from the island.

He put up a hand before she could ask. "Adler's on his way." He gestured to the screen. "Your sister's not far behind him."

Auburn accepted this news with little interest expressed toward the arrival of her twin. He couldn't blame her. Auburn had watched through the eye implant as Oakley used her power to kill. Though it wasn't the killing that bothered Auburn—he'd raised her to understand that death was required to keep order in the world. What disturbed her was the lack of accountability for Oakley's power. To her, Oakley was a wild card in need of control.

His gaze roamed Auburn's face. How different would the two of them seem once Oakley arrived? The physical differences would be evident since they were fraternal twins. Auburn's jaw was a little harder, her eyes a darker shade of blue. But what about their personalities?

They were raised apart—Auburn raised by him and Penna, and Oakley raised by Marcel and Lillian, while she was alive. At the time when the twins were separated, it had seemed an interesting scientific experiment in nature versus nurture. Now, Lumas had to be prepared to win over Oakley's mind. She might not embrace his mission as wholeheartedly as Auburn had. But if she did, the twins would be unstoppable ... and lucrative.

A LONG, fitful night of sleep on the hard wooden planks of the hunting blind had turned Chubs's muscles stiff and rigid. He groaned as he leaned over the edge to examine the ground for the hundredth time today. The jungle sounded normal.

On the lower portion of the tree trunk, deep gouges and dents remained as evidence of Red Grizzly's frustration. When ramming its shoulder into the trunk a dozen times hoping to dislodge Chubs hadn't worked, the creature had kept a vigil for hours. Long past sunset, he still heard the soft pad of its feet and the stray crack of branches as it circled the base of the tree.

Despite the close proximity of RG, he'd fallen asleep until the first rays of dawn woke him. Since then, he'd watched the forest and waited for most of the day. Had the creature left? Or was it stalking him from the cover of the bushes?

Hunched over, he listened to the forest sounds. Monkeys chattering. Birds whistling. Insects buzzing.

His stomach let out a loud gurgle, and he pressed his fists against it to keep it quiet. He'd last eaten yesterday afternoon, not long before Kaleo kicked him out. He needed to hunt, or more correctly, forage since he wasn't an expert hunter.

Dead leaves rustled on the ground about ten yards from the base of his tree. He leaned over farther. A small *Compsognathus*, hardly bigger than a chicken, limped into view. Its leg appeared broken near the ankle. Perhaps it had narrowly escaped from one of the many traps set up by the gang.

The animal whimpered as it trudged along, then froze when it heard Chubs's stomach rumble again. It looked up and tried to scamper away but couldn't move fast.

He smiled. Breakfast had walked right up to him. He slid a knife from the side pocket of his backpack and quietly climbed down the rear side of the tree.

He circled around to the front. The miserable creature had only reached the next tree over. He crept toward it with the knife raised in his hand. Time to put it out of its misery.

The compy hobbled faster, trying to escape.

As he stood poised to strike, a cold sweat broke out on his neck. Something else was here. He backed off a split second before the sharp screech of his prey signaled another predator.

A low growl rolled through the air.

He looked over his shoulder. Red Grizzly stood between him and his sheltering tree.

This had been a trap. He'd underestimated RG, and now it would cost him his life. But he wouldn't die easily. He spun around, swinging the knife in a wide arc.

The blade caught RG on the snout. It howled and snapped its teeth over the blade.

Chubs let go of the handle and raced blindly into the forest. But he had nowhere to go.

He pushed through a curtain of vines, flung a snake off his arm, and kept moving. Branches and leaves thrashed and crashed behind him.

Red Grizzly was coming.

The tangled undergrowth broke free just as a swoosh of air came from behind. A heavy impact propelled him forward.

He screamed as the nine-inch claw pierced his back, then screamed again as his body hit open air. He'd fallen over the edge of a short, steep cliff.

His chest hit the bottom of the ravine first. The impact stole the breath from his lungs. Then, his head smashed on the ground. A flash of pain barely registered before his vision went dark.

CHAPTER FOUR

THE OCEAN LAPPED against the hull of the boat in a rhythmic, soothing motion. They had driven under gas power for about five miles before Cane decided to shut down the motor. Now, they floated at the mercy of the current, waiting for the solar panels to recharge. It was a solid plan. They needed to conserve their available gas in case of an emergency.

Oakley rubbed her eyes and tried to focus on the nautical maps spread on the fiberglass floor. Using his finger, Cane drew a curving line from Costa Rica, around Nicaragua and Honduras, then switched to another map where his finger crossed between Mexico and Cuba, finally landing in the middle of the Gulf of Mexico.

"It's a long trip," he said. "Probably at least a thousand miles depending on where in the gulf the headquarters is located."

The map held a multitude of foreign symbols. She took his word for it since she had nothing helpful to add. She pinched her eyes shut and tried to remember everything Dad had said about the company during her single visit as a child. "It's on some sort of slope with salt."

Cane frowned. "What?"

"I remember my dad saying the office building wouldn't have lasted on land because most of the sediment it's anchored to is composed of rock salt."

He pulled the Gulf of Mexico map closer. "Okay, on a slope off the coast of Louisiana, so not in the deep gulf." He circled a finger near several steep contour lines. "It would have to be somewhere along the Texas-Louisiana shelf before the Sigsbee Escarpment drops off."

For a few minutes, they scoured the small symbols and numbers scattered across the map. Depth of water contours, buoys, and landmarks blended together.

"What is this?" Cane asked.

She squinted at it. Next to his finger sat a small circle. Inside, printed in a tiny italic font, were the letters *AI*.

It had to be Asperten International. At least it was a starting point for where to look. She smiled at him and leaned back against the lower half of the bench seat.

Cane mimicked her posture and nudged her knee with his. "Shouldn't need more than an hour for the solar panels to get us going again. Thank God for a sunny afternoon."

"And for the shade created by the panels." She

couldn't imagine the trip without overhead shelter. They would have burnt in the sun like overbaked cookies. "How long will it take?"

"About three days."

"Three days?" She leaned forward to stare into his face. His one raised eyebrow told her he was serious.

"It's a long way to go, and that assumes we're boating through most of the night."

She blew some errant hairs off her face. They would have to conserve their food, but they could make it. Would Kaleo worry about her during that time? It wasn't like she could text him to let him know this would be a week-long round trip. For that matter, she ought to let her Dad know what she was doing. Could she call him? "Hey, do you have a phone in this tin can?"

"No. There wasn't any point in bringing a satellite phone with me. I wasn't going to pay for years of service that I wouldn't use."

Of course, a satellite phone would still need service. "Does Neve have one?"

He shook his head. "Her family died before the evacuation. She has no one on the mainland to communicate with."

Raptor would have a satellite phone, but even if she would have thought of it, she couldn't have borrowed his. The government would easily track it.

Then, it slowly sank in. This trip would probably take too long. FBI Agent Brooks would want her location secured by an implant soon. When he sent a team to install it and they couldn't find her, he would launch an intensive search.

Cane tapped her arm. "You're sure this is what you want to do? There's still time to change your mind."

She glanced over her shoulder and stared at the rough outline of Extinction Island, visible as a shadow along the horizon. Then, she swiveled to gaze at the open sea in front of them. Empty, yet ... beckoning. The same way that her mother had beckoned her in the dream. A dream that was as real and solid as the fiberglass floor she sat on.

Right or wrong, this trip was her only chance to find out what had been done to her. Hopefully, the FBI wouldn't come looking for her right away. She needed this time of discovery, and Cane did too, even if he didn't realize it yet. Besides, once she discovered the truth, she might determine that she belonged on Extinction Island for the safety of the public. Without looking at him, she gave a firm nod.

<hr>

"OAKLEY LEFT THE ISLAND?" Raptor stared suspiciously at Kaleo.

"Keep your voice down," Kaleo whispered as his gaze darted across the resort dining room. Thankfully, no one was around. The guys in the compound still believed Oakley was dead.

"Sorry."

When Raptor showed up at the compound looking for Oakley, Kaleo could have left well enough alone, but instead he'd confessed. Only problem was, he'd lied to Raptor in the past. "I swear. It's true."

"Why would she do that?" Raptor asked, shifting in the cushioned counter-height chair.

"She had a dream. Something about her mom and finding out what she did at that company."

A small spasm jerked through Raptor's neck. "Is she coming back?"

Kaleo shook his head. Sadness swirled inside him. He'd meant it when he told her not to come back, but an island without her sounded like eternal torture.

"Look, I don't want her here any more than you do, but you know the law. If the government finds out she's gone, or even finds out she left and came back, they will hunt her down and execute her immediately."

Kaleo rubbed his jaw. "Maybe they won't find her."

"They have vast resources."

Silence stretched between them. Those simple words wormed through Kaleo's mind, carving tunnels of fear and regret.

"We can protect her here. You, me, and Cane." Raptor gestured to the verdant view outside the glass doors. "If she's out there, how do we keep her safe?"

He averted his gaze. Telling Raptor any details would endanger him and compromise his duty to the government. But what if he was right? Then the more he knew, the more he could help.

Raptor smacked his hands on the counter. "Of course. She's with Cane. He's the only one who could leave with her. But a former pastor won't be able to hide her from the FBI."

More deafening silence. Despite his confident words, the war was written all over Raptor's face—the same war Kaleo had been battling since she left. Was Oakley safer here or on the run?

His own indecision nearly choked him. Maybe he shouldn't have let her go. Could she really disappear and hide from the FBI forever? The odds were not in her favor.

After five minutes, Raptor offered up a sliver of hope. "We have a little time. I can keep the secret of her disappearance until the medics get here to replace her tracker. But we have to find her before then. Her quest for the truth isn't worth her life."

He didn't respond.

Raptor leaned forward and stretched out his stocky frame, a move meant to intimidate. "Where did she go?"

Kaleo squirmed in his chair, not because of the implied physical threat, but because Raptor was asking him to betray Oakley.

"Don't you care for her?"

His eyes narrowed. "Do you?"

"Like she's my sister." A pleading look crossed Raptor's face. He'd known Oakley before all of this, had worked with her every day. He felt responsible for her too. No matter what his government job required, it was clear he would make the best decision for her.

Kaleo sighed. "All I can do is show you where I saw them last. You'll have to track them from there."

CHAPTER FIVE

CHUBS GROPED for control of his groggy mind in the darkness. As the space behind his eyelids lightened, a sharp pain pricked his upper back.

He opened his eyes to slits. The leaves looked fuzzy as they spread out in a circle from his head. He lay on his stomach with his face smashed into something rough. For a brief second, the pain eased.

He tried to move. The pain returned, even sharper.

Someone, or something, was still cutting into his back. Primal fear gripped his heart as memories flooded in. Red Grizzly had laid a trap for him. By the time he'd realized the danger, it was too late. He should have fallen into unconsciousness and not woken up. But now he was being eaten alive.

Another stabbing pain drew a grunt from him. Nausea rolled through his stomach. He pressed his eyes closed. At what point would the pain overwhelm him again, and he'd pass out? Soon, hopefully.

"Hold still," a gruff voice ordered.

At first, he had the insane idea that the dinosaur was telling him to hold still and be good prey. As the wave of pain washed over him, so did the ridiculousness of that thought. He pushed his eyes open and turned his head.

"I said hold still."

Wait. That deep rumbling voice. Why was Taye Turner—the best tracker from the gang—here with him? Come to think of it, no birds chirped and no breeze rustled the leaves. They weren't in the jungle. So, where were they?

He blinked hard. The fuzzy leaves were variations in the folding of a stained green blanket. His body lay on a cot suspended off a dirt floor. Grubby boards ran along the walls, cracked beams held up the ceiling, and vines crept in the doorway. He was in one of the old shacks that dotted the countryside of Costa Rica, abandoned by those who'd been evacuated. Based on the hazy illumination, it was probably late afternoon outside.

Taye pressed something on Chubs's lower back. Chubs sucked in a deep breath to fight the pain, then swung a hand around, holding a cloth on the wound as he sat up.

Taye stepped away from the cot, arms folded over his chest, his expression unreadable. Chubs faltered as he went over his options. While at the compound, Taye had never hurt or even been unkind to him. In fact, he had a grudging respect for Taye's abilities based on what the other gang members said. Whenever on the hunt for game, Taye prowled around the forest like a stalking panther. Powerful and dangerous. Qualities worth emulating, but also qualities to be wary of. Not to mention Taye was hunting buddies with Kaleo.

"I cleaned the wound," Taye said.

"Thanks." The cloth felt moist, as if it was filling with blood already. His vision clouded at the edges. He lay down on the cot again, pressing the cloth into his cut.

"You need stitches."

Chubs pointed at him by way of asking if he could do it.

Taye shook his head.

"Guess it will heal well enough on its own, then."

Taye studied him. Chubs stared back, fighting the urge to squirm. Finally, Taye dropped his arms to his sides. "I'll find someone."

"Not Misty," Chubs blurted out. She was the only healer at the compound, but he wouldn't let her touch him. That woman would kill him just as easily as heal him.

Taye shook his head again. "No, not Misty. A friend of mine."

Confusion wrinkled his brow. Taye knew other people on the island? And one who was a healer? His mind hazed over, and his eyes grew heavy. He couldn't focus enough to ask any more questions. "Whatever."

Through his half-closed eyes, he watched Taye walk

out of the opening in the shack where the door should have been. Maybe he should play it safe and leave before Taye got back, but he didn't have the energy. His eyes drifted closed. Hopefully, no animals would be lured by the scent of blood and discover him defenseless.

Sometime later, he awoke to a gentle hand on his forehead and a sweet soprano voice asking, "How do you feel?"

A woman with a sable complexion, a few shades lighter than Taye's, light brown eyes, and shiny black hair leaned over him. Though she appeared fifteen to twenty years older than him, she was exotic, petite, and gorgeous.

"I'm Neve," she said.

"Chubs. Beautiful to meet you." He'd meant to say nice to meet you and that she was beautiful, but it had come out wrong. Perhaps he'd lost too much blood.

Taye glared at him from over Neve's shoulder. This was a woman Taye didn't want him to mess with. That made her even more attractive.

Neve twisted at the waist and touched Taye on the arm to get his attention. When he turned to her, his expression opened and softened. So that was why Taye seemed protective. He was into her. Neve didn't give any hint that she'd noticed.

"Can you help me roll him over? I don't want him to tear anything more by doing it himself."

Together, they lifted Chubs and shifted him to his stomach. Neve raised his shirt from behind. Taye moved to the doorway, a greenish cast to his face. "I'll be out here. I'll walk you home when you're done."

"Of course." Neve's voice held understanding.

It was probably the needle and thread that Taye didn't like. Funny how Chubs had lived with him for a year without discovering that information. Seemed like all the men at the compound guarded their reputations. Especially Kaleo, who was the weakest of them all.

Neve smoothed something wet over his back. He winced as the cloth crossed his open wound.

"In a few minutes, this will control the pain a little," she said. "But even if it hurts, I need you to hold still."

A cool sensation spread over his skin. But it wasn't enough to cover the pain when the first stab of the needle bored a hole through his skin. What was she using, a knitting needle? His flesh screamed in protest, but he bit his lower lip hard, causing it to bleed. He would not yell.

He gritted his teeth until she paused for a moment. Better to strike up a conversation as a distraction. "How long have you been on the island, Neve?"

Taye said he would walk her home. Perhaps she lived nearby.

As he'd planned, she held off sewing while she answered. "All my life."

She was a local, not a criminal. No wonder her face held an angelic innocence and her name tasted as smooth and sweet as ice cream on his tongue. A smoldering heat invaded his gut. He hadn't met a kind, gentle woman since coming here. In fact, he'd have a hard time finding someone this perfect on the outside.

"I haven't seen you around."

She laughed softly as she began another stitch. "I don't get out much."

Had she always been protected by men like Taye? An erotic possibility occurred to him. Maybe she was still a virgin. Maybe that was why Taye found her so captivating.

"Where do you live?" he asked.

A long hesitation, during which he tried not to cringe at the pull of the thread on his back. The pain increased as she made her way higher.

Finally, she answered, "I'm not sure I can tell you that."

"Don't I look trustworthy?"

She placed something on his back below his wound. "I've learned not to judge on superficial things like appearance."

The swoosh of something being unspooled was followed by another sharp stab.

She paused for a moment. "I've come to the thickest part of the wound. Five more large stitches before I put on the bandage. Don't move."

He would continue to keep still, if only to show her how strong he could be. She pulled the thread though the holes made by the needle, dragging bits of his skin with it. He grabbed the edges of the cot in tight fists. After she pulled the thread to the end, she pierced him yet again with the broad needle. He suffered through the process over and over.

His anger kept him focused on the source of his misery. All this pain, humiliation, and fear could be laid at the feet of a single person. Somehow, he would make sure Kaleo paid for everything he'd had to endure.

CHAPTER SIX

RAPTOR HAD TRAVELED north until darkness forced him to stop. His mandate and duty—to capture Oakley and hold her until the government could tag her like a head of cattle—broke his heart. But if he let her escape, her life would be in even more danger.

He'd spent the night high off the ground nestled in the crook of a guanacaste tree. Early this morning, the trail led him to a small shack where they must have spent the night. He was probably half a day behind them.

Picking up the pace, he pressed through the trees, searching for the barest of indicators: a snapped twig, a cut vine, disturbed leaves. He moved as fast as his eye could identify the clues. Whenever his mind wandered, he reined in his focus. The madness of the situation ached deep in his bones. To protect Oakley, he had to hunt her.

Except the FBI wasn't the only potential danger for her. Kaleo said she was heading straight to Asperten

International Headquarters, home of Director Lumas Verret. Lumas's company might fund half of Raptor's salary, but he was an ambitious man whom Raptor didn't trust. Too many unusual things could be traced back to him. Like an upturn in the number of dinosaurs with deadly adaptations. Like Adler Calais, who worked for Asperten and who had tried to kill Oakley. Like the parts of Asperten's bunker that were restricted from Raptor—portions Adler had access to. Lumas's true role on the island and the goal of his manipulations were closely guarded secrets.

Several hours later, Raptor broke out into the open where grass grew in clumps between rocks along the top of a sea cliff. Rushing water crashed below. Was he close to whatever boat they had come to find? He peered over the edge. They wouldn't have made it down that way.

Several areas of smashed grass led farther north and then down a steep slope. He followed until the slope broke off in a lower cliff.

At the edge, jagged rocks stuck out like basalt daggers. He had a momentary vision of Oakley tumbling over with Cane jumping in to save her. But on the cliff face below, several large rocks were covered in tiny crumbling pieces, as if freshly worn down by shoes. They must have descended along the rocks, probably to the dark cave at the bottom.

He listened. No voices. Only the turbulent surf.

But he had to be sure. Using the same path, he climbed down to the cave. When he reached the opening, it confirmed his worst fear. If they had been here, they were gone.

Twisting around to the mouth of the cave, he put a hand over his eyes and scanned the ocean. Nothing marred the horizon. They were long gone. He dropped to the nearest rock and let out a slow, ragged breath.

Would Cane go on the run with her? Or would he eventually return to his people at the cave? Raptor faced the real possibility that he might never know what had happened to her.

He pushed the fears away. For now, he could do one thing for Oakley—run interference with the FBI. If the appointed team took a small boat from New Orleans or Miami, the trip might take five days. But if they flew to Guatemala, then set sail from there, it could only be a couple of days. Either way, they would probably arrive before Oakley returned.

A moment of clarity hit him. If Oakley was determined to get to Asperten International, she'd make it. She had a way of bulldozing through every obstacle. That being the case, she would need some help dealing with Director Lumas Verret.

He climbed up the cliff, sat on a large boulder, and dropped his backpack to the ground. He dug the satellite phone out and clicked on the number for Oakley's father, Marcel Laveau.

It rang twice before Marcel picked up.

"It's Raptor." Without waiting for a response, he continued in case their connection didn't hold. "Oakley has found a boat and is heading to Asperten. She may need you."

"She ... What?"

"She's headed for Asperten."

A long silence hung on the line.

Raptor could hear breathing, but the man said nothing. "Any idea why she's going there?"

Marcel didn't answer right away. After several seconds, he said, "I'm not sure."

That was a lie. It was in the tone of his voice. Marcel knew something about this impulsive decision of hers. A decision that seemed odd considering what Kaleo had told Raptor—it was based on a dream about her mother who died many years ago. Why would Oakley want to find out about her mother's work now? It could have something to do with Adler Calais.

"Maybe she'll go into hiding," Marcel said.

Sounded like Marcel didn't believe his own words. Besides, Oakley wouldn't make it on the run unless she cut ties with Marcel and her brother, Eric. That was something she wouldn't do. "If she's going to Asperten, she would probably get there in a few days, depending on the speed of their boat."

"I'm not supposed to be at the research lab this week, but I'll check in to see if she shows up." Despite Marcel's effort to keep his words casual, the underlying hardness to his voice divulged his true feelings.

Raptor tightened his jaw. "Marcel, tell me what's going on."

Another long, painful silence that left him questioning their friendship. They had met ten years ago when Marcel first visited the Lazy Lizard to ask for alligator eggs as part of his research on the chemical reactions involved in reptile reproduction. When Raptor found out that Asperten was involved in cloning dinosaur DNA, he'd requested regular updates from Marcel on the progress.

For years, Marcel told him very little about the research. But then some species of dinosaurs were released on the mainland. The US government took steps to contain them by creating Extinction Island. At that time, the FBI came to Asperten in search of a dinosaur behaviorist. Marcel recommended Raptor for the job.

Over the phone, Marcel breathed out a low reply. "You're better off not knowing, my friend. And if you need to know, it should come from Oakley."

He had a point there. Except Raptor couldn't ask her. It was like an odd game of pin the tail on the donkey where he was randomly searching for something he couldn't identify. "I'll try to keep her disappearance quiet. But I can only do so much. Soon enough, the government will come after her."

"Thank you."

He disconnected the call and stared out to sea. He raised the phone to his ear again to call Calista but then thought better of it. His perceptive girlfriend would pick up on his nerves and refuse to let it go until he told her all his problems. He couldn't afford to lie to her, and he certainly couldn't tell her the truth. As much as she liked Oakley, she would beg him not to throw his future away ... their future.

What was Calista doing now? Probably working on some legal case to help endangered tree frogs or to save the riparian zone for the hippos in Africa. It was inspired work because not many people had the patience to fight through the legal systems in foreign countries.

Calista always did the right thing, even when the right thing was exceedingly hard. Hopefully, she would admire the same quality in him if this situation with Oakley went south. He would jeopardize his job, Calista, and all he'd worked for with his business to keep Oakley safe. But it would make the sacrifice easier if he understood why she'd left.

THE SCREEN MOUNTED on the wall next to Lumas's simple wooden desk caught his attention. The camera covering the three sea-level loading bays had picked up movement. Except for his private helicopter landing pad on the roof, the bays with their short docks were the only way in or out of the building. The area should be deserted since all of the employees who were staying on-site for the week had arrived this morning.

In the second loading bay, Auburn stood against the railing, her loose, dark hair swaying in the wind coming from the open roll-top door. A red warning light brightened the control room, signaling an approaching watercraft.

Auburn's vigil meant it had to be Adler. But how had he gotten back so soon?

Lumas shook his head and rose to make his way to the landing area. He needed a word with Adler.

By the time he reached the docking bay, Auburn had captured Adler in a forceful kiss. As usual, Adler happily took whatever she was willing to give.

A protective emotion ballooned in Lumas's chest. It startled him, stopping his hesitant steps. He'd frowned on their relationship from the beginning. They were both too integral to the company to risk a bad breakup, but every time he debated her poor choice of a boyfriend with her, she shut down and refused to work in the lab. In the interest of his goals, Lumas had capitulated.

"Thanks for sending the helicopter," Adler said as he pulled away from the kiss.

Strange. Lumas hadn't noticed any unusual helicopter activity. The chopper came and went every day to bring mail with only one pilot aboard. Desperate to speed up Adler's return, Auburn must have sent the pilot to pick him up and drop him off at a nearby port. Sneaky of her.

She flung her hair over her shoulder in an effort to keep it out of her face. "It's wonderful to see you, but maybe you should leave again. Dad is still angry."

He waited for Adler to say something romantic, like "I couldn't leave you." Instead, he merely shrugged.

The sunset silhouetted the pair against the wide

opening from the roll-top door. Lumas took a step back and surveyed him anew. The lack of emotion came genetically from Adler's biological father. Odd how he hadn't taken on any of Penna's maternal characteristics. She was a strong woman, but not hard or cold.

Despite their threadbare emotional ties, Adler returned here because after Penna abandoned them, Lumas was the only parent he had left. Stepping forward again, Lumas cleared his throat.

Auburn jumped and had the good sense to look guilty. She opened her mouth to speak.

He put a hand up to stop her. In a firm voice to dispel any argument, he said, "Adler and I need to talk."

She merely nodded and left, probably grateful to be spared a lecture.

He pointed to a long bench and gestured for Adler to sit. Lumas remained standing, enjoying the rare opportunity to tower over the taller man. He paced along the catwalk in front of Adler. "Why would you disobey my orders?"

For a brief moment, Adler's eyebrows lifted as if to question when he'd done so. Under a stern glare, he relented. "She isn't who you think she is."

"Meaning?"

"She's uncontrollable. Not like Auburn."

"So you thought you'd get rid of her when I wasn't looking." The flames of his anger still burned white hot. Oakley had been kidnapped by one of the gang members and blindfolded. When Adler thought Lumas couldn't see, he made his move to kill her.

Lumas had to take a stand here to convince Adler not to act on his own again. "Tell me why I shouldn't end your life for such treachery."

A jaunty tilt of Adler's head. "Because Auburn is in love with me."

He leaned down and let out an undignified snort. "A better reason."

Adler licked his lips before swallowing hard. "Because Oakley doesn't know where Mom, I mean, Penna is. I can continue to look for her on the island. Please, let me find her for you?"

The question hung in the air between them. Silence dragged on as he let Adler stew in a morass of fear. Adler had already done months of searching on the island with no success. Sending Oakley there to draw Penna out had been a desperate effort to find the woman who'd put all this in motion.

"I can still be useful to you."

"Useful is useless when you can't be trusted."

Finally, Adler seemed to grasp the point. His shoulders slumped, and his head bowed a fraction. "I'll do anything to prove I'm trustworthy."

Lumas squatted before him to look him in the eye. "Then, I've got another mission for you."

"Anything."

"Marcel might be a problem." Clasping his hands on

his knees, he held Adler's steely gaze. "I need you to kidnap Eric Laveau."

Adler took another long swallow. Confusion knotted his brow, but he nodded soberly. Kidnapping a child would not be difficult for him. He had the emotional lethargy necessary to do what others could not.

"You leave in an hour. This time, you will receive an eye implant so I can be sure the job is done well."

A hitching breath slipped out before Adler controlled his reaction. Lumas gave a small smile. Adler hated any type of medical procedure, thereby compounding the punishment.

Lumas stared at him flatly, awaiting his response.

Finally, Adler gave a slow nod. "Of course."

Lumas stood and crossed his arms over his chest. Adler had better show complete obedience this time. Otherwise, he'd consider him as one more failed experiment.

CHAPTER SEVEN

THE GENTLE HUM of the electric motor rose just above the crash of breaking waves across the bow of the boat. Oakley shifted on her seat as the arc of the sun caught up with her. Yesterday, she'd spent too much time behind the captain's wheel in her tank top enjoying the abundant sunshine. Now, even with Neve's homemade sunscreen, her meager base tan couldn't protect her from getting a sunburn on her shoulders.

Perhaps she should ask Cane if she could drive the boat more during the evening hours. As it was, on both nights, she'd slept for six hours and helped steer for four so Cane could get some sleep. Without fail, a couple of hours before dawn, the engine would stall because they'd exhausted the charge from the solar panels.

This morning, their progress seemed agonizingly slow, and yet Cane said they were making good time. The vast distance and unchanging scenery were never-ending. And then, there was the question of what they'd do when they arrived.

There were really only two options: knock on the door or break in. Knocking seemed unwise. Someone in that building had directed Adler to kill her best friend to frame Oakley in order to send her to Extinction Island. They wouldn't likely welcome her with open arms and volunteer information.

That left breaking in. But how?

She closed her eyes and pictured the building as it appeared in her dream. Perhaps she could climb onto a catwalk and find a door to break into. Or maybe there was a service entrance down below. She'd just have to wait and see ... and hope they didn't have a lot of security to keep people out. The building was in the middle of the ocean after all. Break-ins wouldn't be much of a concern.

She took a long breath and let the air ease out of her lungs. What if they tried to break in and were caught? Anyone who ran her fingerprints would find out she'd escaped from Extinction Island. Then she'd be executed, and Cane would be charged as an accomplice.

Dashing off to the research lab was a reckless thing to do. But, like all the other times when doubt surfaced, the image of her mother crystallized in her mind. In the beginning of the dream, her mother stood inside the building and swept her arm down a hallway, insisting she enter it. What was down that hallway?

She dropped to the floor for the fifth time to check the nautical chart. Once again, she confirmed the heading, then stood next to Cane to check the compass on the boat's dashboard. They were right on target, moving ever nearer to the passageway leading to the Gulf between the Yucatan Peninsula and Cuba.

"We must have picked up the Caribbean current," Cane said in a gravelly voice. "It may help shave off a couple of hours. I think we'll make it there late tomorrow."

"Great." Her voice sounded just as rough, probably due to lack of water and lack of use. They were drinking as little as possible to conserve the last of their three jugs of water. Plus, they hadn't spoken much since leaving Extinction Island. She had a lot on her mind and in typical Cane fashion, he'd given her space to process.

She left the bow and returned to the shelter of the roof. Cane followed her, leaving the boat on autopilot for a few minutes. His skin couldn't handle much more sun than hers. She gave him the sunscreen—a blend of aloe vera and avocado oil—and looked away while he stripped off his T-shirt and slathered it over his chest and stomach. Not only would it protect his exposed skin, but it would ease the burn he'd suffered on the first day when he'd taken his shirt off for a few hours.

Kaleo's Hawaiian coloring would have fared much better out here, but he couldn't have left the island because of the FBI tracker imbedded in his arm. His crime had cost the lives of two people, and he would spend the rest of his life paying for it. There was justice in that, if one didn't look at how much he'd changed since then.

She pushed down the longing. Kaleo wasn't here. Cane was, and he'd left his ministry to come with her.

"Did you always know you wanted to be a pastor?" she asked.

He cocked his head. His rough-cut strawberry-blond hair draped over one eye. "No. I wanted to be a veterinarian."

"Seriously?"

"I know, right? Funny, where I ended up. Plenty of animals to help. When they aren't trying to eat me." He stared off at the calm water, squinting at the reflection from the sun. "We didn't have any pets because my mom was allergic, so I chased after every animal I could find. Geckos were my favorite."

"A lizard lover. I knew there was a reason I liked you."

He laughed. "Actually, they were my favorite because they were easier to catch than a squirrel or a stray cat."

He had a point. Geckos freeze when confronted. As a kid, she used to slowly creep up on them, then grab them just before they bolted. "Not nearly as cuddly, though."

"True." He pulled his shirt back on before leaning on the railing. "I didn't think of ministry until much later."

"Why?"

A slight frown dipped his eyebrows. "Simply put, I needed forgiveness, and that pushed me into the arms of God."

The somber way he said the word *forgiveness* brought to mind the tenderness of a cherished treasure. She could try to press him, to find out what he'd done to need such forgiveness, but he shook his head and turned his gaze to the floor of the boat. Although it went against her nature, she left the unanswered questions alone. The least she could do was offer him the same space he gave her.

She picked up their last jug of water and shook it, listening to it slosh. A little more than half full. With a sigh, she put the jug down unopened. Since they'd started rationing, she'd grown accustomed to constant thirst. With their careful planning, the water would run out just as they arrived at the research lab. By that time, she might need luck more than water.

FROM HIS AWKWARD position laying on his belly on the cot, Chubs reached for a small chunk of wood and tossed it toward the doorway. He aimed for the three-foot-high stack of branches meant to keep small animals from coming in the opening. He missed, instead hitting the far wall. He picked up another piece and tried again. What else was there to do after all?

Perhaps he should try to sit up today. He'd spend most of the last two days flat on his stomach, waiting for his back to heal. His wound still ached, and now his neck felt permanently crimped in the shape of a twisty straw.

Using tiny movements, he shifted his torso until he rested on one elbow. No searing pain, just a dull ache in his lower back. He slowly swiveled his legs around, sitting up as he did. Although Neve had sewed him up tight, the flesh still felt raw. He stretched, careful to avoid the affected muscles.

Afterward, he pressed his upper back into the wall, leaving his lower back free. Red Grizzly was one nasty female that he would avoid at all costs. At least, he assumed Red Grizzly was a female since the creature was so large. In most dinosaur species, the largest animals were female. Not like humans.

Not like Neve. She was small boned and graceful, similar to Teresa, although their coloring was completely different. Teresa had seemed kind and attentive at first as well. She'd shown interest in him when no one else had. His parents had checked out of his life in favor of pursuing their own. They had always said they cared, but they hadn't meant it. "We love you, Leo, but ... We'd like to come to your football games, but ... We wish we could help with your science project, but ..." There was always a *but* that resulted in them ditching him. Love with no action wasn't love at all.

When he'd met Teresa, she'd made time for him, told him crazy stories about the kids in her classes and treated him like an adult. Their special time together was an oasis of love in his pointless life. She said they were meant to find each other, that she'd never leave him. Then her family got suspicious.

A month later, her husband began asking around school, causing her to break off their relationship. The anger and betrayal had consumed him so much that each muscle fiber vibrated with the need to lash out and destroy. So, he bought a gun from a guy off the street.

He smacked his head against the wall of the shack and cringed at the pain. Come to think of it, maybe he should have killed her family instead of her. That way, there would have been no distractions to keep them apart. But it was impossible to do it over again. Teresa was dead and buried.

Neve was alive and right here on the island.

Movement at the door drew his attention. Neve waved as she lithely swung her leg up to climb over the dam of wood at the door. Her visits were the best part of his day, especially since he couldn't do anything else except sit here, recover, and plan.

Now it was time to put one of his plans into action. He raised his eyebrows and drew his arms into his body to simulate fear. "I'm so glad you're here. It was a long night."

She stopped in her tracks, her expression alarmed. "Your stitches?"

"No, worse. A *Baryonyx*."

Neve sucked in a shallow breath. His mention of the thirty-foot-long predator had achieved the desired reaction.

"Maybe it could smell the blood. It stuck its long, narrow snout in here and rooted around. Then, it tried to bite me."

Her gaze darted to the debris field cluttering the dirt floor.

"I had to throw stuff at it to keep it away."

Her mouth dropped open, and her lovely dark eyes went wide with compassion.

"I don't feel safe here." He rounded his own eyes into his classic puppy dog look. "I was so scared."

She played with the ends of her ebony hair, hesitating. Then, she adjusted the barrette that held the hair off her face.

Perhaps he'd stretched it a little too far, but he was committed. "Can you take me to the place where you stay? It's safe there, right?"

The sweet scent of ginger lily enveloped him as she came to the edge of his cot. "Let me check your bandage."

He complied by laying on his belly once again. He rested his face sideways to keep peering up at her. "You didn't answer my question."

"Yes, it's safe where I live." Her fingers stripped off the tape, followed by the cloth. "I don't think I can take you there, though."

"Why not?" He raised his head a few inches off the cot. "You can trust me. I'm not a bad guy."

After a long pause, she answered while smearing an unknown cream on his wounds. "Because it's not just my home."

So, there were more people like her. More women? Could he be that lucky? It stood to reason a gentle person like Neve would only feel comfortable with others who were as caring as her. "Wouldn't the rest of the people there want me to be safe?"

His line of reasoning threw her. The crease between her brows testified to her indecision. He just had to get her to act on it before Taye came to check on them. Taye would talk her out of this for sure.

"Please, Neve. The dinosaur's teeth bit down inches from my toes."

Still, she hesitated, her concern warring with her fear. He needed to give her a bigger fear.

"If I can't go with you today, then I don't want you to come back here tomorrow." He forced a slight tremor into his hands. "You shouldn't have to see my half-eaten body. That's not how you should remember me."

She reapplied his bandage in silence.

"You've been kind," he tried a different approach. "No one has ever been this concerned about me. You're different from any woman I've met."

Her gaze swung up to meet his, curiosity lighting her eyes.

No doubt about it. He was on the right track. "You make me want to be a better person. If there are others like you, I could learn from them."

Her gaze darted around the room, not settling on anything for several minutes. She was weakening. He only needed to nudge her a bit further.

Shrugging, he let a sigh escape before he spoke. "It's okay. You're right. I don't deserve to be around good people like you."

When she began to gnaw at her bottom lip, he fought to control his smile. He had her.

Time to tip her over the edge. He forced a quaver into his voice. "It's just that ... I have nowhere else to go."

Her face hardened. Had he gone too far? Had she figured him out? But then her firm resolve became clear. She intended to help him no matter the cost.

"I can't carry you there," she said.

The sweet adrenaline rush of victory spread through his veins. He slowly pushed his shoulders off the cot, rolled over, and placed his feet on the dirt. With only a small wince, he stood. "It's okay. I've healed enough to walk as long as we go slowly."

After he put on his tennis shoes, he stood again and leaned on Neve for help in stepping over the branches in the doorway. His back protested at the stretching, but he ignored the pain. He was headed to a safe place alone with a beautiful woman. What more could a guy ask for?

KALEO PUSHED through the last of the tangled trees and broke into the bright sunlight of the open coast. The roar of rushing water filled the air, along with the tang of salt. He spotted Raptor sitting on a massive boulder, staring out at the water. Kaleo moved toward him, but Raptor didn't look over.

"Hey," he said.

Raptor jumped and spun around.

"Sorry. Didn't mean to scare you."

Raptor shook his head. "My fault. I was alone. I forgot to listen closely."

Kaleo didn't bother to tell him how dangerous that was. Raptor knew. Although not many dinosaurs came close to the coast or wandered through exposed areas, some of the other convicts did. Nowhere was truly safe on Extinction Island.

"You've been here since we talked two days ago?" When Raptor hadn't shown up at the compound again, Kaleo had followed the trail here.

"Not sure what else to do."

He sat down on a nearby rock. "You know, I told her not to come back."

Raptor's posture went rigid.

A pulse of guilt raced through Kaleo's gut. "What happens to you if she doesn't?"

Raptor pinned him with an offended stare. "This isn't about me. I would sacrifice to keep her safe. This is about the FBI, specifically Agent Brooks. He's a bloodhound. He'll find her."

Kaleo let the sea breeze blow over them for a minute as the worst-case scenario cemented in his mind. Oakley caught and executed, then Raptor sentenced to Extinction Island for treason. Two lives destroyed for little gain. "You didn't answer my question. I'm guessing you have a life you'd like to go back to."

Raptor's voice came out hoarse. "A girlfriend who is my family. My business. No more or less than what Oakley has already lost."

"One thing I know about her, she wouldn't want you to lose your life."

A long moment passed while Kaleo mulled over their possible options. Raptor didn't move or speak. His gaze stayed firmly fixed on the horizon, hazy pink with the reflection of the setting sun.

Finally, Kaleo blew out a long breath. "I believe we can fix this."

Raptor shot him a side-eyed glance. "Why did she leave?"

The question caught him off guard. "What makes you think I know?"

Raptor raised incredulous eyebrows. Fair point. He wasn't stupid.

Kaleo shifted his gaze to the rocky ground. Telling Raptor about her secret might put him in an even trickier situation. Would he feel compelled to give the information to the FBI? Probably not, if it endangered Oakley. But if she hadn't told him, she must have had her reasons.

Kaleo turned his gaze back to Raptor. The man's entire life was on the line. He deserved to know why. "She needs information on the biological research that is happening or has happened at Asperten."

Raptor ran a hand over his close-cropped hair. "There's something different about her, isn't there?"

He hesitated.

"The tourists' statements always bothered me," Raptor continued as if Kaleo had agreed with him. "The day she jumped into the water to save that boy, the day she lost her fingers, what the tourists said didn't make sense. The gator came after her, she pushed her hand out, screamed, and then the gator rolled over dead. Its first bite was its last bite. I thought the witnesses had been in the sun for too long or that the trauma had messed with their minds."

Kaleo shifted on the rock. Raptor was almost there. Better to let him come to it himself.

"And there's no way she should have survived her encounter with Daric. He was a ruthless serial killer. He chases her into the deserted jungle, and *he* ends up dead. That makes her either the luckiest woman on the planet or a woman who can defend herself."

Raptor glared at Kaleo, almost as if he were angry that Kaleo knew something he didn't. The sun dipped toward the water, coating them in shadows. But Raptor's piercing eyes didn't waver.

"Tell me," he demanded.

Kaleo answered slowly. "She can generate electricity with her hands."

Raptor went silent for several moments. Finally, he spoke flatly. "If I were her, I'd want answers too."

Kaleo gave him a wry smile. "So, let's work the problem. How are they going to tag her again?"

"A doctor from the mainland is on the way to perform the procedure, actually an acquaintance of my girlfriend."

"Can't we tag somebody or something else?"

"I don't think the doctor will be a problem, even though we've never met." Raptor shook his head. "The real issue is that the FBI agent accompanying the doctor will have a picture of Oakley."

That complicated matters. He rubbed at the stubble growing on his chin. "Any idea when they might get here?"

"Maybe as soon as tomorrow."

"Will they come in at the usual landing area?"

"Yes." Raptor gave a sad nod. "It's my job to give them protection and bring them to Oakley."

"What if I gave them protection?" Kaleo put an arm around Raptor's shoulders. A plan was forming, and they had just enough time to talk over the particulars. "Some very isolated protection."

CHAPTER EIGHT

THE ASPERTEN INTERNATIONAL RESEARCH LABORATORY rose from the slate blue water as a metal behemoth. Scaffold walkways wound up the smooth gray walls in layers, dusted with pink by the setting sun. Aircraft warning lights flashed on the highest antennas of the building, but they were green instead of the usual red, which had allowed Oakley and Cane to see the facility from quite a distance out.

Oakley stretched her neck, stiff from three nights of sleeping on the floor of the boat, and peered at the structure. The building sat in the middle of the ocean like a deep-sea drilling operation, except it rested at sea level with no supporting pillars visible. The first steel walkway sat five feet above sea level and wrapped around the south side of the building. On the north side, steel roll-top doors forced the walkway higher on the structure. Distance and the fading light obscured the rest of the building in shadows.

As their boat came within five hundred yards, Cane cut the engine.

"Do you have any binoculars?" she asked.

Cane reached into a cubicle near the steering wheel and handed her a pair. She trained them on the lab, searching for signs of security. No obvious cameras. No exterior guards. Other than a few lights inside small windows, there were no signs of life at all.

Some scientists, like her father, stayed on-site for up to a week at a time, but perhaps they rarely ventured outside. There wasn't much to see out here anyway except the vast ocean.

Was her father working in there now? She had no way to know. Not that it mattered. On his last visit to the island, he'd refused to answer her questions about Asperten. He said he preferred to let the past rest.

She placed the binoculars in Cane's hand and let him take a look.

He adjusted the focus. "If they have cameras, we'd be spotted on the scaffolding."

"What about those huge doors?"

"They look like loading doors. Could be noisy."

"I'm guessing there aren't many people to hear down in the bottom of the building." As the sun sank farther toward the horizon, several floodlights switched on to illuminate the catwalks. "It's also a place without much lighting."

The closest catwalk had a support pole that blocked most of the light from spilling onto the first two loading doors. It seemed like the perfect spot to go in unseen.

Cane put the binoculars away, then turned to her, his green eyes sparkling in the waning light. "Are you ready?"

"I should be asking you. You're not a criminal yet."

He gave a rueful smile. "How little you know about me."

Well, he wasn't a convicted criminal anyway. She fought the urge to press him on the specifics. His stony face meant he wouldn't answer.

"Let's go take a look at those doors," she said.

He nodded but didn't move. "We should wait until the middle of the night. Less chance of people roaming the halls."

She let out a sigh. "You're right."

He pushed the button to engage the solar engine. "We can't anchor. It's anywhere from a couple hundred to a thousand feet deep here. I'll take us north so we can drift south for a while and not use the engine. That should get us to midnight."

"Sounds like a plan." Or at least the best facsimile of a plan they could develop.

As they pulled away from the building, he asked, "What are you hoping to find in there?"

The answer was as simple as needing information about her mother and as complicated as needing to know if evil had been encoded into her DNA. Certainly, there were degrees of evil, weren't there? She wasn't as evil as

Daric, the serial killer whom she'd killed in self-defense, but she had killed people with her bare hands.

She looked at him. "I'm hoping to find the truth."

He lifted a reddish-blond eyebrow. "Adler said the person who created you ... I mean, us ... went into hiding long ago."

"I don't trust Adler."

"That makes two of us. But did it occur to you that you also shouldn't trust anyone in that lab?"

Of course it had. Her stomach rolled over with nerves. "Don't you want to know about your mother?"

He dropped his gaze to the instrument panel. "I want to know about my mother more than anything. But something inside me is saying this is a mistake."

She placed a hand on his arm. "But everything inside of me is telling me I have to do this."

His sea-green orbs were several shades lighter than the ocean around them, but they seemed much deeper. He stared into her eyes, searching, probing her motives until she felt raw and exposed before him. Still, she refused to look away. While she respected his opinion and sensed the waves of trepidation coming off him, she couldn't shake her own conviction.

After several minutes, he gave her a forced smile. It had come down to his will or hers, and again he'd let her make the ultimate decision. Was it because he cared about her, or was there a part of him that wanted answers too? Either way, they would find out soon. She took his hand and squeezed it gratefully.

KALEO KNELT behind a large bush on the spongy ground next to Taye, holding his spear at the ready. They'd waited most of the day for the arrival of the transport boat and had heard the horn blast just in time to get in position. The captain of the boat must have been desperate to drop off his passengers since most of them tried not to dock near sunset. With the waning sunlight, shadows slipped through the jungle foliage. Soon, the twilight predators would be prowling.

Tension coiled in his gut. They needed to put their plan into action before they became a hungry carnivore's next meal.

As a metal ramp lowered from the small boat to the concrete landing pad, he glanced at Taye, who gave a quick nod. He crept closer, pausing at the last leafy bush on the edge of the tree line.

A man dressed in khaki pants and a green polo shirt stepped confidently down the ramp. His shiny bald head and frown lines marked him as being in his late forties to early fifties. His tense demeanor, along with the pistol attached to one side of his belt and the Taser on the other identified him as an FBI agent. The man glanced around several times before gesturing for someone else to join him.

An attractive woman with chin-length curly blond hair and impeccable makeup stepped from the boat. She wore jeans and a pale-pink, long-sleeved T-shirt. At the end of the ramp, she huddled warily behind the agent. Raptor hadn't mentioned the doctor would be a woman.

Both of them seemed expectant and apprehensive. They had planned to meet Raptor who would provide shelter and security. Would they go it alone if he didn't show?

On the boat, a lone sentry leaned against the upper level with his gun pointed toward the jungle. The prison boat would have dropped the people off and left within minutes. Apparently, the officers on the transport boat felt more responsible for their passengers.

Several tense minutes ticked by. Kaleo and Taye couldn't very well take the agent and the doctor by force in full view of the guard. Time for an adjustment to the plan. He held up a fist to tell Taye to stay put.

After smoothing down his T-shirt and brushing off his jeans to look less like a convict, he stepped onto the concrete landing pad, using his spear as a walking stick. Hopefully, these two would attribute his casual clothes to a need for practical jungle attire.

He pasted on an arrogant smile. The only way this ruse worked was if the agent hadn't seen a picture of Raptor.

With a subtle eye on the agent's weapons, he strode up and said in a confident voice, "FBI Agent Fischer and Dr. Anderson, I presume?"

Both of them nodded.

According to Raptor, Agent Jack Fischer had twenty years at the FBI and was married with no children. Dr.

Anderson was a young single doctor who'd been given a huge amount of hazard pay for this duty, and who also happened to be an acquaintance of Raptor's girlfriend.

Agent Fischer narrowed his sparse eyebrows. "Mr. Greene?"

His smile faltered. Raptor hadn't divulged his last name. It could be a trick, but the agent didn't come across as deceptive. He went with it. "Yes. Call me Raptor. Everyone here does."

"Couldn't have picked a better nickname in a place like this." The agent stuck out his hand.

"Nice to meet you." He shook it, then turned to the woman and held his hand out. "I guess that makes you Dr. Anderson."

"Yes, I'm Wells Anderson." As she released him from a firm handshake, she eyed the spear in his other hand.

He stuck the weapon in the crook of his arm. "Don't mind this. It's protection from small dinosaurs and convicts. I try not to bring my Glock out here. If a beast gets me, a different kind of beast will get my gun." He'd never seen Raptor with a gun, so it sounded plausible enough.

Agent Fischer ran his gaze up and down Kaleo's clothes. Skepticism tugged on his mouth.

He needed to get them out of here before Fischer acted on that gut instinct. "Can we get going? I'd like to get to the shelter. Night predators and all."

Several seconds of tense silence ticked by. Kaleo stood

his ground, running his fingers absently along the shaft of the spear.

Finally, Fischer looked up at the gun-toting man above and gave a wave. "Thanks for the lift. Be back in three days to pick us up, or sooner if we call."

Kaleo made a mental note to confiscate the agent's satellite phone when they had control of the pair. He stepped into the trees, guiding them to the right of Taye's hiding spot. "This way, please."

He led them thirty yards from the boat—far enough that the sentry wouldn't hear a cry—before he gave a low whistle. It was the signal for Taye to attack.

Nothing happened.

He had no choice, except to keep walking. Dr. Anderson trailed behind him with Agent Fischer behind her. A few minutes later, he gave another low whistle, keeping it as nonchalant as he could. Much more, and he'd arouse the agent's suspicions again.

Still, he heard nothing.

Had Taye given up and gone back to the compound? Just then, a loud thump came from the end of their procession.

He whipped his head around in time to see Agent Fischer pull out his gun and attempt to fire from his knees.

Taye batted the weapon aside with the handle of his spear, then cracked Fischer on the back of the head. He scooped the gun from the ground.

Dr. Anderson tried to run, but Kaleo grabbed her by the arms. He swung her around and addressed the agent in a menacing tone. "If you listen and follow instructions, you'll stay alive."

A grunt came from Agent Fischer. "You're convicts, aren't you?"

"Don't worry. We only want a ransom. You'll be released after Raptor pays our price." He held Dr. Anderson by the wrists. "Until then, I expect no problems. Problems will get you both killed. Understood?"

Fischer merely grunted a second time. Taye took off the Taser and stuffed it in his backpack with the gun.

Dr. Anderson kicked backward at Kaleo. He easily sidestepped her attempt.

"You can't do this," she exclaimed. "The FBI will miss us if we disappear."

He almost applauded her defiance. "By the time they miss you, we will have this all worked out."

With rope from Taye's pack, they tied the hands of their captives, leaving their feet free to walk. When they were secure, Kaleo looped the rope around the bindings, using the long lead as a leash, which he wrapped around his wrist. Finally, he confiscated their backpacks, including the satellite phone.

"Now what?" Taye whispered.

Kaleo caught his meaning. The deception had taken too long. Deep shadows obscured the jungle around them. Taye's dark skin blended perfectly with the dusk. Kaleo could only see the whites of his darting eyes, but it was enough for a sliver of understanding to pass between them. They couldn't make it safely to the cave tonight.

"The vine keeper?"

Taye nodded and allowed him to take the lead.

"What's that?" Dr. Anderson asked. "Where are we going?"

He bent down to whisper in her ear again. "For your own safety, you're going to want to shut your mouth. Predators have excellent hearing. Plus, you're risking his life." He indicated Agent Fischer. "He'll be the first man the predators pick out, what with his shiny white head and all."

Her terrified expression was genuine. Hopefully, she understood that one wrong move could get them all killed.

The vine keeper was located a mile uphill from the landing dock. Kaleo traveled slowly and cautiously. Fischer was obviously trained in stealth. Dr. Anderson, however, was not.

Kaleo constantly shifted his head, trying to catch the sound of hunting predators in between Dr. Anderson's crunching footsteps. He trusted Taye to do the same from behind.

When they were almost to the shelter, he halted them with a raised hand. Instinct had pricked him, raising goose bumps on his skin.

For some reason, his attention stayed riveted on the head of a ravine twenty yards away. No sounds came from the area, but murky shapes waved in the dim moonlight. Was it the wind rustling the leaves? Or something more lethal?

The moon retreated behind the clouds. He couldn't

make out any distinct forms ahead, just a pattern of movement.

He motioned for everyone to stay put, and then he crept forward a few yards.

A sniffing huff rushed through the silence. He still couldn't see anything, but by the sound of it, a big animal was moving about ten yards away. They would have to skirt around the area to get to their hiding place.

He lifted one foot to step back. The moon peeked out from the clouds, illuminating the massive head of a *Carnotaurus*.

He froze midstep. If he could see the creature, then it could see him.

The *Carnotaurus* dipped its head and bit into something on the ground. Seconds later, it lifted its head.

Kaleo's stomach shuddered as he identified the blue and red pattern of material trapped between the creature's teeth. It was the blanket he'd used when he faked Oakley's death. It was covered in a mixture of blood—his and Oakley's.

As if the creature had instantly tracked his scent, it peered through the trees. A white-hot column of fire exploded from its mouth.

Kaleo stumbled back as heat smothered him. What kind of dinosaur could do that? Running backward, he kept an eye on the creature while returning to the others.

A shaky whisper came from Dr. Anderson. "Is that a demon or a dragon?"

Dragon Demon. Demon Dragon. Whatever. He'd

never seen a fire breather before, but no sense hanging around for another demonstration.

The *Carnotaurus* fixed its gaze on them, its fierce eyes encased in rings of scales.

"Run!" he yelled.

He sprinted into the jungle, running next to Agent Fischer but trying to keep an eye out for the woman. With a flick of his wrist, Kaleo whipped a knife out of his pocket and sliced the rope that bound the man's hands. He glanced back. Taye was doing the same for Dr. Anderson. All of them deserved a chance to escape.

"Follow me!" Kaleo pulled out in front of the group.

At that moment, the two newcomers were much more afraid of the *Carnotaurus* than they had been of Kaleo and Taye. Both obediently fell in step.

Fortunately, the moon stayed out in the open during their flight. They dodged fallen logs, thorny bushes, and hanging branches as they ran.

A hissing roar sounded behind them. Heat melted over his exposed arms and neck, forcing him to pick up the pace. He shot a glance over his shoulder again. Long tongues of flames licked the air behind Fischer, the last man in line.

Up ahead, the forest opened onto a two-foot-wide path. Possibly made by convicts, possibly a game trail. Either way, it would be easier going. He veered toward the path.

At the last second, he caught a glimpse of a tree to the left. He registered the symbol carved on the bark and instantly switched directions. This symbol—a large X enclosed in splayed out lines—indicated a trap involving poison. Definitely not worth the risk. "Not that way!"

The *Carnotaurus* rushed at them, splitting the group apart. Agent Fischer ignored his warning and jetted down the path toward the trap.

Dr. Anderson seemed ready to follow. Kaleo dropped his spear, then wrapped his arms around her waist and dragged her behind a large tree, covering her scream in his T-shirt. The *Carnotaurus* had already zeroed-in on the agent, his intense flight further triggering its prey drive.

Seconds later, a short cry came from down the path.

Dr. Anderson whimpered. Of course, she wasn't used to survival situations. Kaleo exchanged a resigned look with Taye.

There was nothing they could do for the man. Fischer had probably been struck by a poisonous arrow and had mere minutes to live. Unfortunately, those would be agonizing minutes since the *Carnotaurus* wouldn't give up. Perhaps if the dinosaur ate his poisoned flesh, it would also die.

"Is he ..." Dr. Anderson's voice was muffled by his shirt.

"Dead? Hopefully, by now he is."

Kaleo released Dr. Anderson and forced air through his nose and mouth. Another cry, this one an excruciating scream, tore through the air. Apparently, the man wasn't dead yet, but he wouldn't survive much longer.

"This way." Kaleo grabbed his spear and guided Dr.

Anderson away from the path and toward the vine keeper that sat a hundred yards away. Too close to the kill site for comfort, but the *Carnotaurus* wouldn't need to eat again until tomorrow.

They reached the vine keeper just as a mighty roar came from the direction where they had been. He stripped back the camouflaged door, made of small tree trunks draped with vines, and ushered Dr. Anderson and Taye inside.

Before entering, he set the early warning system, a wire connected to a clanging bell. The obnoxious noise usually drove small dinosaurs away. But not the big ones.

The three of them squeezed into the small sanctuary meant for one. He and Taye instinctively sat back-to-back, bracing each other. Dr. Anderson sat on the other side of the lone support pole, trembling. Her arms brushed against the vines, making a faint rustling noise. She jumped at every sound.

Kaleo grabbed her and held her still. Intermittent thumps were coming their way. The ground literally vibrated with each footfall.

When he pulled his hands away from her, he put a finger to his lips, telling her to stay quiet. He retrieved his spear, holding it at an angle because the space was too narrow to lift it straight up.

The thumping drew closer, a consistent pounding akin to a heartbeat, but completely out of sync with his own erratic heart. The bell clanged as the dinosaur broke the trip wire.

Dr. Anderson's eyes grew wider, and her mouth dropped open. Taye covered her mouth with his hand. Kaleo shook his head in warning. *Don't make a sound.*

The bell didn't deter the animal. The pounding steps stopped right outside their enclosure. No doubt the dinosaur had tracked them, possibly straight from their trail where they'd split up. But it shouldn't be hungry. Perhaps it locked on to his scent from the blanket and was just investigating them?

One wall of the vine keeper shuddered. It was meant as a shelter, not a bunker. Under a full assault, the tightly packed trunks held together by wire would collapse.

The dinosaur sniffed right outside Kaleo's portion of the enclosure. Was it standing on the other side of the wall with its horns drawn together in confusion? Maybe it would simply walk away when it didn't sense movement.

The billowing sound of rushing air came through the spaces between the tree trunks, and a draft of heat blasted his skin. The smell of burning leaves nearly choked him.

His gaze darted around the space. None of the trees or vines inside were on fire.

Smoke filled the vine keeper, but the tree above them must have taken the brunt of the flames. He pulled up the bottom of his shirt and put it over his nose and mouth, gesturing for the others to do so as well. Taye let go of Dr. Anderson's mouth, but she didn't make a sound.

They listened to the crackling of the tree burning for several minutes without any other noise. The creature had to be out there still. Why hadn't it gone away? The more smoke that filled the area, the more he agreed the name Demon Dragon fit this creature well.

After what seemed like forever, the crackling noise subsided. Only the trunk was smoldering now. Several more minutes went by.

Finally, stomping strides shook the ground again. It was retreating. Demon Dragon had left them in their hiding place.

He lowered the shirt from his face. The air in the vine keeper was barely breathable, but they couldn't go anywhere else. Too much risk of running into the creature again.

In hopes of sleeping, he let his full weight lean against Taye, who copied his posture. Dr. Anderson wrapped her arms around the support pole and lay her head against the wood, even though she showed no sign of being able to sleep. The adrenaline would likely keep her awake for hours.

Taye drifted off quickly, but sleep wouldn't come for Kaleo either. The image of Agent Fischer running for his life replayed in his mind over and over. When he closed his eyes, the agent's agonized scream ripped through his eardrums. Even though he hadn't directly killed Fischer, that man wouldn't have been at risk if Kaleo hadn't intervened. Just one more body to weigh down his already guilty conscience.

CHAPTER NINE

OAKLEY STARTLED when Cane placed a hand on her shoulder. She hadn't been sleeping—her racing mind and roiling stomach wouldn't let her—but she had been staring at the stars in a daze. She sat up from their makeshift bed, consisting of two blankets on the floor with folded-over life jackets for pillows, and stretched her stiff muscles.

"We floated past the building about half an hour ago." He moved to the captain's chair and turned on the engine. "We still have plenty of solar charge left, so we can approach slowly and quietly."

Cane maneuvered the boat northeast for thirty minutes. As they approached, he didn't speak. Thankfully, he didn't ask her again if she was ready to do this. In the dead of the night with floodlights shining from the lab like the bulging eye of a cyclops, she might have said no.

Smoothly, he guided the boat to the north side of the building and cut the nearly silent motor twenty feet outside one of the large doors. In the weak beam of the nearest floodlight, she stared at the metal door, similar to a garage door, that was partially submerged in the ocean. The outside of the door held no mechanism for opening it.

They could circle around to see if there were more boat docks on the opposite side, but additional boating increased the chances of someone spotting them. Maybe the door had a latch on the bottom? To find out, one of them would have to jump in and swim underwater in the darkness. It should be her since she couldn't drive the boat as skillfully as Cane.

"I'm going in." She stripped off her sweatshirt and her long sleeve T-shirt, leaving on her jeans and a white tank top. Lastly, she removed her hiking boots and socks.

"Take this." Cane held out a flashlight. "It's waterproof."

She grabbed the light, gave him a wave, and jumped into the cold water. The shock of the chill on her sunburned skin stole her breath. As she surfaced, she sucked in the warm, humid air and threw her wet ponytail over her shoulder.

Clutching the flashlight in one fist, she swam to the door and ran her hand over the metal. The surface was slick up to two feet above the water line because of the shifting waves. She tucked the flashlight under her arm and used what little leverage she had to anchor her hands in the crinkles of the door. She shoved with all her might.

The door didn't move.

She slipped the flashlight into the back of her jeans and tried again, kicking against the water to push harder.

Still no movement. Either she wasn't strong enough, or something was preventing the door from opening.

She slid both hands down the wet metal in the center of the door, searching for any obstructions. Nothing.

She did the same for the left side with the same results. But on the right, just below the waterline, she discovered a small circular protrusion. She probed it with her fingers for several seconds before ducking underwater to get a look with the flashlight.

Her heart sank.

She swam back to the boat where Cane reached down to pull her up. As she dripped on the floor, she gave him her assessment. "It has a key lock embedded in the bottom."

"And here I left my picklock set at home," he replied sarcastically.

Normally, she encouraged his sarcastic side. This time, she frowned at him while she worked the problem. "It must unlock from the inside automatically because they wouldn't go underwater with a key every time a supply boat arrived. If I can break it, I can probably swing the door up."

"Break it with what?"

"I don't know." Their supplies were mostly food, water, flotation devices, and maps. It wasn't like a boat needed a crowbar. Still, she searched the boat for anything helpful and came up with nothing.

She slumped onto the bench seat in defeat. Then, it hit her. The automatic locking mechanism would be electronically driven, at least on the other side of the door. Maybe they unlocked it via Wi-Fi or maybe with a button inside. Either way, she could probably short-circuit it.

But the idea had one major flaw. The previous times that she'd used her electricity underwater, she'd burned herself. Water caused her power to disperse in unpredictable directions. Some of it would come back at her.

But what if she could find a way to direct it? Her gaze fell on the container that held the nautical maps. It was a long cylindrical tube wide enough for one of her hands to fit inside. It might direct her power, but then how would she protect the skin on her hands?

Socks! The cotton would act as a buffer against the current. Of course once the sock got wet, it would conduct some electricity, but it had to be better than nothing. She dug through the backpack of clothes they'd brought and pulled out her spare pair. If she cut out the toes, she could slip her fingers through. She fisted the material in her right hand as she sliced them with their only knife.

Cane watched her in confusion. Ignoring him, she stuffed the socks and the knife in her pockets. She wouldn't be able to hold the flashlight; she'd just have to go without. Finally, she held the map tube close to her chest, once again braced for the chilly water, and jumped in.

Holding the map tube awkwardly in one hand, she swam for the door. Once there, she fumbled with putting the sock glove on while treading water and holding the tube under her arm.

When her right hand was covered, she pulled the knife from her pocket, held it in her fingertips, and slid her arm through the map tube. Good thing it wasn't longer because her short arm could barely reach through to the end. She held her other hand in the open air to keep it from transmitting current through the water.

Now for the hard part, controlling the flow. She tried to dredge up memories of her mother attacking her and then Daric attacking her. But her mind kept pushing those memories under. They were too painful.

Eventually, she focused on the only other thing that could bring her emotions bubbling to the surface—Kaleo's kiss. She pictured his eyes, dark with desire, and his tanned, stubbly jaw as his lips neared hers. The heated pressure of those soft lips had melted her heart. She filled in the details of the scene. How she'd run her hands along his strong arms, drawing him closer. How he'd pressed her firmly against his chest, overwhelming her with his restrained power.

Her insides smoldered, and she channeled the heat, pushing it from her core, into her arms, and down to her hands. Her fingertips shot electricity through the handle of the knife. Would it be enough? To be safe, she slid her fingers down to the metal blade, ignoring the slight pain.

The map tube and makeshift glove did their job for the most part. The majority of the electrical force from her right hand was directed at the lock. Her fingertips and palm warmed and ached a bit, but not much electricity arced back to burn her.

She concentrated on keeping her hand still until her fingers went numb. When she had no more spark left to give, she pulled back. After stuffing the map tube under her arm and the rest of the items in her pockets, she shook her hands out, and then tried the door. It gave a slight creak and slid quietly up to the top. It must have been well oiled.

Inside, dim lighting illuminated another steel catwalk running alongside a metal dock. Definitely a loading dock. The perfect place to park their boat.

She swam back to Cane, and he helped her into the boat. She gave him a triumphant smile while shaking off as much water as she could, since they didn't have a towel.

He drove the boat in and tied it to a steel support pole. They could try to lower the door again, but it was better not to. They might need to make a quick getaway.

She tugged on her shoes and T-shirt before climbing onto the gangway and surveying the large area. Two identical docks sat behind the other rolling doors. Beyond the docks, crates and cargo bags were stacked in neat piles along two walls.

A quick perusal of several stacks revealed mostly food and medical supplies like tubing, needles, and protein enzymes. Pretty typical for a research lab.

She ignored the rest of the containers. The holding area wasn't what they needed to search. The biological lab would likely be on one of the upper levels.

At the end of the storage area, a dark hallway led deeper into the facility. Maybe they would find stairs through there. She turned to grab the flashlight from the boat.

Cane already held it up with a cautious smile. "I still can't believe we're doing this," he whispered.

With a nod, she let him lead. Before entering the hallway, he stopped and shone the flashlight along the corridor for several seconds before proceeding. The area appeared to be deserted.

They passed several doors, all of them locked, and all of them with strange plaques. *Stress Testing. Controlled Mating. Diseased Genes.*

Obviously, some sort of research happened down here, even though glances through the windows didn't reveal labs, rather small empty rooms with plain white walls. She trailed behind him as the hallway widened a few feet.

The doors switched to cages with vertical bars. She peered inside one. It was full of hay, grass, and broken wood.

Just when she was about to move on, scratching noises made her turn back. A scaly head poked out from behind a pile of hay. In the low, blue light coming from the corner of the cage, the animal's white teeth sparkled.

Down the hall, she heard the scrape of claws on wood. A low screech sounded, followed by a deep rumble. The concrete floor vibrated from movement in a cage to their right.

Her heart rate picked up as she walked a few more steps. These cages were full of dinosaurs. A lot of dinosaurs. So, this was where the creatures were created. Had the scientists genetically modified all of them?

No matter how fascinating the answer, she wasn't after a herd of dinosaurs. Her mother—the woman who had helped to create her and tried to destroy her—had lived and worked in these halls. Her research had been a secret. Either Dad had no idea, or he knew and wouldn't talk about it. Perhaps he was afraid that if Oakley knew the truth, she'd never speak to him again.

She passed Cane to continue down the hallway. The stairs to the main level had to be around here somewhere.

The farther she walked, the more her mother's presence seemed to envelop her. In the dark recesses of this place, her mother had made the life and death decisions that resulted in Oakley's genetically altered life.

THE SECURITY ALARM was silent in the rest of the building, but it pulsed an insistent whine in Lumas's private quarters. He bolted upright in bed. Someone had broken in. It had to be Oakley.

After a glance at his personal security monitor, he dressed quickly and made his way to the control room, nodding to the guard on duty who stood alert and ready for action. "I'll need your help with these intruders in a minute. Let's allow them to look around first."

The guard followed him inside, then retreated to the edge of the room. Lumas sat at the computer that controlled the wall of security monitors. He pulled up the feed from the DNA Zoo—Auburn's pet name for her experimental area in the bowels of the building—and smiled at the image on the screen. Oakley peered inside cages as she walked down the hallway, accompanied by the man from the cave.

In hindsight, it might have been better to bring her here in the first place rather than have Adler send her to Extinction Island, but it had been worth the risk to fully awaken her power and possibly determine Penna's whereabouts. Besides, if she hadn't gone to the island, he wouldn't have discovered this mysterious man.

Oakley moved through the DNA Zoo with feline grace, similar to Auburn. What other similarities did they possess? Twenty-five years earlier, it had been Lumas's idea to split Lillian's twins apart. Feisty, dainty, and beautiful, Lillian had been the most gifted geneticist he'd ever met, other than Penna. The two women were a perfect duo, except where Penna was cool under pressure, it didn't take much to destabilize Lillian. Genius and insanity weren't two sides of the same coin, more like adjacent coins that were constantly bumping up against each other.

Splitting the fraternal twins became Lumas's quirky experiment. If Oakley was raised by Lillian and Marcel, would she turn out to be brilliant and emotionally unstable like her mother? And if Auburn was brought up by Lumas and Penna, would she embrace his severe philosophy? Lillian had agreed to the separation, probably because she felt overwhelmed by the prospect of parenting one child with special abilities, much less two. Never one to challenge Lillian's strong personality, Marcel reluctantly went along with her wishes.

For ten years, Penna and Lumas made it work, raising Adler, Auburn, and Elliot, Penna's autistic son from another relationship. But when Adler lost control of his emotions and killed Elliot, it caused Penna to abandon them all.

Oakley and Auburn would soon be reunited as the intellectual, if not literal, progeny of Penna. In her absence, he would make sure they worked together to continue Penna's legacy.

Auburn entered the room, her reflection shining on one of the monitors. She was dressed in sweatpants and a yellow T-shirt. The nagging alarm emanating from his room next door to hers must have woken her. Good thing the other twenty employees who were staying over for the week slept on a middle floor and wouldn't be awakened by the nighttime visit. She placed a hand on his shoulder.

He grasped it. "My dear, I need you to get rid of their boat. We can't let her escape."

"Understood."

A single quiet word. As a scientist, she valued efficiency, even in her communication. She left the room without another comment.

At these times, Auburn reminded him of Penna, but

with one clear difference: he'd raised Auburn to appreciate the beauty of dominance. His weekly lectures on how order and control were necessary for a productive world had shaped her views. No need for genetic predisposition. He'd guided and molded her mind into a block of obedient granite. She fully embraced the ideals he'd taught her. When the time came for him to twist those ideals a few degrees, it wouldn't faze her.

He squinted again at the security monitors. This man was an unknown variable. Their surveillance had revealed his ability to poison with his hands, but where had it come from? Where had *he* come from? For a week, Lumas had searched the old files for any possibility and came up with only one. That information would be his leverage when he spoke to the mystery man.

He stood, smoothed the wrinkles out of his button-down shirt, then changed his mind and tugged it from his jeans. A casual look would seem less threatening.

As he slipped from the control room, he snapped his fingers at the guard. The man knew what to do. He would keep to the shadows until called upon.

They quietly descended the stairs, a genuine smile crossing Lumas's face. Time to reconnect with his long-lost experiment, waiting for him in the DNA Zoo.

CHAPTER TEN

HALFWAY THROUGH THE STRUCTURE, the hall divided into two smaller corridors, branching in opposite directions. Each were dimly lit by gray overhead lights. Each had a curve that hid everything beyond. No stairs were in sight. She hesitated. To follow them both, she and Cane would have to split up.

He made the decision for her. "You go right. I'll go left. Check to the end of the hallway, then meet back here to report what we find." Gallantly, he handed the flashlight to her. "I want to be able to see you."

She took it and mumbled her thanks. As she headed down the hallway, she continuously swung the flashlight back to look at him. He would disappear around his curve before she reached hers.

Animals grunted and groaned from behind metal bars on both sides. Her tennis shoes padded softly on the marble floor. She still scanned every enclosure. Maybe she'd find a storage room with old files down here in the basement of the lab.

A loud screech blasted through the quiet. She jumped back. The nearest dinosaur rammed into the bars of its cage. She gaped at the snarling snout of a *Velociraptor*.

The dinosaur screeched again. It was making too much noise. She moved out of its sight line and hummed softly, hoping to soothe the animals. Surely, the builders had placed a lot of insulation between this floor and the quarters above. Her father stayed here every other week. He wouldn't be able to sleep if he could hear the intermittent cries of dinosaurs. Was he here now? Even if he was, she wouldn't know where to look for him.

So far, this corridor contained more of what they'd already seen. Captive dinosaurs in various-sized cages. Some sleeping, others pouncing on leaves or sticks, most of them sniffing at the bars as if trying to identify the newcomer.

Glancing back, she searched for Cane. He moved slowly, peering into what she assumed were more cages. As if he felt her eyes on him, he twisted to look at her. He gave her a thumbs-up.

She returned the gesture just as a loud clanking sound broke through the air. The noise originated between them. Something moved down from the ceiling, accompanied by the whir of rollers on a metal track.

At the head of the hallway, a large steel door slid down from the ceiling. Cane's silhouette disappeared as the door slammed to the floor. She ran back down the corridor, fighting the urge to scream.

"Cane." She kept her voice controlled and soft.

No answer.

She pushed on the door. It wouldn't budge.

There had to be a mechanism to open it somewhere. She searched around with the flashlight and discovered a keypad. It needed a code. Frustration boiled in her veins.

From the other side of the door, she heard him calling her name, also trying to stay quiet. What had triggered the door?

Behind her, a firm footstep clacked. She spun around.

In the center of the hallway stood a man with dark hair, graying at the temples, and a goatee that had gone entirely gray. He was slender yet muscular for his age, probably in his fifties, with a confident, authoritative posture.

"I wanted to talk to you alone." His silky, smooth voice drifted over her like a cool fog.

She tucked a strand of hair behind her ear. "Who are you?"

A smug smile flashed over his face before he controlled it into something more amiable. "I'm responsible for your life, so I guess that makes me your father."

Bitter bile rose in her throat. "I already have a father."

He clasped his hands behind his back. "Of course. Marcel is a good man. And yes, he donated the original biological material, but he didn't make you who you are."

She took a step back, torn between fascination and fear. Did this man hold the answers she sought?

"My name is Lumas Verret. I'm the director here."

Goose bumps erupted across her arms. He was the man her father had warned her about. Did he mean to say he was the one who manipulated her DNA along with her mother? Oakley examined the hard set of his jaw and the arrogant tilt to his eyebrows. Did this man know why her mother had tried to kill her?

A simple thought broke through her confusion. "How do you know who I am?"

This time his smile was guileless from the outset. "You are one of my most stunning achievements."

She squared her shoulders and took a step toward him.

He didn't step back. "I'm not afraid of you."

So he knew what she could do. But how, when she'd barely figured it out herself? The answer hit her fast—Adler Calais. Her dad had said he was an employee here. Was he more than that? He'd demonstrated no extra abilities to her but said they both had enhanced pheromones.

She pulled her focus back to the man in front of her. Lumas could probably answer all of her questions, if he chose to. Maybe honesty would get him talking. "*I'm afraid of me.*"

He blinked at her for a moment before speaking. She'd caught him off guard. "Would you blame a *T. rex* for killing a *Velociraptor?*"

She shook her head. What was his point?

"They're both predators, Oakley. Given the right motivation, every human being is a predator."

"I don't believe that."

He gestured to her small physique. "With most predators, you'd be at a disadvantage. I've reversed that for you."

Her eyes widened. Did he expect her to thank him for this deadly skill? This power was the whole reason Adler had framed her and sent her to Extinction Island in the first place. On the other hand, her power had saved her from Daric, and before that, from an alligator and a *Velociraptor*. She wouldn't be standing here without it.

She cleared her throat. No matter how she felt about her power, she needed answers in order to move forward. "My mother. What part did she play in this?"

A loud clang came from the door behind her. Cane was trying to break through the steel.

Lumas's eyes focused on the vibrating door. He frowned. "Let's get you settled into a room first. Then, we can talk."

She stood her ground. "Answer me now."

A slow shake of his head. "I'm afraid I have to deal with your friend at the moment."

He pivoted a quarter turn to the left and gave a two-fingered gesture to the shadows of the hallway. A burly man in a black uniform stepped out concealing a device in his hand.

Before she could react, two barbs launched out and connected with her arm. Current seized control of her body. The tingly feeling was both a welcome friend and an evil stepmother. All the muscles on her right side clenched, quickly followed by her left.

She fell to the ground. Her head smacked hard, but that was the only source of pain. Weren't Tasers supposed to be painful? Her breathing continued unabated, her stomach felt fine, and her brain seemed as sharp as ever. She just couldn't move anything from her neck down.

As she lay there, waiting to discover what they would do to her, a weird, logical conundrum surfaced. How could a Taser immobilize her if she was able to conduct high amounts of electricity herself?

CHAPTER ELEVEN

LIFE in the cave for the last two days had been a little slice of heaven. On the zip line trip into the cave, the harness irritated Chubs's injured back, so each day Neve rubbed ointment into his abraded skin. Her lithe fingers stroked his back and eased the ache in his flesh, but her touch created a new ache—a longing deep in his gut, especially for her. If only he could touch her in the same intimate way without fear of her rejection.

The strange aloe smell from the cream mingled with Neve's particular scent of ginger lily, probably from the white blossoms she tended in a pot by the cave's entrance. He sneaked a peek at her over his shoulder. Her silky dark hair was pulled into a ponytail with a few wisps hanging loose. Her cocoa-bean skin was flawless with one small imperfection, two shallow concentration lines creasing her forehead, the only indication that she was about twenty years older than him.

That wasn't an issue. He'd always been into older women. And Neve had several key differences from Teresa. While Neve was reserved and shy, Teresa had pursued him and manipulated him. When he'd been with Teresa, she always had the upper hand, but here, Chubs could take what he wanted ... well, if he could get rid of Taye and Kaleo long enough.

Perhaps he had a chance to succeed now that he finally grasped the magnitude of Kaleo's secret. Neve had let it slip that Oakley lived here. Although she wasn't here at the moment, this was the place where Kaleo had sent her after faking her death. But Kaleo hadn't been protecting just Oakley, he'd been protecting everyone here, with Taye's help.

It was clear why. This cave was as close to paradise as a convict could ask for. Secluded, naturally suited for captivity, and two women to choose from—Neve and Oakley, whenever she returned.

From what he could tell, the people here looked up to a man named Cane, who wasn't a convict. Chubs had seen the man briefly on a few boat landing days, and he was tall but not as strong as Kaleo. Cane also wasn't here now, which meant this place was ripe for a takeover.

He groaned as Neve hit a sore spot. The small testy dinosaur in the corner raised its head and growled. They'd given it a name, Cody, and treated it like a pet. Ridiculous. As far as he was concerned, the only good dinosaur was a dead dinosaur. When he took over, Cody would be the first thing to go.

He should make a move soon, before Cane returned. Why wait for Oakley when Neve was right here? But he needed to be sure of his strategy. In this condition, one of the four men here could incapacitate him with a hit to the back. He wouldn't repeat the same mistakes he'd made at the resort compound. This time, he'd be ruthless.

On the other hand, why should he take over the cave and live in obscurity while Kaleo lived in the best room at the resort? If Kaleo was desperate to protect these people, maybe he'd trade their lives for his position as leader of the gang ... for his own life, actually. Because if Chubs could prove Oakley was alive, the gang would kill Kaleo for faking her death.

Neve patted him on the shoulder to let him know she was finished. He flipped over and picked up his shirt from the floor. He didn't put it on right away. Maybe she'd notice his rock-hard abs and muscular biceps.

When Neve failed to look his way, he put his shirt back on. He'd have to work harder. But eventually, she'd come around.

A commotion sounded near the front room at the mouth of the cave. Neve finished washing her hands and headed to check it out. He followed.

Peering over her head, he saw Taye taking off the zip-line harness. When their gazes met, Taye's dark eyes went almost black.

"What's he doing here?" Taye growled at Neve.

She squared her shoulders. Not such a pushover after all. "It was no longer safe for him at the shack."

Taye didn't respond. He merely tugged on the pulley to return the harness across the chasm.

As Taye turned to Neve, he softened his gaze. "Let's talk alone. I'll explain what's going on."

She nodded, and the two of them whisked past him into the second chamber of the cave, where he had just been alone with her. Having Taye ignore him was worse than the initial anger. The overt slight burned as if Red Grizzly had sunk its claws into his chest instead of his back.

He moved to follow them, halting when a terrified scream came from the mouth of the cave. A woman sped across the zip line, screaming the entire way. Obviously, someone had pushed her. He couldn't blame her. The possibility of a three-hundred-foot drop to the jungle floor could be frightening.

She landed on shaky feet. For no other reason than to touch another woman, he grabbed her hips and helped her unhook the harness.

"Thanks," she said.

"Anytime." Someone else tugged on the other end of the rope, urging him to send the contraption back. He released the harness and engaged the pulley. How many people were visiting today? Not that he was complaining. Adding another woman to the mix could only help his odds. This one had kinky blond hair and dark green eyes.

At the woman's questioning look, he pointed over his shoulder where Taye and Neve had gone. She twisted her lips indecisively and then folded her arms over her chest.

As the other person moved along the zip line, Chubs went to pour a glass of mango juice, intending to offer it to her. When he turned back around, he almost dropped the glass.

Kaleo was unhooking the harness from his wide frame. Muscles bulged against his T-shirt as he swiped the harness to the side where it hit the rock wall.

Chubs took an involuntary step backward before shoring up his courage. Kaleo could have killed him rather than kick him out of the compound. No reason to think things had changed.

Kaleo marched toward him. If the glare had been a sword, Chubs would have already been disemboweled. "What are you doing here?"

He forced his feet to hold their ground. "Neve brought me. She told me it was a safe place where I could heal."

"Not safe from me."

Chubs flinched but didn't back down.

"She doesn't know you like I do." Kaleo stepped closer, bringing him toe to toe with Chubs. "If you hurt anyone here, I guarantee you won't live to regret it."

"Neve wouldn't want you to talk to her guest like this."

Kaleo broke the space between them and fisted his shirt. With the other hand, Kaleo grabbed his cheeks and squeezed tight. He winced but refused to pull away. It would only make things worse.

For a few seconds, Kaleo drilled him with a glare.

"You will not hurt these people or tell anyone else about this location. Do you understand?"

In a full-on fight, Kaleo had the advantage of more muscle and more experience. Chubs briefly entertained the idea of shoving him backward over the ledge of the cave. If only he could watch big, bad Kaleo scream all three hundred feet to the bottom of the chasm. But the fantasy died quickly. They weren't close enough to the edge.

He nodded with gritted teeth.

Kaleo released him as Taye and Neve came back to the front room. The pair glanced at the blonde briefly before turning to Kaleo. Taye nodded to Kaleo as if answering an unspoken question. All this silent communication pricked on Chubs's nerves.

Taye gripped the harness, preparing to leave again.

"We should take Chubs with us," Kaleo said.

"He's injured. He needs to stay." Neve crossed her arms to show it was already decided.

He smiled at her protective stance. This meant she actually wanted him around.

Without looking at Chubs, Taye came back to Neve. He slid a hand down her arm. "Be careful."

"I will." She grabbed his hand for a flash of a second.

Jealousy flared white hot, but Chubs kept his face passive. They wouldn't leave if they knew his real motives.

"Oh, wait," Neve said. "Take Cody. He deserves a little freedom."

Taye strapped on the harness and scooped the dinosaur into his arms, then gave her a lingering look before leaping from the edge.

A few minutes later, the harness came back. Kaleo strapped himself in. On the edge of the precipice, he stared directly at Chubs. "Remember what I said. Anyone gets hurt, and you'll wish Red Grizzly had finished the job."

He swallowed hard at the threat. No doubt Kaleo meant it.

After they left, Neve didn't use the pulley to reel the harness back. Instead, she addressed all of them standing in the room. "I'm afraid we're stuck here for a while. I can't tell you exactly why, but Dr. Anderson needs to stay here. Kaleo is taking the zip-line harness off the line so no one can leave and no one can get to us. Don't worry. We have plenty of supplies."

Chubs stood there in shock, looking at the empty zip line. He hadn't bargained on becoming a prisoner when he'd convinced Neve to bring him to the cave.

Then again, things could be worse. He watched her slender backside walk away one moment, and the next, he shifted to appreciate Dr. Anderson's tight jeans and bouncy curls. If he had to be stuck somewhere, he could definitely make the best of this.

THE CONSTANT HUM of the forest filtered in through the windows of the tree house. Kaleo shut the wooden hatch in the floor, then went to the window opposite from the cot where Raptor sat. The man's face showed signs of stress from letting Kaleo and Taye handle the kidnapping part of the plan, but they'd all agreed he couldn't be involved for his own safety.

"The doctor is safe at the cave," Kaleo said as he flipped around and sat on the windowsill.

Raptor ran a hand down his face. The tense lines eased. "And the agent?"

Raptor wouldn't like this part. "A *Carnotaurus* killed him."

The stress lines returned, deeper now. No matter how much death surrounded them, it wasn't easy to bear the weight of a man's lost life.

He crossed his arms over his chest. "Have you ever seen a *Carnotaurus* shoot fire from its mouth?"

Raptor nodded. "A few were located on the western coast about a year ago. Last spring, their hunting grounds were deserted. I went looking for them but assumed they'd all died out."

"Apparently not all of them did."

He stared over Raptor's shoulder in the direction of the sea. Even though the view was blocked by a wall and miles of trees, he could almost hear the lapping waves. Oakley was out there on the open ocean, hopefully safe, with Cane. At least she would be safer there than she would be on an island full of flesh eaters.

Did Raptor feel the same way? Needing her to come back and yet wanting her to stay away? Raptor's concern for her wasn't romantic, more sisterly, but no less earnest.

Kaleo shifted his gaze to look at him. "She's innocent, you know."

"I know."

"She doesn't deserve to be here."

No answer, just an eyebrow twitch.

"But you're still hoping she comes back?"

Raptor stayed quiet for several minutes. Finally, he shook his head. "I wish she didn't have to."

Kaleo stood and paced to the open window. She shouldn't come back, but his heart argued for her return. Each day, he relived their time together. Her slender body pressed against his chest, the silkiness of her hair under his fingers, and the soft wetness of her lips when he claimed them. But guys like him, who had stolen lives, didn't deserve to have a life. He deserved a lonely existence on this island, not a future with Oakley. Besides, what kind of future would she have here?

The room marinated in silence for several long minutes. Finally, Raptor picked up a satellite phone from the cot beside him. He pressed a few buttons, then held it to his ear. The person who answered must have started talking without pleasantries because he listened for a while.

Eventually, he spoke in a clipped tone. "Brooks, I don't have the team."

This was the next part of the plan. Raptor had to make a report to FBI Agent Noah Brooks.

"I tried to meet them at the transport boat, but by the time I got there, the boat had left, and they were gone."

Mumbling came from the phone, but Kaleo couldn't make out the words.

"Well, I didn't pick them up, no matter what the officer from the boat says." He sounded suitably insulted. After a brief pause, he lowered his voice. "I think someone may have taken them before I could get there."

The loud reply rattled from the speaker. "Taken by who?"

"I'll find out."

Raptor listened for a few more minutes. When he ended the call, he dropped the phone to the cot and hung his head. "I bought us a few more days."

Kaleo nodded as if this was good news. But it was nothing more than a temporary reprieve. A Band-Aid for the time being. Now they needed to figure out what to do next.

CHAPTER TWELVE

AFTER TASING HER, the guard had scooped her up and carried her to a sparsely furnished room where he deposited her on a bed with a white comforter. His deft fingers had removed the barbs from her arm and took the knife from her pocket. He'd left her alone, lying there, waiting for the last of the tension to ebb from her muscles.

As the cramping subsided, her arms and legs became as limp as wrung out dish rags. But her body wasn't her biggest concern. Lumas said he needed to "deal with" Cane. Did that mean Lumas would hurt him? Kill him?

She drew her arms into her chest, suddenly cold. She couldn't handle it if Cane died. He was only here because of her. To support her. And he was the one person who understood what she was going through. The only one who could relate to her struggle to find her origins. And the only one who understood, without words, the sorrow in her heart.

She pushed her weak body to a sitting position and looked around. The room had three stark white walls with no pictures, giving it the impression of a hospital room. Except not many hospital rooms had an entire wall of clear glass overlooking the hallway that was interrupted only by an opaque double-bolted glass door. Despite the comfortable bed, this was a prison cell.

For a half hour, she explored the room, searching in every cabinet, most of which were locked, and every drawer, which were all empty. Finally, she sat cross-legged on the bed and closed her eyes. She wouldn't learn anything trapped in here. How could she get out?

For that matter, how had she ended up here? Her body created its own electricity. Shouldn't it have accepted the Taser as a free recharge?

A few minutes later, a bolt twisted in the lock. Her eyes flew open. The frosted door hid the identity of the figure outside. The second lock twisted, and the door slid into the wall, revealing Director Lumas Verret.

His nonchalant stride belied the strain evident in his eyes. "How are you?"

Such an innocent question. If only she could answer with a fist to his upturned nose. She rubbed at the place on her arm where the barbs had pierced her skin, then she held it out for him to see the angry red marks. "I'm confused."

He gave a slight smile. "Your muscles and nerve endings are aligned to carry a high electrical current traveling in a single direction, that is, out from the electrocytes in your core. But electricity delivered from the outside will seize up your muscle tissue as it would in any person. However, the current doesn't penetrate your organs, thanks to a fatty layer surrounding them, or make it past the layer of insulation at the base of your brain. That makes the Taser effective for controlling you without endangering you or putting you in pain."

He made the process sound benevolent, almost kind. Her snark reared up, but she wouldn't challenge him just yet. He knew more about her physical abilities than she knew herself. "Where is Cane?"

"In another room. Don't worry. You will see each other soon. I felt you both needed to rest after your journey."

He felt. The fact that he controlled everything about this situation sparked her anger. Electricity buzzed in her nerves, but she held the pulse inside.

Her gaze scanned the hallway beyond the glass wall of her prison room. She'd come here for answers. Out there, she might search for hours without finding them. She focused on Lumas again. He seemed to have plenty of information to go around. "You knew my mother."

He retreated to a wooden bench in the corner to sit, then folded his hands in his lap. The door stayed ajar as if he was daring her to try to escape. But she wouldn't be so rash. Besides, Lumas's open and eager expression kept her rooted to her spot. He wanted to talk, and she would give him the opportunity.

"Your mother, Lillian Hebert, worked for me along

with a woman named Penna Gallardo. They were a team. Lillian continued to work here until her accident left her brain unusable."

He dipped his head in Oakley's direction. Was he trying to tell her he knew she'd caused her mother's accident? It didn't matter. She wouldn't discuss it with him.

His eyes searched her face. "Marcel told me she slipped in the tub. Terrible concussion."

She stared blankly at him.

He unfolded and refolded his hands. "I allowed you to live with Marcel and Lillian, hoping your power would develop in a natural setting, but then it didn't."

He'd allowed it? The sentence was spoken with such self-assurance, such arrogance. No doubt he spoke the truth. This man had wielded control over her parents. But how? Did he have a hold over her father still? It would explain Dad's strange behavior when he'd come to visit her on the island. He'd seemed afraid at the very mention of the company.

"You have a logical mind and a tendency to compartmentalize. We designed you that way. Unfortunately, Marcel's influence seems to have softened your naturally strong personality."

Her fingertips burned. If she could get her hands on him, she'd show him exactly how strong her personality was. But he hadn't come unarmed. The top portion of a Taser stuck out of his pants pocket.

"After your mom passed away, you locked your power inside," Lumas said. "Of course, we couldn't leave you that way. To reverse the course of your life, extreme measures had to be taken. We sent you to Extinction Island because you'd turned away from your true self."

His confession jolted her heart. It *was* him. He'd given Adler permission to kill her best friend. All because he thought she needed to use her powers. Powers that could kill. A blast furnace of anger burned inside her. She fought to control it, to keep it below the surface. It wouldn't bring Monica back. To get answers about her past, she had to stay calm. She gritted her teeth. "My mother made me this way?"

"Yes." He paused for a moment. "And Penna Gallardo. All that you are, and all that your friend is, can be traced to small changes in base pairs, a sort of cut-and-paste of information."

An icy shiver ran down her spine. How did he know what Cane could do? No one except Kaleo, Taye, and Neve knew.

"DNA manipulation was your mother's job. Penna told her where and what to modify. It's not as simple as kindergarten cut-and-paste. It's more like an artist using a thousand brush strokes to create a striking landscape." He gazed at the ceiling as if searching for the right words. "If you think of DNA as a template for a painting, merely having the instructions is not enough to create the masterful landscape. A painter must layer in colors in the proper places at the correct time to create the effects of depth and scale. So it is for the geneticist, who must trigger the DNA instructions to happen at certain times and in specific sequences to affect the expression of the genes. The true artistry was all due to Penna. Genes were her paintbrush, enzymes her paint, and your body was her canvas." The edges of his eyes turned downward as he met Oakley's gaze. "When Penna left fifteen years ago, the work stalled."

Then her mother was only partly responsible for her deadly skill. Penna had created more of her, but for what purpose? She wasn't buying the story that she was the artistic dream of a geneticist. "What were you trying to do with this manipulation?"

"Exactly what we did. We created you with abilities that are normally only seen in animals."

"For what reason?"

He hesitated several seconds before answering in an even voice. "To ensure a peaceful future for the world. A fighting force with special abilities has won the battle before it begins."

But a small group of people with abilities wouldn't make much of a difference on a worldwide scale. Perhaps he had made more like her and Cane. Tall, muscular Cane would make a fine soldier, but what kind of fighting force consisted of petite women like her?

She gestured with a flat hand to her head, indicating her height. "What gives, then? Shouldn't I be as tall as an Amazon?"

An almost fatherly smile broke across his face. "Your size and stature weren't a mistake. After we created Adler, Penna and I both agreed that women were less intimidating and, therefore, more suited to peacekeeping. Women with power, of course." He shrugged and gestured toward the door. "Your friend is a surprise to me. I'm still trying to figure out how he came to be."

"Is Adler like us?"

"The first generation. He doesn't have any true abilities like you. His pheromones can ingratiate people to him, but that's about all he has."

She scowled. "That and a bitter, sociopathic personality."

Lumas gave her a reproachful look as if she'd spoken ill of a sibling.

"We're not related, are we?"

He laughed. "Not genetically, no."

She narrowed her eyes at him. Adler and Cane couldn't be more different. Cane had the same pheromones as Adler, but a completely different personality. How could those two men have been made for the same reasons? Perhaps the answer to that question came around to why Cane was a surprise to Lumas. Did someone create him behind Lumas's back?

Before she could ask, he stood and gestured to her. "I'd like you to see something. If you'll come with me."

He'd tasered her to get her to the room and was now asking her permission to leave. Weird. Didn't he worry that she would zap him as soon as they crossed the threshold? Perhaps he understood her powerful need for the truth. As long as he continued to provide information, she would stay compliant.

She nodded and slipped off the bed. She followed him out the door, through a long hallway, and up a flight of wooden stairs to a small office with a metal door. He punched in a code on its keypad and it slid open.

As she entered, she took in the piles of messy paper everywhere. Frayed posters hung from two walls. One of them displayed an image of DNA superimposed on top of what looked like a view of the ocean from this facility. On another, a cartoon of a psychiatrist sat across from a strand of DNA that reclined on a couch. The caption underneath read "DNA Analysis." This room was biology nerd heaven.

He looked around fondly. "For someone with such an organized mind, Penna had real-world organizational issues."

Her mind reeled. *Penna's office.* She inspected the place again, almost as reverently as him. Penna hadn't been her biological mother, but apparently the woman had influenced every part of her DNA. For better or worse, Penna had been like God to her genes.

"She left fifteen years ago, and I've been searching for her ever since," he said wistfully. Then, he stepped backward. "I'll give you some time alone. It's a long shot, but if you happen to find anything that might help me to locate her, I'd appreciate knowing."

He closed the metal door. The click of the lock soon followed. He wasn't letting her go free, but she didn't want to escape right now. Not until she learned everything she could about her origins. Hopefully, Cane was okay, wherever he was.

Myriad stacks of printouts covered every available surface. The documents probably spanned years of research. In theory, the ones closest to the computer would have been the most recent and most important to Penna.

Oakley swiped a layer of dust off the rolling chair and sat. They had truly left this room undisturbed for fifteen years on the off chance it held clues to Penna's location. Lumas was clearly dedicated to finding her.

In the stack to the left of the computer, she found lists of status entries for genetically manipulated dinosaur embryos. The location column for each specimen was designated "on-site." She took that to mean those embryos had been housed at the research lab. Other columns consisted of jumbles of letters and numbers that she couldn't decipher. Possibly genetic information.

To the right of the computer, another stack contained similar information. She shuffled through the papers, stopping on one that displayed an additional column labeled "Dinosaur Specimen." The paper was partially crumpled as if someone had tried to throw it away, but then retrieved it at the last minute. Each specimen was listed as being located in Costa Rica. Most of the species names were familiar: *Tyrannosaurus rex, Edmontosaurus annectens, Triceratops prorsus, Dimetrodon borealis.* For a few, the genus was familiar, but not the species: *Carnotaurus ignis, Saurosuchus mutatio, Velociraptor sinuanimi.*

But there was one she couldn't place at all: *Morbusaurus irazu.*

That genus wasn't on the list posted at the boat transport dock on Extinction Island. And if her limited knowledge of Latin could be trusted, morbus meant *illness.* What geneticist would name a dinosaur essentially Sick-asaurus? On the chance it meant something, she folded the paper and stuffed it in her jeans' back pocket.

She continued to search through the other stacks in a concentric circle outward until Lumas came back hours later. Disappointment swirled in her gut. Most of the papers were records on dinosaurs, not people. And other than the one small anomaly, she hadn't found anything else unusual. Her right eye burned, and she rubbed it. Maybe it was all the dust.

As Lumas entered, the hopeful look on his face brought a twinge of pity for him. She'd worked with Raptor for only a year before being sent to Extinction Island, but if he had disappeared without a trace, she wouldn't stop until she found out what happened. Still, the fact that Lumas had Oakley searching for clues in Penna's own office meant that she might have disappeared on purpose. Perhaps she didn't want to be found ... at least not by Lumas.

"Anything interesting?" he asked.

"Not sure. There is so much stuff."

His features drooped. "Well, it's dinner time."

"I'd rather keep looking." Even so, exhaustion had

started to creep up on her. She hadn't slept the night before the break in.

"Later." He nodded toward the door. "After your long trip, you need to eat."

Her stomach rumbled at the suggestion. No harm in having dinner before she came back to search.

As they walked to her cell, the many questions she needed to ask floated around in her head. In particular, an explanation of the DNA manipulations performed on the dinosaurs. Some of the comments mentioned electricity and cyanide—not surprising—but others had been more concerning. Things like tetrodotoxin and LTNF. Tetrodotoxin was a poison, but what was LTNF?

Lumas had told the truth about the nature of the research. That much was clear. Penna had used her success with the dinosaurs to inspire her genetic manipulation of people. She'd been on the cutting edge of illegal research with no one the wiser since it happened in the middle of the ocean. Was she a crazed scientist who manipulated people just to find out if she could? Or did she truly believe that modified people would make the world a better place? Maybe she'd simply gotten in over her head. Perhaps fear of what she'd done had caused her to leave.

At Oakley's cell, a tray of steak and potatoes waited for her, accompanied by a glass of wine. Her mouth began to water at the smell of the beef. She'd eaten plenty of meat on the island, but dinosaur meat couldn't compare to the marbled delicacy in front of her.

Before she attacked the food, she turned to Lumas's retreating form. She needed to ask the most burning question on her mind. "Are there more of us?"

A slow breath in and out. He didn't want to answer, but he tossed the words over his shoulder anyway. "One more that you haven't met."

Her heart rate quickened. "Who?"

"Your sister." He slid the door shut as her heart leaped into her throat.

⬛

FOR PEACEKEEPING. The words tumbled around in Cane's mind without finding a crevice to cling to. From experience, anytime someone claimed to want power for peacekeeping purposes, the opposite was their real aim.

Director Lumas Verret, as he'd introduced himself, appeared sincere with his peaceful demeanor and calm posture, standing with his hands clasped behind his back. But a warning twinged inside Cane's gut. The tiny speck of wisdom that he relied on to make decisions had never let him down. Lumas wasn't being completely truthful.

"Oakley is fine?" he asked.

Lumas had already assured him of this. Hopefully, on that matter, the man was telling the truth.

Cane paced back and forth near the head of the plush white bed. He was supposed to find answers together with Oakley. Not be separated as prisoners. Still, Lumas's face held no malice, merely curiosity.

"What do you know of your mother?" Lumas asked.

He stopped and squared his shoulders. "She was a single mother to me, her only child."

"Don't you mean, her only adopted child?"

A shudder ran up his back, and he steeled his spine to keep it from showing. There was only one reason for Lumas to look into his adoptive mother—Lumas knew of his abilities. Had Oakley told him? He tightened his jaw. What had Lumas done to her to get her to talk? "I want to see Oakley."

Lumas frowned. "I'm sure you do. All in good time. I thought I might answer more of your questions first."

He narrowed his eyes. For the last twenty minutes, Lumas had portended to answer questions, and yet the answers generated more questions. Lumas stood only a foot away from a gas mask hanging on the wall—another indication that he knew what Cane could do—otherwise he might have been tempted to put Lumas to sleep. Besides, Cane hadn't used his power to knock someone out in a long time. He might kill Lumas by accident.

"I've looked into our records, and I have a theory. I believe your biological mother worked here almost twenty-six years ago."

Cane's eyes widened. "What was her name?"

"Eloisa Bordeaux."

He opened his mouth to respond, but no words came out. His mother's name was Eloisa. Just hearing the name melted a hard spot in his heart.

When Lumas continued, it was with the gleam of a

man who kept secrets. "She was the first technician to work with my geneticist, Penna, even before Oakley's mother. Penna and I had explored using Eloisa's embryos as base material because she was brilliant, but before we had any successful implantations, Eloisa left. She'd taken a pregnancy test just before leaving that was supposedly negative. It never occurred to me that she'd lie."

"You're sure?"

"As certain as I can be. We will take samples to compare, but it's the only way to explain your gift."

Again, the ghost of a shiver skipped down his spine. Lumas knew everything about him, putting him at a disadvantage.

"There's still one thing I don't understand," Lumas said. "Tell me how you ended up on Extinction Island."

No way would he divulge the truth. If his mother had kept her pregnancy a secret, then it was probably for a good reason. He wouldn't tell Lumas that she had left him a clue pointing to Extinction Island. He rolled his shoulders in a stretch to buy time for an answer, since he also refused to lie.

Lumas lost patience with him. "I'm the reason Oakley was sent to Extinction Island."

Cane kept his face passive. He'd guessed as much. Someone at Asperten had to control Adler.

"I have reason to believe Penna is on the island." He pressed his lips into a tight line. "It's too much of a coincidence to find you there as well."

Cane licked his lips as he formulated a half truth. "I

came to the island to teach the prisoners about God's grace."

A slow nod. "You know a bit about grace, I think. After the unfortunate incident in your hometown."

His throat went dry as the image of a young boy's lifeless, strangely red face floated in front of him. He turned away from Lumas in case his grief showed in his expression.

"I'll be honest with you," Lumas said. "Penna had great success in the beginning. Adler, Auburn and Oakley, and some interesting modifications to embryos, but then nothing. She began to put all of her energy into modifications to the brain. Much more difficult, and much more trial and error involved. I was busy with the children and thought we had plenty of time to create more. Just when I started to complain about Penna's lack of progress, she was gone."

Cane flipped his head around to catch any betraying eye twitch or facial tic. None were evident. Lumas appeared to be telling the truth.

"As much as I want to believe she's still alive, I might be fooling myself." Lumas let out a raspy cough. "That's why I need you. Both of you."

"For what? Blood samples? To be human lab rats?"

A quick shake of the head. His eyes bored into Cane's. He enunciated one shocking word. "Procreation."

Cane let out his own strangled cough. *Procreation.* The man couldn't be serious.

A cheeky grin. "You could do worse."

He wasn't joking. Cane's heart rate soared, and not solely from the craziness of the idea. Almost involuntarily, he let the scene unfold in his mind. Sweeping a hand along Oakley's cheek, tilting her chin up, and tasting her full lips. Her sweetness would be a prelude to deeper, more intimate caresses. His insides warmed, and his knees felt weak.

Lumas took a step toward him and narrowed his eyes. "If you want me to tell you for sure who your mother is, you should consider my request."

Was that a threat? Did Lumas plan to stop divulging information until Cane did what he wanted?

Lumas pointed a finger at the door on the other side of the room. "Feel free to clean up in the shower before I take you to see Oakley."

As Lumas left the room, Cane ran his hands through his hair. What was he going to do? There were many things wrong with this line of thinking. First, the Bible taught that sex was for marriage only. It seemed unlikely Lumas would allow them to get married before consummation. Second, he still hadn't determined if his feelings for her were due to their pheromonal connection. And finally, Oakley obviously had some sort of feelings for Kaleo. Could Cane betray their friendship to pursue his own desire for her?

CHAPTER THIRTEEN

RAPTOR CHECKED the time on the satellite phone. Fifteen minutes before his appointment with Kaleo. Just enough time to call Agent Brooks back in private. It wasn't that Kaleo couldn't hear what Raptor needed to say, but the mention of Oakley's name seemed to tear him up. Raptor would spare him the pain when possible.

While he waited for Agent Brooks to answer, he sat on one of the cots in the tree house sanctuary.

A clipped voice answered. "Brooks."

"It's Raptor Greene with an update."

"Go."

"One dead, one missing. I believe some inmates kidnapped Dr. Wells Anderson and FBI Agent Jack Fischer, after which Agent Fischer was killed by a large, meat-eating dinosaur. Dr. Anderson's whereabouts are unknown. I'll keep searching for her."

A few seconds went by. The unusually clear connection allowed him to hear the *tap, tap, tap* of a pen on a desk.

"No," Agent Brooks said. "Resume your search for Oakley Laveau."

"But—"

"Dr. Anderson accepted the risks. We aren't giving up on her entirely. You can look for her as soon as Ms. Laveau is found." Raptor tried to interrupt, but the agent continued. "I will not have the first escaped inmate from Extinction Island on my watch, Mr. Greene. You need to make sure she is secure."

If only Agent Brooks knew. Raptor cleared his throat before responding. "Yes, sir."

"I'll send another doctor out with several agents this afternoon. They will be there in two days."

"Understood." Raptor turned as someone began climbing the ladder to the tree house. Kaleo was early. "Two days," he repeated for Kaleo's benefit. After hanging up, he explained, "Another crew is coming."

"Did he suspect you?"

"Hard to tell. If he did, I probably wouldn't know." He let a long sigh leak out of the corner of his mouth. "It will be so much harder to prove her innocence while she's on the run."

Kaleo gave a wry chuckle. "You think anyone cares about guilt or innocence once you're here?"

"I think Brooks would care." Even as he said it, doubts wormed into his mind. Agent Brooks coordinated with Asperten International, the company at the center of the genetic manipulation of the dinosaurs. Would the agent believe Asperten might have stepped over the line into human manipulation—or even further, framed Oakley for murder to send her here? It was a stretch.

"Where's Taye?" Raptor asked.

"Prowling our territory. We've had several sightings of Red Grizzly, and one of our hunters, Orion, was burned by Demon Dragon."

"The *Carnotaurus* who can spit flames?"

"Yeah. Taye is hunting for evidence of either one, hoping to find their nesting grounds so we can take them out."

Raptor's naturalistic side flinched a little at systematically killing off species, but he firmly believed human life ranked above animals. What these guys were doing was essentially self-defense. "Let's go."

The tree house was merely a safe meeting place. Their mission today was to check on those stranded in the cave, especially Calista's friend, Wells Anderson. If he couldn't vouch for her safety, his girlfriend might want to kill him.

They didn't speak much on the way. Once they reached the cave, Kaleo reattached the harness and worked his way, hand over fist, up to the cave. He sent the harness back, and Raptor got the advantage of the pulley system being hooked up again. He slid onto the ledge to the sound of voices raised in argument.

Kaleo was yelling at Chubs, "Don't look at her that way." He looked at Neve. "Has he touched you?"

She moved between them. "No. He's been a perfect gentleman."

For his part, Chubs held his hands up in surrender, the picture of youthful innocence. "I wouldn't hurt her."

The words may have been appropriate, but his tone was the whine of a petulant child. Raptor put a hand on Kaleo's shoulder. "Chubs knows better than to mess up his last chance." He glared at the kid. "Right?"

Chubs nodded quickly. "Right."

"Then get out of here and leave her alone," Kaleo said.

Chubs backed away, heading to the other end of the room.

"How is the prisoner?" Raptor asked Neve.

She pointed to the area farther inside that they used as a kitchen. "She's doing fine. Though she's not too happy with you."

Of course, she wasn't. Via Calista, he'd asked her to come to help him find a way out of tagging Oakley, but then the plan had changed. Wells had been kidnapped by inmates, stalked by a dinosaur, and left as a prisoner in a cave. She probably hated him by now.

He found her in the kitchen, washing dishes in the rough-cut rock sink. At his footsteps, she looked up briefly.

"How are you?" he asked.

She ignored him, supposedly absorbed in the mundane task.

"How about I start again. I'm Raptor, and I'm sorry."

"I'd say nice to meet you, but I'd rather punch you in

the teeth." She dropped the dish into a nearby bucket. Her shoulders slumped. "Why did you have Calista ask me to come?"

He could list off the reasons: Because Calista said he could trust her. Because she was already on the FBI approved medical professionals list. Because her recent association with CADRE, Citizens Against Death Row and Execution, made her willing to help. Instead, he simply said, "Because an innocent girl here needs you."

She slowly turned around to face him, leaning her hip on the sink. "The one I'm supposed to tag."

He nodded.

Her skeptical look didn't fade. "How does that lead to kidnapping me?"

"I was buying time."

Horror crept into her expression. Her eyes watered. "A man died not ten feet from me."

His gut pinched at what he'd put her through. "I'm sorry. That wasn't supposed to happen."

She put her fists on her hips. "'That wasn't supposed to happen' could be the motto of this place."

Didn't he know it. Nothing here ever went as planned. "How was Calista when you left?" He'd only talked to her the day that he asked her to call Wells. She was used to his erratic schedule and bad phone connections, but this time he hadn't called her on purpose. She might hear the fear in his voice. Then he'd end up confessing everything he was doing to protect Oakley, and all he'd done to endanger their life together.

"Working tirelessly for the animals. She didn't want me to come, but she asked anyway because of you. You know how she feels about the separation of dinosaurs and humans."

He smiled. "Yeah, she barely tolerates me coming here. I really am sorry to bring you into this. I needed someone on my side." He proceeded to explain Oakley's situation, beginning with the murder that Adler had framed her for and ending with her leaving the island to search for answers. He was necessarily vague regarding her abilities.

"So, you brought me here *not* to tag her?"

"Sort of. I need to know if there's a way around the tracker. Can we implant one that's removable? Can it be programmed to register as active when it's not? What about setting up a signal that mimics a tracker?"

She took in all of his ideas, shaking her head at each one. "No to all of the above. The tracker must be in contact with muscle tissue or blood at all times. If it's removed without safety precautions, it will send a slug of poison throughout the patient's system." She took a breath. "Programming is proprietary and closely guarded by the FBI. I know how to safely remove one and install one. That's all the information they give me."

"I get it."

Wells uncrossed her arms. "She's really innocent?"

Raptor nodded again.

"I'll do what I can to help. I've got two trackers from

the FBI agent's backpack. Maybe I can reverse engineer one."

"I appreciate you trying." He took a step toward the other room. "You're safe here. Please, be patient. I'll come back to get you soon."

He returned to the main room, leaving Wells to finish her task. He found Kaleo and Neve huddled together, whispering. They looked up at him for a beat before continuing their discussion.

Kaleo glanced at the corner of the room. Raptor followed his gaze. Chubs sat alone on a cot, glowering at both Kaleo and another man sitting nearby who was probably only a target of his anger because Kaleo hadn't asked the man to leave like he had Chubs.

"It will be a few days before we can visit again," Kaleo said, his voice low so only they could hear. "Taye and I need to track down Demon Dragon, and Raptor has to prepare for the other FBI agents who are coming. I think we should kick Chubs out now."

"I agree," Raptor said.

Neve took a long look at Chubs before answering. "I think he needs more time to heal. Just a few days."

"You've given him enough compassion," Kaleo challenged.

Neve's lips curved in a mysterious smile. "God is infinitely compassionate, dear Kaleo. No limits at all."

"Taye will not be happy when I tell him."

A pretty blush rose on her cheeks, but she said nothing.

"If things become too difficult here, take the back way out and come find me."

Raptor wrinkled his brow. What was the "back way out" of here? He'd have to ask Kaleo later. At least Neve and Wells had an escape route if necessary.

Kaleo pointed at Chubs and raised his voice. "Keep your hands to yourself."

Once again, Chubs put his palms out, face up. Raptor didn't buy his plaintive look. However, Neve was the queen of the cave. If she wouldn't kick him out, there wasn't much they could do. Cane would have allowed her the same latitude.

As Raptor strapped into the zip-line harness, he felt the weight of his choices pressing fully on his shoulders. Not only was he not helping Oakley at the moment, he'd also endangered Wells. He wasn't a praying man, but Cane was. Hopefully, those prayers were keeping Oakley safe right now.

▭

"NEVE, WOULD YOU CHANGE MY BANDAGE?" Chubs infused his request with all the sweetness he could muster.

"Of course." Dutifully, she picked up her medical kit and walked with him into the men's quarters.

He had the cave back to himself again. The other men here didn't possess the hostility of Kaleo or Raptor, or even Taye, for that matter.

He lay facedown on his cot. No one had followed the two of them into the men's sleeping room. They were alone. Though he'd been able to get her alone at various times in the last several days, she had yet to pick up on his hints for something more. Or at least she wouldn't acknowledge them.

As her delicate hands swept over his skin, his mind went to erotic places. Even the stinging rip of the tape being removed heightened his arousal. Did she want him too?

The new woman, Wells, stuck her head in the room. "Do you need help, Neve?"

"No, I've got it."

Wells was beautiful in her own way. She just didn't satisfy him like Neve did. Too young. Too much frantic energy. Where Wells pushed and prodded, Neve took the time to be gentle. Where Wells chattered on, Neve listened patiently. Where Wells bustled about, Neve exuded calm peacefulness.

"How is it feeling?" she asked.

"If I say better, are you going to kick me out?" Hopefully, she heard the tremor in his voice. He hadn't been this attached to a woman since Teresa.

"Whether you stay or not will be Cane's decision when he gets back."

"Why?"

"This place is a refuge for those who have turned from their old life and become new. Since he is our pastor, he will determine if that is the case for you."

The same guy who was close with Kaleo. That wouldn't do. Kaleo would make sure Cane didn't let Chubs stay.

He twisted his neck to get a peek at Neve. Her loose hair fell forward as she worked. Several silky strands tickled his back. He couldn't leave her now. Not when he'd just found her.

Before any of them came back, he would have to make his move. If he took control of the cave by then, the matter would be settled. Cane wouldn't attack to regain control. After all, the dude was a pastor.

And hopefully, Kaleo and Taye wouldn't risk people's lives once Chubs had full control. Question was, how would he take over? He'd have to be patient. Wait for the right opportunity.

Neve finished with the bandage and swept her fingers along the edges. She might have been trying to make sure the small amount of tape she'd used had stuck to his skin—tape was a valuable commodity since they couldn't easily make more—or she might have been lingering to touch him longer. He'd take the chance to find out.

Rolling to his front, he captured her hand and kissed the back of her fingers. She gasped and tried to tug them away. He held fast.

"Thank you for everything," he said.

She nodded and tried once more to reclaim her hand. He let her go. The flustered flush creeping up her neck said it all. She was fighting the attraction, but she wanted him too. Maybe he could convince her to run away with him.

But they didn't need to go anywhere. At least not until Kaleo was willing to trade the resort compound for the cave. Until then, this place had many amenities. Water, toilets, protection from both human and animal predators. Next to the resort, this was a good setup.

His first order of business was to intimidate or incapacitate the four men on-site—Henry, Justin, and two other guys whose names he hadn't bothered to learn. Justin was in his midfifties and stooped over from a bad back. Not much of a challenge. Henry, however, looked to be around thirty and in solid shape. The other two men might have been late thirties to early forties, but they seemed like wimps who followed Neve's instructions as if she were Saint Mary. What on earth could they have done to earn a death sentence?

Henry usually hung out along the sides of the cave where he wove ropes from thick fibers. Come to think of it, Henry had been doing so yesterday when Kaleo and Raptor came to visit. Maybe he'd overheard something useful. Wouldn't hurt to ask.

Chubs found Henry in the main area, sitting near the edge of the cliff. He sat next to the man and gazed out. A shimmer of vibrant green waved from the valley floor as if it were a lake made of leaves.

"What are you doing?" he asked.

For once, Henry didn't have anything in his hands. He merely stared out at the landscape. "Nothing."

"Crazy, how many people come and go when we're supposed to be on lockdown. Don't you think?"

A half-hearted shrug.

"Did you know the stocky guy that came earlier?" Chubs asked. Raptor had visited the resort compound from time to time, usually bringing chocolate in exchange for information.

"Never seen him before." Henry shifted to face Chubs. "Wells called him Raptor. Perfect name for around here. I need a dangerous nickname like that."

He ignored the implied invitation to brainstorm. "Did you hear what either of them said to Neve?"

Henry slanted his eyebrows. "You shouldn't bother with Neve. Taye would be all over you."

"Hey, man. I just want to know when our captivity might end."

"I thought you wanted to stay here."

"Well, yeah, but that's different than being trapped here."

Another shrug. "Not for a while. Kaleo said that he and Taye had to hunt down some crazy carno and wouldn't be back for a few days."

What type of *Carnotaurus* required elimination? He opened his mouth to ask, but then ignored the impulse. He had to stay focused. "You're sure they said they wouldn't be back soon?"

"Yeah."

"What about Raptor?"

"He said something about the FBI coming. Didn't

sound like he'd visit soon either. I'd get comfortable here if I were you."

Chubs fixed his gaze back on the vast lake of trees. When Henry did as well, he let a smile spread across his face. Maybe he didn't have to be patient after all. The timing was perfect. He planned to get comfortable here ... with Neve right beside him.

CHAPTER FOURTEEN

OAKLEY WOKE the next morning with a familiar pit of anxiety in her gut. In the last three weeks, she hadn't stayed anywhere long enough to consider one place home. Each time she awoke, she had to grapple for her location.

Glancing around the stark white room, she worked to accept her situation. A prisoner to a man she'd just met. Sadly, that was nothing new. At least no immediate danger threatened her. No dinosaurs hovering nearby. And no hardened killers stalking her every move.

Instead, the cozy smell of toast drew her gaze to the nightstand. Butter melted at the center of the bread, mingling with a dollop of jam. A glass of juice sat next to the plate. She scooped up the orange juice first and took a long drink. As she bit into the toast, she fingered the edge of the serving tray. It sat in front of a partition in the wall. Someone had shoved it through and closed it, just like in a jail cell.

After devouring the food, she went to brush her teeth using the toothbrush she'd found last night before she dropped into the bed. Then, with nothing else to do, she sat on the bed, pulled the blanket over her knees, and tugged the experimental results sheet from her pocket. She held it low so the camera in the corner of the ceiling couldn't see what she was doing.

According to the location column, this entire list of dinosaur specimens had been let loose in Costa Rica. She ran her finger down the date column. The timing was off. Work on Extinction Island had started seven years ago. The last entry on this sheet contained a date from fifteen years ago—probably right before Penna disappeared. Penna and Lumas had released dinosaurs on the unsuspecting Costa Rican population long before the US government transformed it into a sanctuary. Probably to test their hybrids.

The light shining in from the hallway dimmed as someone stood in front of the door. The figure appeared as a shadow fumbling with the locks.

She put the paper back in her pocket but didn't get up. The person stood there for a few minutes, then gave up on the locks and moved to the clear portion of the wall. She raised her head and sucked in a quick breath. It wasn't Lumas. It was her father.

She ran to the glass. "Dad!"

"Oakley, dear." His voice came through muffled. "I was going to come in, but then I realized I shouldn't."

"Why not?"

He shot a quick glance at the camera in her room. "Lumas wouldn't approve. And he'll know if I come in. Listen to me, you shouldn't have come here. You have to leave. Find a way to get out."

"How do you propose I do that?"

"I don't know." He ran his hand through his thinning hair. "But I can't help you."

Of course he could help her. He was roaming free. There had to be something he could do.

His attention darted down the hall as if he heard something. "I have to go."

"No." She pounded a fist on the glass, but he was already moving down the hall. "Come back."

He disappeared around a bend as tears welled up in her eyes. She crawled back to bed with a heavy heart.

Several hours later, another shadow crossed the doorway. She jumped up. Had her father returned?

No, this person was smaller. A woman about her size with similar dark hair. Oakley shoved the contraband paper she'd been examining under her leg and then under the blanket while the woman unlocked the door and slid it aside.

Oakley blinked at her. The woman's features mimicked her own, though not quite the same. Her first step inside the cramped room caused Oakley's heart to pound. It was like looking in a mirror except with a few slight differences. Darker blue in the eyes. A flatter chin. A more defined widow's peak at the hairline. But in the mire of shock, other subtleties were hard to pick out.

They stared at each other in silence for a few moments. Clearly, this woman was related to her, but they had never met. Her mother and father must have had another child. One that they had kept from her.

Her sister. Lumas had been serious.

The woman frowned. "Dad didn't tell you?"

"No." Her answer came out as a croak. He hadn't said a word about this when he'd come a few hours ago. The last time she'd talked to her dad before that would have been almost two weeks ago when he'd taken the visitors' ship to the island. At that time, he hadn't told her much of anything.

"He likes to surprise people." Her tone sounded chiding, not truly irritated.

Oakley puckered her brow in confusion. Dad hated surprises and rarely did anything out of the ordinary. He was bound and defined by his habits. Then again, he had surprised her today.

The woman slid over to lean against the wall. "I was supposed to wait to talk to you until Dad finishes with Cane."

Something wasn't adding up here. It was Lumas that had wanted to meet with Cane. Dad didn't even know of Cane's existence.

With their resemblance, this woman had to be her sister, the other gifted person Lumas had mentioned. But it was clear now that she referred to Lumas as her father. How was that possible?

"He will probably be mad. But I had to see you for

myself." The woman's eyes hardened, giving the impression she didn't like what she saw. "I'm Auburn. You're my twin."

The icy note to Auburn's voice chilled the air between them.

She cleared her throat. "To clarify, I'm Auburn Verret. I took the name of the only father I've known, same as you."

Oakley mentally ran through the conversation she'd had with Lumas. He said he allowed her to live with Marcel and Lillian. He never confirmed that Marcel was her biological father. She looked—actually both of them looked—a lot like Lillian. "So, you're the biological daughter of Lillian Hebert and ..."

Auburn crossed her arms and dipped one eyebrow. "Marcel Laveau. That's what it means to be a twin. Good thing we're not identical because you're a little slow."

Her relief clashed with her irritation at the harsh words. What had she done to cause her sister to dislike her before they'd even met? *Her sister.* She had a sister to introduce to her younger brother, Eric.

"Perhaps you're just not good with your words? They say the older twin has better communication skills."

Disbelief percolated through Oakley like fizzing bubbles, making her head spin. She'd gone from being the oldest and only child of Marcel and Lillian to the youngest twin. Maybe Auburn was right because she could find no words to describe this joy mixed with dejection.

Auburn's face softened as if she only now realized how confrontational she sounded. "Dad ... I mean, Lumas, has been good for me. He's directed and disciplined. Marcel is anything but. He floats along, trying to please Lumas, to please the women in his life, and to keep the peace."

A surge of anger pulsed through her. How dare Auburn judge him? Her father—their father—was more than the placating man Auburn portrayed him to be. She didn't bother to disguise her sarcasm. "Keep the peace. Isn't that what Lumas says is his goal?"

"Of course. That requires strength and the ability to fight when necessary."

Auburn's supreme confidence rubbed her the wrong way. Since being sentenced to Extinction Island, Oakley hadn't been confident of anything. "Why did you come in here? This obviously isn't a sentimental family reunion for you."

"Dad thought we should meet."

She folded her arms across her chest. "There's more to it than that. Isn't there?"

A momentary hesitation before Auburn answered. "I wanted you to see me and how I support Lumas." Another brief hesitation. "And Adler."

The lift of her chin and the way she spoke Adler's name was telling. She and Adler were a couple in some sense. How ridiculous.

"Some things will be asked of you," Auburn went on. "Things that can help redeem your past. To bring life out of the death you've delivered. Cane will help you understand."

"Understand what?"

Auburn's expression turned stoic. "Lumas has expressed to him what needs to be done. I'll send him to talk to you soon."

Two could play at that game. She pasted on her most disinterested face. "What makes you think I'll listen to Cane?"

Auburn tilted her head, giving Oakley a side-eyed look. Oakley shifted on the bed under the scrutiny. Still, she held her face immobile.

Lifting a single delicate finger, Auburn said, "If you agree to be open to whatever Cane proposes, then you can ask me what you really want to know, and I'll answer."

She bit her lip. Either it was the pheromones or a twin thing, but Auburn knew exactly where to press on her already raw emotions. She blurted out the one thing she desperately needed to know. "Do you have special abilities?"

"Yes."

A long silence stretched as Oakley waited for her to explain.

Finally, Auburn let out a long sigh. "I have a structure akin to quills underneath my hair." She turned around and flipped her locks up in back. Stubby tips of fibers, several times thicker than her hair, stuck out an inch from her scalp. "I can pull these out to throw them or under extreme duress I can shoot them out like a porcupine, although they aren't made from keratin like a porcupine's quill."

"What are they made of?"

"Collagen, a harder type of protein. Consequently, they are less flexible and shorter than a quill."

"So, they're poisonous?"

"Tetrodotoxin, the poison found in a puffer fish."

"Why don't you poison yourself?" It was a question she'd meant to ask Cane as well. Thanks to Lumas, she now grasped why she didn't electrocute herself.

"Our bodies have safeguards. My case is a little different." She raised both eyebrows. "In your boyfriend's case, he produces a peptide that acts as a buffer to protect him from hydrogen cyanide. You'll be happy to know I've confirmed through your blood sample that you have the same immunity to hydrogen cyanide."

Oakley yanked up her sleeves. Sure enough, a small red spot on her left arm indicated the area where blood had been taken. Lumas must have put drugs in her dinner last night. No wonder she'd slept so well.

"Great," she answered.

Auburn pushed off the wall and slid toward the door. "If there's nothing else, I'll go so you can see Cane. Remember, you agreed to listen to what he says."

"Wait."

Auburn halted.

"One more question. Why do you hate me?"

Auburn took another step. She paused with a hand on the transparent door frame, her expression superior, much like Lumas's from last night. "When you have a problem, you seem to be fine with using your powers to kill. As if it's the only solution. I see your inability to find other solutions as selfish and reckless."

She passed through the doorway, then the cloudy door slid shut, locking with two clicks.

In the sudden silence, Oakley battled with her twisting gut. She couldn't deny the accusation because she'd been accusing herself for weeks. What kind of woman left a trail of bodies everywhere she went? But in the middle of treading water in her sea of guilt, confusion rose above the waves. How did Auburn know she'd killed people? Cane hadn't told Lumas, had he?

CANE LAY on the bed in his plush cell, his gaze focused on the clear glass wall, trying to work through the facts. Oakley had walked by his cell about an hour ago. She was alone and walked with a purposeful stride, like she owned the place. Despite him yelling her name, she hadn't looked his way. Perhaps they'd soundproofed this room.

Since then, her possible whereabouts had consumed him. What was she doing? Why hadn't she come for him? He closed his eyes to pray that she would reappear.

When he opened his eyes, he let out a surprised laugh. The figure of a woman stood outside his opaque door. Her long dark hair swept back and forth as she worked at the electronic lock. She was breaking them out!

He hopped up from the bed just as the door slid away. "I can't believe it. How did you—"

Shock reverberated through his chest. The woman who stood before him looked much like Oakley—same dark chestnut hair, sapphire blue eyes, and angled cheek bones—and yet, it wasn't her. The chin was wider. The lips a bit thinner. While still beautiful, this woman didn't carry the vigor and intensity that Oakley did.

He took a step forward. Maybe he could slip past her. "Who are you?"

"A friend." She held up a Taser, the wicked prongs barely visible inside the black casing.

"You don't look too friendly."

"Just a precaution. My father sent me to come get you. He wanted me to remind you of your conversation yesterday."

He squinted at her. She'd said her father, but from the context, she had to mean Lumas. If Marcel Laveau was Oakley's father, shouldn't he be the father of this woman who was her spitting image? Cane pushed away the puzzle as the conversation from yesterday came flooding back. Lumas sent this woman here for a purpose. Probably to illuminate Cane's options. If he didn't convince Oakley to procreate, Lumas might try to force him to procreate with her look-alike.

Perhaps Oakley would be willing to pretend to comply until they could find a chance to escape. A tiny pinch of hope ignited in his gut. Dare he pray Oakley would be more willing than he thought?

Guilt followed quickly on the heels of his hope. *Dear Lord, help me to follow your path in this, not mine, not Lumas's.*

The woman swiped her arm toward the door. "I'll take you to her."

He couldn't suppress a shudder as he moved past this woman who hadn't revealed her name. Had she presented herself to Oakley yet?

"And don't get any ideas," the woman said. "I've got a boyfriend. You've met him, actually. It's Adler."

His eyes widened. Adler? The man who had framed Oakley for murder? That relationship wouldn't end well for this woman.

He followed her out and around the corner to a nearby cell with a glass door similar to his. But this door had one distinction—a manual system of locks. No fancy electronic locks for Oakley to short-circuit. Lumas was taking no chances.

The woman flipped two deadbolts to open the door. She allowed him to enter and then closed it behind him. Two clicks sounded as the deadbolts locked into place.

Inside, Oakley lay on a white bed dressed in the same dirty jeans and teal T-shirt she'd worn yesterday. Her face appeared freshly scrubbed, and her loose hair shone coppery in the bright lighting. She must have taken a shower as well.

She sat up and leaned against the headboard, her expression a tense mixture of relief and confusion, probably much the same as his.

He went to her and sat on the foot of the bed. "Are you okay?"

"Other than a small bump on my head from falling while being tased, I'm fine."

"Let me see." He stood to gently probe the back of her head. The lump was about the size of a nickel. Her hair felt like silk under his fingers. "I'm no Neve, but I think it will heal just fine."

She captured his hand and motioned for him to return to sitting. "I see you met my alter-ego."

He nodded. "Did you know that she's dating Adler?"

"I guessed as much." Her eyes searched his with a hint of guilt, if he wasn't mistaken. She hesitated before speaking. "I have to ask, did you tell Lumas that I killed people on the island?"

"Of course not. I haven't told anyone."

An ocean of relief poured from her cells, washing over him in a calming wave. The strength of the pheromones that passed between them sometimes caught him off guard.

"I'm sorry. I didn't think you would. It must have been Adler, then." She brushed her loose hair behind her ears. "Did Lumas tell you about Penna Gallardo?"

He nodded as she released his hand, his skin already cooling due to the absence of her warm contact.

"Lumas says she created us for peacekeeping, but I think it's to fight." Her eyes turned down. "I've seen what a difference breeding can make. Back home, I would go on calls with Raptor to rescue alligators. Many of them were scarred and mutilated from years of being stuck in a dog-fighting pit. The last challenge the dog had to face was a six-foot alligator. Those dogs were bred to never give up, to keep attacking no matter what."

He dipped his head to look into her eyes. "We are hardly fighting dogs."

"Aren't we?"

She had a point, though a limited one. Even a peace-keeping force needed muscle behind its benevolence.

"Did he tell you what he wants from us?" she asked.

His mouth went dry. How could he phrase it? *Lumas wants us to be intimate. We're supposed to create some baby peacekeepers.* It sounded ridiculous.

When he didn't answer, she went on. "He's the reason I was sent to the island. He wanted me ... correction ... he still wants me to find Penna. Yesterday, he let me snoop around in her office."

She pulled a folded sheet from her pocket and slid it over to him underneath the blanket, obviously trying to hide it from the camera over her shoulder. He lifted the edge of the blanket and peeked at the paper. It was a list of species.

"They were sending dinosaurs to Costa Rica long before Extinction Island was created." She lowered her voice to a whisper, and he leaned closer to hear. "This is the last list of dinosaurs printed out before Penna disappeared. I recognize almost all of the genus names from my vertebrates class, but the last one is an odd entry."

He chanced another glance. *Morbusaurus irazu.* "How so?"

"There isn't any dinosaur or ancient lizard that I know of with that genus name."

He matched her low tone of voice. "But Penna was creating new dinosaurs. Why would you recognize them?"

"Yes, there are plenty of species names that are unfamiliar. But in every other case, she kept the genus name of the dinosaur consistent. Plus, I'm sure *Morbusaurus* is not on the official list of dinosaurs displayed at the transport-boat dock. Does it mean anything to you?"

She fiddled with one of her fleur-de-lis earrings. The flitting of her delicate fingers distracted him. To focus, he set his eyes on the stark white comforter and the edge of the list beneath. "Irazu sounds like a name I've heard on the island." He rubbed the stubble on his jaw as he rolled the name over in his mind. "I think it's a volcano, maybe ten miles from the cave."

He glanced up at her. She bit her lower lip, her perfect white teeth dragging across the smooth skin. It nearly drove him to distraction again. He cleared his throat.

"What about the rest of the stuff on here?" She snaked her hand under the blanket to retrieve it, then handed it to him while sliding closer to block the camera's view with her back. The scent of lavender wafted around him. Though she'd probably used whatever soap the bathroom contained, the lavender suited her.

He forced his gaze to the paper that was littered with columns. The headings tracked along the top: Location, Species, Chromosome Modified, Recombinant DNA Strand Used, Success/Failure.

Under the last column, most of the entries had data in the form of an *S* or *F* to indicate the status, all except for one—the same entry she had asked him about. *Morbusaurus irazu* had a capital letter *A* underneath the Success/Failure column. He sought out the index key, tracking with his finger as he searched.

When he found the definition, his stomach did a somersault. *A* stood for *Acantilado de Espiritu*. In Spanish, it meant ghost cliffs. The wording was an echo of the last communication his adoptive mother had received from his biological mother.

She picked up on his shock. "What do you know?"

He let her read the index key, then he handed it back. "Put it away."

She complied, folding the paper into quarters and slipping it into her pocket.

He motioned for her to stay close so he could whisper. "I haven't told you the whole story about my birth mother. I didn't know her name. Lumas seems to think she was Eloisa Bordeaux who worked here. When I was ten years old, she contacted Amy, my adoptive mother, and said she had to go away for a while. She recited two lines of a poem for Amy to copy down and then asked Amy to give it to me when I became an adult. I've always believed she left me those lines as a clue because she wanted me to search for her. It's the main reason I came to Extinction Island."

"What was the poem?"

He recited the lines from memory, having lost the original paper in his first trek through the jungle. "Search for the fire along the coast that's rich. Brave the disease lurking in the ghost cliffs."

Oakley tapped a finger on her chin. "I can see how you got Costa Rica from rich coast, but what about the last part?"

"In Spanish, *Acantilado de Espiritu* means ghost cliffs."

Her brow scrunched up as she took in his words. "The status listed for the mysterious dinosaur. Are there ghost cliffs near the Irazu volcano?"

"I don't know. We'd have to ask a native, like Neve." In fact, he'd already asked her in general about ghost cliffs. She hadn't heard of any, but now that they had a possible location, something might make sense to her.

Oakley stared over his shoulder at the locked door as she whispered, "Lumas would probably let us go if we told him we knew where Penna might be."

"Maybe, but then we'd lead him right to her. If she and my birth mother are trying to hide, they must have had a reason." He sucked in a tense breath and slowly let it out. There was no keeping the truth from her any longer. "Besides, Lumas isn't keeping us here just to find clues that might lead to Penna. He wants more."

Her gaze darted to meet his. "He told you something?"

A quick flick of the eyebrows to let her know she was on the right track. "Good thing you're sitting down." He let out an uncomfortable cough. "He wants us to ... uh ... in his words ... to procreate."

"What?" Her voice was at full volume. She leaned back, and her head fell against the headboard.

He couldn't interpret her expression, but the punch of her shock came through her pheromones. Was the idea of being with him so terrible? He ran a hand over his face. He wasn't thinking straight. Sex outside of marriage was off limits. He shouldn't be wanting this at all.

Finally, she spoke in a flat tone. "Before Auburn left, she told me to consider whatever idea you brought to me."

Auburn had to be the name of her doppelgänger. "Is she?"

Oakley nodded. "My twin."

"From your father and mother?"

"Yes. She calls Lumas dad, but my father is her biological father." She huffed out a breath. "A confusing family tree that it seems they want me to expand." Her mouth opened twice before she managed to say something more. "What are we supposed to do? You're a pastor, for heaven's sake."

He bristled at that. "Pastors are men too."

"Yeah, of course, but we'd have to get married, right? I'm not ready to get married."

"Me either. However, I don't think Lumas cares much

about a commitment. He's looking to create more people like us, which means he won't give us much time to transition from friends to lovers." Cane leaned in and tried to lighten his voice. "Painful as it might be, we should give him something to make him believe we're considering the idea."

The pink flush on her cheeks told him his words had the desired effect. She was thinking about kissing him and gave no indication that it would be painful. But would she allow it?

She moistened her lips. His gaze tracked the movement of her tongue.

Her blush deepened.

A torrent of sensation flooded his body as his awareness of her grew. He could drown in the depths of her blue eyes. He tried to draw up concern for Kaleo's feelings, but his friend's image came as a fuzzy and indistinct shadow.

It was only a kiss after all.

Slowly, it dawned on him that the charged flow of desire between them originated only partly from him. An undercurrent of longing came from her. Maybe it was the pheromones that made him so sure of her feelings. Or maybe it was the subtle parting of her lips.

Tentatively, he placed a hand on her cheek. He leaned forward, cutting the distance between them to a few inches.

Her eyes widened, questioning and seemingly as drunk on this sensation as him.

He leaned the rest of the way and brought his lips gently to hers. The electricity hit instantly. He tangled his hands in her hair, brushed them down her cheeks, and then cupped her chin.

For an instant, she responded, but she pulled away much too soon. The fire between them cooled. Her questioning gaze morphed into panic. "I can't ..."

He shifted to get up from the bed. It wasn't hard to guess the reason. There was more than just the two of them in this room. Kaleo's shadow hung over them.

She pushed herself up into him, her cheek brushing his cheek, her breath tickling his ear in a soft whisper. "There's another way. I think I can get us out. Be ready at midnight."

Her close proximity nearly overwhelmed her words, but he forced his brain to process them. She knew a way out of here. Escape should be their main goal. His mind agreed. Too bad, the rest of his body had its own agenda.

CHAPTER FIFTEEN

UNDERNEATH THE FLUFFY COMFORTER, Oakley worked the pieces of the broken alarm clock apart. Even though her room was illuminated solely by a safety light from far down the hall outside, she still needed to hide. Perhaps Lumas had night vision on the camera behind her. Best to give him as little warning as possible.

She used one of the broken plastic pieces to cut the outer sleeve from the long power cord. The process required more persistence than brainpower, causing her mind to wander back to the kiss. Was it only a few hours before? Her body warmed at the memory of Cane's lips on hers. When she'd let go and given in, her body had responded. And why not? Cane was kind, patient, and handsome. She remembered how the smattering of freckles across his cheeks seemed to disappear as his face heated with desire.

The hunger coming from him had affected her in a

visceral way. Biologically, even chemically, she and Cane existed on the same wavelength. And yet, she missed Kaleo. Her chest ached just thinking about him.

Ugh. How could she possibly have feelings for both of them? Perhaps she shouldn't trust her own heart, especially given that her previous boyfriend had cheated on her with her best friend.

The last of the plastic coating dropped from her fingers to the bed, exposing bare copper wire. She coiled the wire several times around her right index finger, leaving a tail of about six inches. Then, she threw the blanket off and patted her front jeans pocket for the nail she'd pried out of the bed frame earlier. According to her study of electrical forces in second-year physics, she needed a coil of copper wire, something iron, and a power source to make an electromagnet. Thank goodness all science majors had been forced to take two years of physics.

She slipped her hand in her front pocket to cover the wire and strode casually to the door as if curious about a noise outside. In the dim light, she peered at the two deadbolts installed backward. From inside, a key was required, but she hadn't seen Auburn or Lumas with a key. Probably the outside part of the lock used simple metal knobs. All she had to do was flip the metal knobs to unlock the deadbolts.

She positioned her body to hide her actions and withdrew the nail. She then pulled out the wire and coiled the tail around the head of the nail. Finally, she pushed the nail against the side of the metal lock. Hopefully, she could generate enough current for it to travel through to the locking mechanism on the outside.

To stir up her electricity, she unearthed a traumatic memory from a few months ago. A gator named Blackie had taken the last two fingers of her left hand. She focused on the image of its gaping mouth advancing toward her in the water. The sharp serrated teeth. The scream she'd let loose. The horror of thinking she would die.

When the spark vibrated inside her chest, she pushed the fear and pain out through her right hand. The electric shock leaped from her fingers in a rush, zapping her, and forcing her to let go. The nail flipped over and fell to the floor. She picked it up, recoiled everything, and tried again. This time, she attempted to sustain a slow simmer, directing the electrons the way she would pour water into a cup. She pressed the nail onto the lock and moved it in a slow circle.

Nothing happened. It wasn't enough power. She needed to keep the flow both steady and strong.

Although she had always been more interested in bioelectricity, now she racked her brain to remember the mechanical information from that physics class. The strength of electromagnetism was a function of two things. What were they again? The number of coils and the power of the source. Those were the only variables.

Still keeping her back to the camera, she unwound the wire from her finger, secured her grip at the base, and rewound it into tighter coils, ignoring the bite of the wire as it cut into her flesh. She also added closer coils around the nail until she'd used the entire wire.

Ready for another try. She had to dredge up the memories that still brought her emotions boiling to the surface. Her mother's face arose, pinched with determination as she'd held Oakley underwater in the bathtub, intent on killing her. But Oakley pushed the memory back down. She couldn't go there. Nor would she picture the deaths of the two people she'd killed on the island.

As if it had a life of its own, the memory of Cane's lips on hers jumped to the forefront of her mind. An effusive warmth pooled in her chest. He'd been hesitant, gently coaxing her into the kiss. She hadn't worried that her kiss would kill him, though she had no reason to think it wouldn't. Somehow, her fear had evaporated away, not like with ...

Kaleo. Their first kiss came roaring up with an insistent forcefulness. Instead of gentle persuasion, Kaleo had claimed her lips as if he'd branded them with his desire. Her fear of losing control had shot through her muscle fibers and mixed with her passion until she'd felt drunk on a cocktail of sparking nerves. The sensation was all-consuming in a way that had nothing to do with pheromones, and everything to do with the man who had squeezed every ounce of longing from her heart.

A steady flow of power raged down her arm to her hand, causing the wire-covered nail to vibrate. She sucked in a breath to regulate the stream.

After a few seconds, she twisted the head of the nail, moving it in a slow arc.

The first bolt slid in tandem. But a slight hitch stopped the deadbolt at the vertical position. She nudged it harder, and it slid completely to the opposite side.

One down, one to go.

She placed the nail over the other lock, closed her eyes, and brought Kaleo into her mind again. He was framed in moonlight on the night when they'd faked her death. His taut body hovered over her as she lay on the ground. His golden-brown hair fell forward, brushing her face as he kissed her. Before he'd left her there, his dark eyes pierced her with a look of craving and hunger that set her soul on fire.

As if waking from a dream, she raised her eyelids and twisted the nail in a circle. The deadbolt clicked open, and the door sagged against the frame. It was unlocked!

She gently slid the door to the side. No alarm sounded.

If she could find Cane and get them out of here quietly, Lumas wouldn't know they'd escaped until morning ... as long as no one was monitoring the cameras.

She dropped the wire and nail in her pocket, then set out to find Cane. When Auburn brought him in, they had come from the right. She turned that direction and trod softly down the hall, her boots almost soundless on the marble floor.

Twenty minutes of searching brought her to his cell, the last one nearest the stairs with an electronic keypad for a lock. Using the nail, she pried off the outer covering to expose the wires that linked the buttons together. She would need a large pulse for this. Wrapping her fingers around the bundle of wires at the base of the unit, she brought back the memory of Daric with his fingers squeezing her neck.

The resultant jolt of electricity fried the wires and singed the fingers of her right hand. She rubbed them together as she used her left hand to slide open the door.

Cane was waiting and wrapped her in a tight hug. "Nice work. How did you get out of your cell?"

"Same, but different. We should go."

They crept down the stairs to the lower level without running into anyone.

At the base of the stairs, the sound of movement set her on edge. Mostly the stirring of dinosaurs. She kept her ears alert anyway.

When they reached the loading dock where they'd left their boat, she sighed in defeat. It was empty. Either Lumas had moved it, or he'd let it drift away. Cane put a hand on her slumped shoulders.

"What now?" she whispered.

He pointed with his thumb back the way they came. "Maybe Lumas moved it to another loading dock on the other side."

She nodded and let him take the lead. At this point, what did they have to lose?

He led them down the hallway past the area where they'd been captured by Lumas. Farther along, they discovered more cages, alternately filled and empty. She tried not to make eye contact with any animals inside. Best not to disturb them and cause them to make more noise.

Passing by one cage gave her goose bumps when the distinct odor of bitter almonds reminded her of Cane's deadly power. At another one, they jumped back from the cage when a tongue of fire shot out at them.

After what seemed like a mile, the hallway dead-ended in a human-sized metal door. Cane tested the handle. Locked.

The lock required a key in the handle. She pressed her ear to the door and heard sloshing water. This opened to a dock. It would be an entrance door, so the lock on the opposite side probably also required a key. Opening it wouldn't be as easy as sliding a piece of metal.

But they had nowhere else to go, unless they wanted to go upstairs and invite Lumas to recapture them. Cane either shared or sensed her frustration because he unclipped a nearby fire extinguisher from the wall and slammed it against the door handle. She winced at the loud ping of metal on metal.

The handle dented but didn't budge.

He slammed the extinguisher into it again, harder. The handle clattered to the floor.

She held her breath. Had it worked?

He dropped the fire extinguisher, stuck his fingers in the empty spot, and pulled the door open.

She resisted the urge to let out a joyful cheer and

followed him through the door, joining him on a solid platform. To their right, a set of stairs climbed up. To their left, an arched opening led to a metal catwalk. The soft swoosh of the ocean came from beyond.

She followed him through the archway to a loading area almost identical to the one where they'd arrived, except this one contained two boats. One vessel was similar in size to their missing boat but much newer. The other sat high on the water and was double the size. The hull looked big enough to contain another level below deck.

"Which one do you want to take?" she asked.

He pointed to the bigger boat. "That one would be faster, but it may take more fuel in addition to the solar panels."

"I vote for faster."

Apparently he agreed, because he didn't argue. He punched the control panel to open the roll-top metal door. The rollers creaked and groaned as the door lifted. Had someone heard the racket? How long before they were discovered?

He snagged keys from the hook under the dock labeled B. "Grab any gas cans you can find."

While he dragged several from the nearby corner, she jumped on the smaller boat and cannibalized the spare gas from there.

He climbed partway up the ladder. "Pass them up to me, and I'll throw them in."

She did as he asked, her tension mounting with every

second. No alarm had gone off, but someone might have heard them break the door open. She found a camera tucked into the corner of the ceiling. Maybe someone was on their way to stop them right now.

After she'd passed up the last can of gas, she looked around for anything else they might need. She grabbed a duffel bag marked "survival pack" and a clear unmarked jug that looked like water.

She unwound the rope securing the boat to the dock and climbed the ladder as Cane started the engine. The noise spiked her anxiety even higher. She breathed deep. They needed to get out of here. Funny, how she'd been so excited to arrive not even two days before.

The boat crept backward under the metal door.

Fast movement drew her gaze to the gangway.

Her breath caught in her throat. Adler raced down the catwalk and punched a button on the control panel. The metal door began to drop like a stone.

The boat was only halfway through. Both men seemed to realize the stakes at the same time.

Cane punched the throttle to the limit.

Adler drew a gun.

She ducked down, avoiding a shot that didn't come. As they cleared the door, she peeked over the dashboard.

Adler stared after them, his gun hand limp by his side. It was the reverse image of when she'd arrived on Extinction Island two weeks ago. Back then, Adler had looked eager and expectant. Now, the fury on his face left her with no doubt. He would pursue them.

▭

LUMAS FROWNED at the security camera image of Adler rushing frantically up the stairs to his office. As if Lumas didn't already know about the breakout. Adler was smart, just not a good strategist.

The door crashed open. He looked calmly at the sweaty man.

To his credit, Adler figured it out at once. "You let them go."

"Of course. That's why they're not still in one of my cages."

"Why didn't you tell me?"

"No time. She tried to hide it, but she discovered a clue in Penna's office. Something we overlooked." He gave a careless shrug. "I'll give her a little more time to find Penna. If she doesn't, then I'll have you capture her and keep her at the island site. Auburn's thinking of visiting the island anyway."

Adler raised his eyebrows at that.

Lumas frowned again. "She's tougher than you give her credit for."

"Spoken like a man who hasn't spent much time on Extinction Island."

He let the comment pass like a leaf floating lazily down the river. On the island, off the island. With Penna or without. He didn't care what it took. For too long, Adler had been his only operative. It was time to get this program back on track. "Have you have secured our insurance?"

"Yes, the boy is sleeping below in a cell of his own with the promise that his father will be here to see him in the morning."

"Good." Lumas stared off at the ceiling. "Penna could teach Auburn so many things. It's worth the risk to find out if she's still alive." He snapped his attention back to Adler and, with a wink, asked an obvious question. "Did you realize which boat she took?"

Adler thought for a moment before he broke out in a grin.

He returned the smile. "The package below deck will be quite a surprise for our dear Oakley."

CHAPTER SIXTEEN

OAKLEY AWOKE ALONE on a cot below deck. Cane must have already gone up top. This ship was outfitted with upgraded features, including autopilot, so last night, he set their course and told her they could both sleep below deck. They'd chosen adjacent cots and drifted off to sleep quickly.

All through the night, they'd periodically checked topside for pursuit. They appeared to be in the clear, but the new day might make them easier to find.

She glanced up at a wall clock. It was after eleven. She'd slept too late, but it was probably fine. If there was a problem, Cane would have come to get her.

She used the cramped bathroom. Privacy, what a luxury. On their trip to the lab, they'd had no onboard bathroom. Instead, they'd stopped once a day for her to use the ocean as a bathroom. But on this trip, the boat was well stocked with water, and hopefully there would be some food in the survival pack she'd grabbed.

When she came out of the bathroom, she scanned the small area crowded with stuff: navigational equipment, diving tanks, magazines on fishing, and a laptop computer. Despite the organizational issues, this area seemed like it would be bigger from the outside. Perhaps whatever lay beyond the locked door next to the bathroom took up a fair amount of space. They'd discovered the small door late last night when they were too tired to explore further.

She tried the unusual recessed handle on the door again. It wouldn't budge. Maybe there was a key around here somewhere. She'd have to look around after checking in with Cane.

She climbed the stairs to find him squinting at the complex dashboard. "All clear?"

He glanced behind them. "No boats visible, and no sound of an aircraft."

Satisfied, she dug into the survival pack. Inside was plenty of dried food, protein bars, and chewable vitamins. Then, her hand closed around a handle. She pulled out a tranquilizer gun. She hefted the pistol-sized weapon in her palm. Underneath lay empty cartridges that looked like squat, clear syringes. Could be useful if they ever found drugs to put in them.

She placed the gun back in the bag and stood. "Are we still on track?"

He pointed to the controls. "I believe so."

She rolled her shoulders to stretch her tense muscles.

Though they still didn't see anyone behind them, neither Lumas nor Adler would let them go without pursuit. If nothing else, she and Cane were part of Lumas's old-fashioned way of creating peacekeepers. He would continue to send Adler to Extinction Island. To find them. To drag them back.

Even if Lumas truly had noble goals for his peacekeeping force, she would have resisted the recruitment by force and manipulation. She deserved to make her own decisions. If they found Penna, maybe they'd get a little more information on Lumas.

She nabbed a protein bar from the duffel bag and sat with her feet kicked up on the comfy bench. They were safe, for now. The sea breeze ruffled her hair, easing her stress. Several minutes of silence ticked by.

From the corner of his eye, Cane watched her. When she caught him looking, he quickly averted his gaze. The elephant in the room—or rather standing in the boat, squashing their toes—couldn't be more obvious. Still, she refused to bring up their kiss.

She finished the protein bar and threw the wrapper back in the bag. "Want me to take over for a while?"

He didn't look at her. "I'm good."

"Need anything?"

"Nope."

Okay, so much for conversation. He might be waiting for her to broach the subject. She settled back to listen to the steady whoosh of the boat cutting through the water and the tinkle of tiny crashing whitecaps. The discussion would be just as awkward for her. Let him wait.

SINCE YESTERDAY, Chubs had run through various scenarios. A few subtle comments to Neve, and her subsequent reaction, confirmed what Henry had told him. Kaleo and Taye would be gone for several days. It was time to take action.

First, he had to subdue Henry and the three other men in the cave. For that, he would need a weapon.

He spent several hours yesterday searching the little-used rooms in the cave without appearing to be on a search. Between rooms, he moved gingerly as if still in pain, keeping up the ruse for Neve.

Today, he'd search the only area left—farther down the cave tunnel where Neve told him Cane normally slept. But he couldn't disappear for too long.

He waited half the day for the perfect opportunity. Finally, Neve and Wells decided to clean the tattered rugs in the living area. Piecing one large rug at a time into the small sink for scrubbing took all their attention. He silently crept toward the tunnel, then slipped through the archway while both women had their heads bent over the sink.

As he entered Cane's small room, he wrinkled his nose at the musty odor, probably due to the increased humidity deeper in the cave. Along one wall sat a cot and some storage containers. On the other, a desk with no drawers balanced on the irregular rock surface. Piles of books rested precariously on top.

He couldn't hit those guys with books to knock them out. Surely, the leader of this group would keep some protection at hand.

He rifled through the storage containers. The one on top held blankets and more books. The middle one had an assortment of old clothes. Chubs let out a low growl as he moved to the bottommost container.

More clothes, what looked like a scrapbook, and an old mirror. He set them all aside. Underneath, a flannel shirt covered the bottom of the container. Why did this guy keep every bit of clothes he'd ever owned?

Just to be thorough, he grabbed the shirt to pull it out. A solid thump sounded as it released an object from its folds. He lifted the shirt the rest of the way out. In the bottom lay a small pistol next to a low-profile cardboard box. It was a 20-round box of ammunition.

His heart rate soared. Almost reverently, he loaded half a dozen bullets into the weapon. He hefted the weight of it in his palm for several minutes. Not as powerful as the rifle he'd brought to school to execute Teresa, but more than enough to garner some respect.

He stood and stuck the weapon in the back pocket of his jeans. Neve may have brushed off his hints of interest so far, but she wouldn't be able to ignore him any longer.

The tunnel from the pastor's room to the front area was like a journey of rebirth. He had persevered through his trials and survived a Red Grizzly attack. Now his reward was imminent. He emerged in the living area with more anticipation than he'd had in a week.

Neve stood at the sink, still struggling to soap up a rug, while Wells supported the rest of the material. He watched her for several long minutes, in no hurry to claim his conquest. The swell of her breasts pushed at her T-shirt as she lifted the rug. Several hairs swept along her temple, having escaped her messy bun. Soon, she would be his.

"Neve, I need to talk to you."

"Okay, just give me a minute. We're almost done with this one."

He sat on a wicker stool to wait. Wells shot him curious glances, but Neve didn't look at him again.

When she finished, she pushed the stray hairs off her forehead and strode over to him. "What do you need?"

The other guys were resting in the men's quarters, so he tilted his head toward the back passageway. "Can we talk in private?"

She nodded and followed him. In this area, they were hidden from Wells's prying eyes, and yet not secluded enough to make Neve nervous.

Her petite face turned up to gaze into his eyes. He tried to memorize her features, to imprint her forever in his mind, but he didn't need to. He'd have the real thing to look at every morning and night.

"What's going on?" she asked.

He blinked. He was getting ahead of himself. "I need to tell you something, if you'll just bear with me."

"Okay?"

Using two fingers, he traced a line down her arm. She stepped back but didn't protest. "You are the kindest, gentlest woman I've ever met." The words didn't sound strong enough now that he was finally saying them. Still, he pressed on. "I need you more than I've ever needed anyone."

Her eyes went wide. She took another step back. "I'm sorry. I can't."

He grabbed her wrist before she pulled out of reach. "This isn't all in my head. I know you feel something for me."

She backed away, stretching her arm between them when he didn't let go. "The only thing I feel for you is God's compassion. Hasn't anyone ever showed you compassion?"

He pursued her a step. "This is more. I know it is."

"No," she said in a biting tone she hadn't used before.

His heart reeled in confusion. She'd taken such good care of him.

The only thing I feel for you is compassion. She meant sympathy. She felt sorry for him. The words stung, slicing through his heart like shards of ice. She'd only been kind to him because of her god. She'd used him to make herself seem like a caring person. To convince everyone that she was such a wonderful woman to take care of the sick and injured criminal.

Now she'd toss him aside ... just like Teresa had.

Rage bloomed bright and fiery inside his chest, a healing salve to the stinging words she'd just delivered. She couldn't treat him like this. He ground out his reply through clenched teeth. "You won't leave me."

Neve tore her wrist from his grip and darted toward the front room. He grabbed her around the waist as she hit the archway.

They tumbled to the ground.

Neve grunted as he fell on top of her. His first instinct was to ask if she was hurt. But she didn't care about hurting *him*. She'd led him on. Acting as if he was special when he meant nothing to her. She was just like Teresa. Beneath her velvet skin hid the soul of a selfish monster.

She wrestled with him. He allowed her to flip to her back while keeping her underneath him.

Despite his anger, his gaze locked on to her lips. He needed to taste her.

She turned her head away. He followed her movement and brought his lips to hers. She fought, but not enough. The sweet pull of desire washed over him, drowning the fury. He needed more.

When he pulled back for a breather, a scream erupted from Neve's throat. He pressed a hand over her mouth. Hopefully, the others hadn't heard.

A few tense seconds later, Wells came around the corner holding a smaller version of the rug they had been cleaning earlier. Her eyes went wide, but she didn't look surprised. More determined.

Before he could stand up to deal with her, she threw the rug over his head and tackled him.

He fell to the solid floor, taking the brunt of the rock on his shoulder. Instantly, Wells's weight released him. He scrambled to his feet while struggling to throw off the rug. Finally, he thrust it aside and cleared his vision.

Both women had disappeared.

He swiped a hand to his back pocket. The reassuring coolness of metal brushed his fingers.

They couldn't have gotten far. Leaving the gun in his pocket, he passed through the archway and moved down the nearest hallway to check the women's quarters.

Empty. Of course, they would have gone straight to the men's quarters for help.

As he pushed aside the curtain and strode into the living room, he practically barreled into Justin.

Justin spread his arms. "Hey, what's going on? Neve says you attacked her."

Chubs eyed him. He could play this in two different ways. Either match Justin's diplomatic approach or take it up a notch. He'd been waiting for days for this opportunity and no longer had the patience for diplomacy.

In one long stride, he met Justin where he stood, simultaneously snatching the gun from his pants. He struck quickly, giving Justin two hard whacks to the head with the butt of the gun.

Justin crumpled without a sound. Hopefully, no one in the other chambers would have any idea what happened. He took the time to tie Justin up with fishing wire, just in case he hadn't killed the man, and dragged his limp body to the corner of the room.

As he stood, he glanced around. Silence covered the cave like a blanket. No fearful whispering. No sound of people moving around.

He approached the curtain to the men's quarters, then carefully peeled it back as if the drapery might bite him. The visible portion of the room appeared empty. But he couldn't see around the corner where the room took an abrupt turn.

Cautiously, he moved through the dimly lit space. A slight smoky smell lingered in the air from when someone had extinguished the candles.

He shifted toward the back part of the room. With the gun hanging from one hand, he crept past empty cots.

A scraping noise came from behind him.

He whipped around. Henry leaped at him from beneath a cot that had been draped with a blanket. The man held a metal baseball bat high, ready to strike.

Instinct kicked in. Without considering what a ricocheting bullet might do if he missed, he fired the gun at Henry.

But he didn't miss.

A bullet hole pierced Henry's abdomen, cutting through the fabric of his gray T-shirt. Henry swayed for a minute before dropping to the floor. The baseball bat clattered and rolled haphazardly on the rocky surface.

Chubs followed the progression of the bat until it stopped in the middle of the room. From underneath a nearby cot, a pair of terrified eyes stared at him. A shuffling noise came from yet another cot where his gaze met a second pair of frightened eyes. He'd found the two final men. Neither made a move for the bat.

"Come over here," he directed.

They complied easily, not interested in experiencing Henry's fate. He forced them to tie each other up with the fishing wire.

A wheeze came from Henry's lips. The wound continued to bleed out in a dark stain that covered the lower half of his shirt. He would be dead within minutes. At least he'd fallen on the corner of a blanket. The cleanup would be simple.

With all of the men secured, he resumed his search. Where had the women gone?

When he came to the end of the men's quarters and found nothing, he doubled back and searched again. Still, no women. Had they found a way to use the zip line without a harness? Certainly, they both wouldn't have jumped to their deaths rather than be with him?

A quiet scraping brought his focus back to the rear of the men's quarters. He moved to the wall just before the angled turn. The sound stopped.

He examined the wall. A shadow of movement flickered from a narrow band of rock. He'd overlooked it before. An uneven crack, maybe eight inches wide, nearly invisible in the dark basalt.

The sweet scent of ginger lily filtered from behind the crack. His frustration mounted as the awful truth became clear. Though Neve was short and Wells was tall, both women were fine-boned. Both could squeeze sideways into this crack. They'd had a safe room in the cave all along.

He shoved his arm in up to the shoulder to feel around. Someone scratched him from elbow to wrist. He let out a curse word and pulled his arm out, swiping the blood onto the floor.

A primal growl came from deep in his gut. He'd need twice the opening to fit through. The women were here, not more than two arm's-lengths away, but he couldn't get to them.

Charging back to Henry's now-dead body, he grabbed the baseball bat, then ran at the wall, determined to strike out at the offending rock. Common sense stopped him a few feet short with the bat suspended in the air. The ceiling hung low in this part of the cave. What if the rock above the crack had the effect of a supporting beam for the rest of the structure? He might tear it down, only to have the whole cave collapse on his head.

It wasn't worth the risk of burying them all alive. He dropped the bat and sat down on a cot. The women couldn't stay in there forever. Dehydration and hunger would drive them out eventually.

An idea came to him. In the meantime, he'd make sure they would have no interruptions.

After finding what he needed in the kitchen, he went to the cave entrance. He hefted the thick butcher's knife in one hand, then switched his grip. Why risk ripping open his newly healed back by twisting too much. Using both hands, he gripped the knife, reared back, and struck out at the metal zip-line cord.

The knife stuck halfway in. He jiggled it until it came free.

He raised it and struck again, cutting clean through. The cord whipped down to dangle against the rocks of the opposite cliff. *Let's see Kaleo and Taye try to take this place back now.*

CHAPTER SEVENTEEN

KALEO ROLLED his shoulders to ease the tension building there and bounced in his squat to relieve his tired legs. He and Taye had endured many cramped situations for the last two days while stalking Demon Dragon; however, none compared to the squat he'd had to stay in for the past half hour. The newly arrived FBI agents had picked their campsite wisely—at the top of a hill with visibility on all sides because of the sparse growth of trees. The unusually spongy ground in this area wouldn't support most species of trees and was also the reason they were forced to squat rather than sit on the moist ground.

It was odd for the agents to create a campsite at all. There were only three agents and a doctor. Why not stay at the fortified lab where Raptor stayed?

Perhaps they wanted a location closer to where they thought Dr. Anderson disappeared. Or perhaps they were so arrogant as to believe they could handle the dinosaurs and convicts without aid or a fortified shelter.

But Kaleo and Taye weren't here to engage the agents. When they had ventured to the tree house for their meeting with Raptor, he hadn't showed. Upon leaving, they'd heard voices and come to investigate. These men must have shown up in the middle of the night.

Off to one side of the camp, Raptor argued with an FBI agent while two other agents worked on the other side, pounding in stakes for a metal framework. Kaleo strained to hear their conversation but could only catch snatches of it in between the clanging blows. He motioned to Taye, and they retreated to the tree house.

About ten minutes later, Raptor joined them, looking harried. He sat on an empty cot and wiped a layer of sweat off his face.

"Who was that nice gentleman you were talking to?" Kaleo asked.

Raptor narrowed his eyes at the sarcasm. "Special Agent Gabe Glaser. Expert manhunter and partner to deceased Agent Jack Fischer."

His heart thudded in his chest. "You mean, the Agent Fischer that Demon Dragon ate?"

"Yep. At the moment, he thinks Dr. Wells Anderson may be responsible for the death."

Kaleo blinked at him. "Why? Didn't you tell him about us?"

Raptor shrugged. "I tried, but Special Agent Glaser had already found out about Wells's ties to CADRE, which she only recently joined. She wouldn't have been on the list to come here if they'd have known she was part of a group opposed to the death penalty." He blew out a breath. "The agent believes she came down here to free prisoners by deactivating their trackers. He believes Agent Fischer tried to stop her, so she killed him and assumed the dinosaurs would eat the evidence."

"Quite a theory. At least Wells is safe at the cave." He pulled Wells's cell phone from his back pocket. "I guess they will be looking for this once we turn it back on."

Raptor gave a wry smile. "Exactly what I was thinking."

Kaleo pocketed the phone and stood. "I'll make sure it keeps them busy for a while."

Though they probably wouldn't gain much from all this stalling, he needed to keep the FBI off their back for Raptor's sake. Oakley would want him to protect Raptor. The cadence of her name, even said in his own head, brought a pinch of longing to his heart. Hopefully, she'd gotten away, never to return, but he'd also give anything to hold her in his arms again. The chasm between those two realities was an immense canyon cutting through his heart.

He shook off the melancholy thoughts and climbed down the ladder from the treehouse. With Taye following, he turned south, the same direction they'd come from earlier in the morning. Hunting wouldn't be easy at this time of day, but maybe they'd get lucky.

An hour into their hike, Taye stopped him with a

hand on his shoulder and pointed at the ground a few feet away where matted grass formed a rough ring. Well, not exactly a ring, more like the faint outline of a large footprint. They were in the right territory.

Kaleo tugged out his whip, and they both settled down behind some bushes to wait for prey. Not long after, a juvenile *Hadrosaurus* wandered close to their blind.

He struck out. The tip of his whip hit the animal across the neck, gouging out a large hole. He repeated the strike to open the gash wider. The animal dropped to its knees, spraying blood and leaves up in an arc. Blood continued to spurt out with each of its heartbeats.

Taye jumped up to finish the animal with a spear through the lungs.

As it lay dying, Kaleo fished the cell phone out of his pocket and turned it on. Still seventy percent battery. His original plan was to put the phone in the animal's neck, but the chest contained the prime cuts of rib meat. Even better. He twisted the spear in the *Hadrosaur's* chest to make a larger opening, then shoved the phone into the gaping hole. Hopefully, something larger would take the bait.

THE CLOSER THEY came to Extinction Island, the more tense Cane appeared. They'd spent yesterday and today in almost total silence. Oakley's vow to let him bring up their kiss had led to a charged atmosphere of awkwardness.

She sat mute under the solar canopy, watching the ocean and searching for signs of pursuit. With a baseball cap on his head that they'd found in the survival pack, Cane manned the controls of the boat, even though he didn't need to, thanks to the autopilot.

When he finally broke the spell of their silence, she jumped a little in her seat.

"Are you sure you want to go back?" He threw the words over his shoulder.

Where was this coming from? The entire trip was about finding the person who'd manipulated their DNA. Now that they knew it was Penna, they had to try to find her, and all signs pointed to Extinction Island. Kaleo's words from more than a week ago came floating into her mind. *Don't come back.*

He meant to protect her. If she came back, she might not get the chance to escape again. But what kind of future would she have if she didn't know where she'd come from or what they'd created her to do? Her right eye twitched again. She absently rubbed it.

At her continued silence, Cane faced her and pressed on. "The government will hunt you down and implant your tracker again."

True. But could she run and never look back? Never see Dad or Eric or Kaleo again? And what about Raptor? He'd probably pay the price for her disappearance.

"I can't run. I have to know exactly what she did to

me, how messed up my genome is." She held her left hand out to mark one extreme. "There's you." She held her right hand out far to the other side. "Then, there's Adler. Somewhere in between is me. I need to know where I fit on whatever scale of evil that Penna used to create us."

He scoffed. "You're no more evil than I am."

Of course, he'd see the best in her. "Says the saintly pastor."

He bristled.

"I'm sorry. Sometimes, I can't help the sarcasm."

He shook his head. "That doesn't bother me. What concerns me most is that you do the same to yourself."

She blinked at him several times. "What do you mean?"

"It isn't just me you push away. Inside, you hold back from yourself, afraid to go too deep, afraid of what you'll find."

"Because I'll find a killer."

"Yes, you've made the choice to kill." His sea-green eyes bored into hers. "But you are much more than the sum of your choices."

This time, she shook her head. "It's not that simple."

"Isn't it?" Before she could formulate a response, he continued with words that froze her brain in its tracks. "You think I haven't killed before?"

No, it couldn't be true. This loving, gentle man wouldn't have hurt someone, much less killed them. Not this man who'd come to Extinction Island to find his birth mother and tell people to live for God. A nervous flutter went through her stomach. Unless he came for a different reason.

"I'm not wanted for murder if that's what you're thinking. I got away with it, which is probably worse."

He dropped onto the captain's chair backward, his chin coming to rest on top of the headrest. For a moment, he stared at her, deciding something.

His next words came out in a rush. "I was ten. My power had already surfaced. I'd killed squirrels and rats up to that point, mostly to impress my best friend, Sam. One day, shortly after Christmas, Sam found a stray dog. It had dirty, matted fur, and ribs that stood out like twigs beneath its skin. The poor thing would do anything for food."

He took a shallow breath. "Sam wanted me to kill the dog. I couldn't do it. Squirrels and dogs were different to me. Sam got angry and said he'd do it himself if I was too scared. Before I could stop him, he grabbed a large rock and slammed it into the dog's skull. The dog fell down, stunned. I clasped my hands over my ears, trying to block out the sound as Sam hit the animal five more times before it stopped moving.

"When Sam stood up, triumphant, a burst of anger exploded inside my head. The anger traveled through my body to my hands."

Her stomach soured at the direction of his narrative. A lump formed in her throat.

"The swirling poisonous mist shot out at Sam. He tried to run, but within seconds he couldn't breathe. His face went red. He collapsed and made gasping, choking noises. I pushed more mist at him until he went still."

She tried to swallow the lump in her throat, but it wouldn't budge. "Then, what did you do?"

"I ran away, leaving Sam and the dog lying side by side in a field near his house." Cane ran a hand over his shaggy hair. "I discovered much later that his face went red because the oxygen stayed in his blood, unable to penetrate his cells. The coroner determined Sam's death was an asthma attack so severe that he didn't have time to use his inhaler." He swallowed hard. "Sam might have been cruel, at times, but he didn't deserve to die."

For several moments, she stayed silent while processing his words. He was a murderer, like her. Rather than comforting her, this knowledge reinforced her fear that evil was encoded inside them ... even inside Cane. In a gentle voice, she said, "We were created to kill. I feel it deep inside. Don't you?"

He shook his head. "DNA manipulation may have given me the *power* to kill, but I can control it. I choose how to use it."

His perspective held a certain appeal. But her heart argued against it. Choices were an indecipherable mix of outside pressure, personal conviction, and feelings—the latter two being subject to a genetic connection. She would likely feel and believe a certain way because she was genetically programmed to lean in that direction.

Of course, she had choices. As had her mother. But

bad choices seemed to run in families. How could anyone say there was no genetic component to it?

After a long silence, she replied quietly, "I wish I had your conviction."

He turned back to the dashboard to stare out at the sea. Not long afterward, she retreated below deck. Once again, the locked door beckoned her. She'd tried several times already to unlock it, with no success.

The door didn't have a normal handle. Instead, a square plate lay flat against the fiberglass with a metal pull lever, not unlike an airplane bathroom door handle. The lever would pull out, but the door wouldn't open. The keyhole looked like it took a full-sized key. She'd searched the cabin thoroughly for one but found none.

Letting out a sigh, she stepped up to the door and tugged against the latch. Like every other time, it didn't budge. Was this some sort of safe room to protect passengers from pirates? Not likely. A safe room wouldn't help if it took too long to get in there yourself.

Stepping back, she tried to judge the size of the room based on her imagined dimensions of the boat. The side by the bathroom could be as long as ten feet. The width looked even bigger but was blocked by the two rows of cots. On that wall, a framed picture of a *T. rex* skeleton hung. Unusual choice for a boat, but this *was* Lumas's boat.

Maybe there was another entrance behind the cots. She moved Cane's cot out of the way and subsequently bumped the picture with her elbow. It swung side to side.

Something shiny winked at her from underneath. She yanked the picture down.

A silver circular knob stuck out a half-inch from the wall. Next to the knob, a small pewter sign had been drilled into the fiberglass: *Pull for Viewing*.

Viewing what? She grabbed the knob and pulled.

A mailbox-sized part of the wall slid to the right, exposing a wide hole into a dimly lit room. A flash of quick movement made her jump backward. The nails-against-chalkboard screech of a raptor sent ice shooting through her veins.

"Cane!"

The panic in her voice, and probably the screech, brought him running. "What?"

She pointed with a trembling finger. He drew up short, his eyes bulging.

Sharp teeth snapped at the air outside the viewing window. The raptor had flipped its head sideways, trying to get at them. Two of its lower teeth on each side stuck out in an arc, giving it a fang-toothed appearance. This was a different type of raptor. One that probably couldn't close its mouth completely on a normal day.

Avoiding the random slicing of its teeth, she slid to the side and put her hands on the little window. "Help me."

Together, they pushed the raptor's snout out of the way inch by inch and shoved the window closed. A satisfying click sounded as the cover moved into place. When they let go, the window stayed shut.

She pressed a shaking hand to her chest. "Didn't think I'd find so many teeth in that little room."

"I guess we know how they transport the smaller dinosaurs to the island."

"Can you hear it in there?"

They both went silent to listen.

Cane shook his head. "The room must be sound-proof." He began to pace. "It probably has a built-in water source, which would explain the extra jugs of water sitting around. But they would have to feed it." He stopped pacing to look at her. "What should we do with it?"

She squared her shoulders. They didn't have a key for the room or any meat to feed it. "Let it die in there."

"Of starvation? Wow, the dinosaur whisperer has grown cold."

Though his tone was teasing, a note of truth rang through it. Neither one of them had lived up to the expectations of the other.

CHAPTER EIGHTEEN

SPECIAL AGENT GABE GLASER tugged on his gloves and stared down at the remains of his partner's body, trying to dispassionately assess the carnage. The whole of Agent Jack Fischer had a blackened appearance as if it had been charred. His stomach and intestines were gone, likely devoured by dinosaurs. The rib cage showed evidence of gnawing from large teeth. His head remained the least affected with only scratch marks and nicks on his cheeks, probably because the head contained the least amount of meat. His thighs had deep areas of missing flesh, whereas his ankles and calves remained relatively untouched.

Gabe snapped several pictures with his phone before covering the body again with a sheet. The other agents would place Jack on a stretcher for eventual transport back to his family.

The stump of an arm stuck out from underneath the

sheet. One of Jack's big, meaty hands had been ripped off completely. Gabe swallowed through a thick throat. Those hands had gripped a handgun as Jack and Gabe qualified together during training at the police academy. Those hands had dealt round after round of poker on long stakeout nights. Those hands had played racquetball with Gabe most Wednesday nights for years.

He didn't deserve to die like this, especially not six months before retirement. Jack's wife, Sharon, expected to have her husband out of dangerous duty and back into civilian life. No one had informed her of the tragedy yet. Gabe had kept it quiet until he could confirm it. Truth was, he hadn't believed it himself until just now.

He pushed down the simmering rage and focused on the facts. Raptor said he hadn't met the boat when it arrived. And yet, it was he who'd showed Gabe where to find Jack's body. Had he stumbled across it by accident as he'd said, or had someone told him where it was? He gave the appearance of cooperating, but something seemed off.

Gabe blew out a breath and focused on his training.

Start at the beginning. Four days ago, Jack arrived with Dr. Wells Anderson. They met someone, apparently not Raptor but who must have claimed to be Raptor, then Jack ended up dead a mere mile away. Without a forensics team, time of death couldn't be determined, but given the locus, it was probably the same night or early the next day.

Guilt welled up inside him. His partner had died horribly, violently, while he'd slept peacefully in his own bed on the mainland.

He lifted the corner of the sheet to give the body another once over. A red mark on Jack's ankle caught his attention. It was a puncture wound, smaller and more pinpoint than the others. He looked around on the forest floor. Nearby, several jagged pieces of metal were scattered among the leaves. He picked one up in his gloved hand, admiring the tapered edges.

Definitely made by human hands. Come to think of it, someone had carved a strange symbol on a tree about five yards away. It could mark the location of some sort of ritual. Had Jack died solely from a dinosaur attack, or had he walked into a deadly ambush and was left here for the dinosaurs to finish? It was impossible to tell. On an island full of killers, someone could have planned it to look like a random attack. Even Dr. Anderson.

Gabe slipped the metal shard into a plastic evidence bag as his mind continued down the rabbit hole of other possibilities. Perhaps an opportunistic criminal killed Jack in order to rape Dr. Anderson? Or maybe Jack discovered something about her, causing her to eliminate him? Her association with CADRE, though recent, couldn't be ignored. Citizen's Against Death Row and Execution had orchestrated bloody demonstrations in front of the White House, released recordings of attacking dinosaurs over the loudspeakers at crowded malls, and last year, had designed a mechanized dinosaur replica to scare children at the Easter Egg Hunt on Capitol grounds. They hadn't resorted to violence before, but every organization had its fanatical members.

Perhaps Dr. Anderson was a fanatic. Perhaps not. Either way, he'd find her and learn the truth of what happened. He owed Sharon Fischer that much.

He searched the area for several more hours. The only thing of note was a partially charred enclosure made of branches. He crawled in cautiously and found nothing at all. Not even ashes to indicate the disposal of evidence. He crawled out more confused than ever.

The satellite phone in his backpack emitted a sharp tone. He dug it out to read the notification. A smile broke the tension on his face. Dr. Anderson's cell phone had just come back online. This could be the break he needed.

After organizing the transport of Jack's body back to camp, Gabe turned his attention to finding the cell phone. Stealth was paramount on this mission, so he grabbed one agent—the oldest one—to back him up. In his early thirties, Agent Dean Sykes was young enough to have stamina and brawn, but old enough to follow instructions as ordered.

Given the general fascination with dinosaurs, there was no shortage of agents volunteering for the few missions necessary on Extinction Island. Even so, the FBI typically sent the youngest, most inexperienced agents. Probably because they had less family to miss them if they didn't return. Unfortunately, Jack had been at the wrong place at the wrong time, having just dropped a prisoner off at the dock, so his superiors had asked him to go. Otherwise, he wouldn't have been here either.

Five miles and several hours of hard jungle travel

brought them to the edge of a clearing. Gabe walked cautiously while peering at his satellite phone—an oversized version of a regular phone with specialized programs for tracking worldwide. Dr. Anderson's cell phone remained motionless forty yards ahead of them, on the other side of the clearing.

Gabe raised a fist to halt Sykes. Snuffling and panting noises came from an unseen area beyond the trees. The rest of the jungle was silent. Tree trunks for the last mile had shown the same scorching found on the burned enclosure and also on Jack's body. They had to be close to the dinosaur that fed on him.

A glance over his shoulder. Sykes was dancing on the balls of his feet impatiently. Gabe shook his head to tell him to stop. If he didn't exercise some self-control, they both might be dinosaur bait.

Gabe held his breath. A few moments passed with no noises up ahead. The twittering of birds hadn't returned, however, so his senses stayed on alert as he motioned for forward progress.

They crossed the grassy area, tranquilizer rifles at the ready. On the other side, he halted behind a thick tree to check the location again. Only ten yards away now. If not for the dense foliage, they'd be able to see to the animal already.

No way around it, they'd have to go back into the jungle. He signaled ten and then forward again. As they proceeded, he avoided leaves and sticks in order to travel silently. He scanned bushes and trees for a trail, but it was no use. Much of the vegetation had been trampled as if many animals used this area. Hopefully, they weren't walking into a den of some sort.

He reached out and fingered a soot-covered leaf on a bush. Somehow, this charring led back to an animal. But how?

A quick vibration on his phone let him know the target was on the move again. Rustling noises and quick bursts of breath came from the trees ahead.

He signaled to take cover, then dashed to his right and behind a large tree trunk. Sykes stood frozen, only partially hidden by a small bush. Gabe motioned again for him to take cover.

He finally reacted by ducking down, but it was too late.

From the tree line, a gigantic dinosaur charged out, teeth bared. It resembled a *T. rex* with the addition of two menacing, six-inch horns stuck to its head.

Sykes panicked. Rather than stay behind the bush, he ran across the open field. He dropped the rifle as his arms pumped, and he picked up speed.

But his sprint wouldn't outrun a dinosaur. Gabe tracked the target, made allowance for the creature's speed, and shot a tranquilizer dart into its thigh.

The dinosaur roared at Sykes as if he'd done it and then let out a long stream of fire from its mouth. Gabe gaped at the scene for a split second. He'd never seen a blast so intense from anything other than a flamethrower. This thing was some sort of fairy-tale dragon.

Anguished howls poured from Sykes's mouth. The agony brought Gabe back to his senses. The man was still running. The backs of his arms were black, and his hair was on fire.

The dinosaur had slowed, but not stopped, its pursuit. One dart obviously wasn't enough. Gabe raised his weapon, sighted, and let another one fly. It hit the animal behind the ear hole, causing it to turn as if looking for an enormous mosquito.

Almost in slow motion, Sykes went down, limbs flailing.

Fortunately, the dinosaur had begun to exhibit the effects of the drugs. It swayed on its feet for several long seconds before collapsing next to Sykes, its teeth only inches away from the agent's feet.

Gabe lowered the weapon and cautiously approached. No movement from either party. The dinosaur would survive. As for Sykes, who knew? Angry pus-filled blisters were forming on all of his exposed skin.

For a few seconds, Gabe looked back and forth between the two of them. A glance at his tracking app confirmed it. Dr. Anderson's phone rested inside the belly of this beast. He wasn't supposed to kill any dinosaurs while on this mission, but if he split this one open, he'd find out if it had killed Jack and possibly Dr. Anderson. No one would know.

Sykes's moan effectively sealed his decision. If this man had a chance to live, Gabe would help him. He rigged up a stretcher with three long branches and some rope, then began the arduous process of dragging Sykes back to camp.

As he left the dinosaur behind, his investigative mind ran through the facts again. Dr. Anderson's phone had only just come back online. Was it a glitch in the communication satellites? Or had someone recently turned it on? Perhaps she'd turned it on right before she was eaten? Except the only body he'd found was Jack's. No Dr. Wells Anderson. No Oakley Laveau. The absence of these women spoke volumes. He hadn't figured out the puzzle yet, but a growing suspicion hardened in his gut. If he found one, he'd likely find the other.

OAKLEY AND CANE had gotten good at avoiding two things: discussing the dinosaur in the safe room and dealing with the issues between them. Perhaps they could exist like this until they got back and not confront what had happened at the lab. She couldn't get that lucky, could she?

Last night, they'd used up a lot of their gas reserves to allow the boat to continue running on autopilot while they slept. This morning, Cane had said the gamble paid off. Only one more day left at sea.

Cane had spent most of the day standing at the wheel, leaning against the captain's chair, ignoring her. For her part, she was hyperaware of his movements, even the shallow level of his breathing. Not that his revelation about having killed his friend made her afraid of him. Quite the opposite. It had made him seem more real. From the moment they'd met, she'd unconsciously put him on a pastoral pedestal. Now, he was no longer out of reach. Cane truly was just a man.

"Let me take over for a while," she said.

His shoulder brushed hers as he gave her the captain's chair. An indecipherable ripple of emotion traveled through her stomach. She took up his previous posture, leaning against the seat, though not quite sitting. There was no need to grip the steering wheel because the autopilot did a better job keeping them on course than she would.

Glancing over her shoulder, she scanned the horizon for other boats. They appeared to be alone, but Adler was back there somewhere.

"Do you think they can track the boat?" she asked.

"Yeah, it probably has GPS on it. From our heading, they already know we're going back to the island." Cane's right hand tightened into a fist. A few seconds later, he relaxed it. "What if we did something unexpected? I could steer the boat to shore right now. We'd end up north, maybe in Honduras, then we could just disappear."

Not going back meant giving up on finding Penna. She would never know the extent of what Penna and her mother had done to her. More importantly though, she'd be deserting Kaleo and Raptor. The FBI would be all over Raptor, thinking he'd helped her escape. She opened her mouth to speak, then held her tongue. One look at Cane's face silenced her. He was asking for more reasons than just to protect her. He wanted her to run away with *him.*

After a deep breath, her words came out in a shaky whisper. "I can't."

"It's because of him, isn't it?" His tone held no venom, only sadness.

Clearly he didn't mean Raptor. She opened her mouth again, and again the words refused to fall from her tongue. No matter how she answered, she couldn't lie to him. He'd know the truth. Probably knew it now.

"I need to hear you say it."

She cleared her throat and spoke in a gentle voice. "I think your interest in me is from the pheromones."

He lowered his voice almost to a growl. "Don't tell me what I feel."

"Sorry." Her voice sounded weak even to her own ears. "You and I have a connection I haven't experienced before. You seem to know everything I feel. And I get feelings from you too. What you ... um, I can't come up with a better word ... *emanate* is pure and good."

A tiny curve graced his lips. It fled the second she spied it.

"Is this because I'm a pastor?" He narrowed his eyes at her. "Because God made me a man first."

"I have no doubt about your testosterone levels." Hopefully, her teasing words hid the heat creeping into her cheeks at the memory of their kiss.

He spoke his next words quietly. "Who would you choose?"

So much for avoiding this conversation. Cane wanted an answer, better yet, he deserved one.

Another silence fell as she tried to conjure the right words. When she answered, it was as if she was pressing her way through a thick swamp. "With you, I'm off balance and examining everything inside, all of my motives, my desires, my beliefs. That's good and helps me grow, up to a point."

He stared at her with no emotions that she could discern.

"But with Kaleo, I'm centered and ready to take on the world. Around him, I feel powerful. Even when we can't be together, I belong with him."

Her heart wilted as Cane seemed to deflate. She kept her gaze focused on him until he looked at her. His normally bright sea-green eyes were dull with disappointment.

"I'm sorry."

"It's okay. I'm never completely alone."

He meant God, of course. But he deserved to find a woman to make him happy, even though that woman wouldn't be her. Problem was, he'd have a tough time finding one on Extinction Island.

CHAPTER NINETEEN

A FULL DAY of tracking the *Carnotaurus* over a two-mile spread had led Special Agent Gabe Glaser to a canyon and one colossal pile of feces. Obviously, this dinosaur had the foresight to defecate into a ravine to keep feces away from its den.

He'd taken on the tracking job alone because Agent Dean Sykes had died within hours of arriving back at camp. Gabe wouldn't risk any more of his agents on this hunt.

The steaming pile stood as high as his waist and gagged him with the odor of decay. Somewhere in there lay Dr. Anderson's phone. He wasn't looking for it as much as he was looking for bones and clothing as evidence of digestion.

He tied a handkerchief around his mouth and nose, donned thick gloves, then got to work. Using a long, curved stick as a rake, he combed through the pile in layers. Anything hard he laid to the side.

Several times, strips of what looked like cloth got wrapped around the stick. He placed those aside as well.

It took several hours to properly sift through the dung. Once he'd finished, he walked away to take a break and clear his nose. He removed his gloves, traversed a short distance to a creek, and rinsed his upper arms clean.

Afterward, he put the soiled gloves back on and returned to his treasure pile. He started with the hard items. Many were animal bones. These he discarded.

Dr. Anderson's phone popped up in the middle of the pile. He wiped the plastic off as much as possible and slipped it into an evidence bag.

In total, he found only two human bones—a finger bone and a rib—which he treated with care. He held them up to his own body. They were a close match and therefore too big to be Dr. Anderson's or even Oakley's. They probably belonged to Jack. He placed them in a separate evidence bag.

The clothing turned out to be the hardest to identify. The items had so much feces covering them that he couldn't determine the color. He took them to the creek and washed them off, revealing bits of denim and strips of a forest-green shirt. The jeans could have belonged to anyone. The shirt was likely Jack's. The security officer from the boat said he had been wearing a forest-green polo when he'd arrived, and bits of the shirt had been left on his body.

Dr. Anderson had last been seen in a light pink, long-sleeved T-shirt. He found nothing matching that description in the dinosaur's feces.

Gabe stripped off his gloves and tossed them to the ground. None of Dr. Anderson's bones. None of Dr. Anderson's clothing. It could mean she was eaten by another dinosaur, but why then would her phone be inside this one?

He tapped his finger on his chin as he rolled through the possibilities. Maybe she killed Jack and faked her death so she could help Oakley Laveau flee without being tagged. He shook his head. A right-to-lifer like Dr. Anderson probably wouldn't kill one person to save another.

Perhaps Oakley arranged for someone to pretend to be Raptor, then she killed Jack and kidnapped Dr. Anderson. In exchange for her freedom, would Dr. Anderson have promised to help Oakley get off the island? Through CADRE, she could have connections to people with boats. If so, he might be too late. Oakley could be streaming across the ocean away from the island right now.

Or maybe Dr. Anderson had simply run away from the dinosaur attack and was hiding in the jungle.

There were too many variables here. But considering that an imposter met them at the boat, Jack's death was looking less and less like an accident and more like murder. When the truth came to light, Gabe wouldn't bother to arrest the people responsible. Most everyone here had already had their day in court. He'd have no qualm about carrying out their sentence and executing them immediately. And if Dr. Anderson tried to get in the way … well, he couldn't be responsible for her safety.

SINCE YESTERDAY, the tension between Oakley and Cane had dissipated. Within hours of the discussion ending any romantic relationship between them, Cane seemed to accept her decision. In fact, he'd returned to the peaceful man she'd met weeks ago.

He talked more about his childhood than he had before. He'd grown up happy, except for the incident with the boy he killed. The trauma didn't cause him to repress his power, as her trauma had, but it forced him to learn how to control it. For years, he continued to practice on wild animals until he'd worked out exactly how fast the poison dispersed in the air and how to keep from releasing it involuntarily.

He told of how he struggled with anger when his first girlfriend had cheated on him. He confronted her, and she laughed in his face at his gullibility. In his anger, a small amount of hydrogen cyanide leaked from his fingers. Thankfully, he'd controlled his hands before the poison killed her. She passed out and woke up with a migraine headache, but she'd survived and went on to make other guys look like fools.

After that story, Oakley had given him a sad smile. If

only she wouldn't have been one more woman in the line of heartache for Cane. Maybe he should consider Neve. Though she was probably ten years older, she'd been his main companion for the last several years.

"Land ho!" Cane turned from the captain's wheel, a combination of relief and trepidation on his face.

"Really?" She jumped up to stare out the front of the boat. Sure enough, a gray lumpy mass burgeoned along the horizon. *Costa Rica.* Or more correctly, Extinction Island. Her heart ached at returning to the shackles of her prison. But her search for answers started here and, hopefully, would end here.

A muffled cry from below deck startled her. "Did you hear that?"

Cane nodded, and his brow wrinkled.

The vessel shuddered as a thump sounded beneath their feet. Since they'd closed the viewing window two days ago, they hadn't heard any evidence of their fang-toothed reptilian stowaway. The dinosaur had to be getting desperate from starvation by now. "I'll go check it out."

Cane looked like he wanted to argue, but if they were coming close to the island, he'd need to be at the wheel. Autopilot wouldn't dock the boat. He gave her a sideways look. "Be careful."

She took a tentative step down, then bent at the waist to scan the area. The door was still shut and locked. The viewing window was still securely closed.

Another thump rolled through the air, followed by a

gnawing sound as if a thousand rats were eating through the walls. The noise centered on a space near the floor. She continued down the stairs.

As her feet hit the bottom deck, a metal grid slid across the floor toward her. She bent down and grabbed it. A ventilation grid.

She dropped to her knees to look under Cane's cot. At the base of the wall, a thick gray-green tail stuck out from the hole where the grid must have been. Far from lying on its back preparing to die, Fangtooth was fighting to get out.

The tail disappeared, quickly replaced by a sideways snarling and snapping mouth. Instinctively, she backed away, even though it couldn't reach her ... yet.

The teeth scraped and rubbed along the sides of the opening. The dinosaur wasn't trying to reach her. It was trying to make the opening bigger.

"Cane, we've got a problem!"

His feet clomped down the steps in between growls and snarls and snapping pieces of fiberglass. Already, wads of foam and chunks of the wall were sliding across the floor.

"Fangtooth is coming out."

He didn't respond, merely tugged her arm backward. Once they were topside, he looked first at her, then over her shoulder at the fast-approaching land. "I think we'll make it to shore before that thing gets out, but it could be close." He swiped a line of sweat off his forehead. "I don't want you down there with it for too long because your scent will probably make it work harder to get out, but go back down and gather up whatever you can for supplies."

She obeyed, clinging to the railing as Cane revved the engine higher. A quick glance under the cot told her the dinosaur could now stick its entire head through the opening.

With shaking hands, she grabbed the duffel bag that held the dart gun. She threw in all the food they had left and zipped it up, then she raced back up the stairs to the sound of more thumps. Fangtooth was ramming its wide shoulders into the wall, straining for freedom.

At the top of the stairs, she slammed the hatch door closed. Unfortunately, it couldn't be locked from the outside, but the latch would slow the creature down a little.

A wave of relief washed over her when she peered ahead. The island was much closer. Distances on the water were hard to judge, but it looked like it was a few hundred yards away.

She clutched the duffel bag tightly to her chest. The fiberglass deck vibrated, either from Fangtooth's desperate blows or the stress of the engine running at full speed. The only thing worse than being trapped on an island with hundreds of bloodthirsty dinosaurs was being trapped on a boat with one.

Cane pointed straight ahead. "We probably won't have time to dock in the cave and climb out. I'm heading for that tiny beach over there."

"But then it will follow us onto the island. Can't we sink the boat and swim?"

"To sink a boat takes time that we don't have. Even if I cut the engine, it will still make landfall somewhere."

A loud crack came from below. Was she imagining the worst-case scenario, or was that the wall of Fangtooth's enclosure breaking apart?

Cane pushed her toward the side of the boat. "You might be right. I think we'll need to swim."

Several long scraping noises. The cots being pushed aside?

More scraping. Then, right near the hatch came the tick of claws on fiberglass. Fangtooth was completely out now.

A thump vibrated the covering hatch, followed by the sound of something falling down the stairs. The raptor likely had trouble keeping traction on the small steps.

With her gaze focused on the hatch, she backed away to lean against the railing, but Cane couldn't move unless he let go of the wheel.

She dared to glance over her shoulder. They were about a hundred yards out. They needed maybe a minute to make it to shore. But then what? The beach was open and exposed. They'd be better off in the water, assuming raptors couldn't perform some version of a dinosaur doggy paddle.

She opened her mouth to suggest they jump just as the hatch crashed open.

"Go!" Cane yelled.

Fangtooth's clawed feet slid on the slick floor. Its wide eyes focused on the person closest to it—Cane. She couldn't jump and let him sacrifice himself for her.

The raptor slid, but quickly regained balance. It moved slowly and menacingly toward Cane.

"You have to jump!" he yelled.

"Not without you!"

Her shout confused Fangtooth for a brief second. It peered at her with piercing pea-green eyes. After deciding she didn't pose a threat, it continued to stalk Cane.

With its focus on him, she circled around behind while setting the bulky duffel down on the bench. By the time she reached Fangtooth's flank, it was poised to pounce, its tail stiff, every muscle tense.

As Fangtooth leaped at Cane, she grabbed the tail, simultaneously trying to summon her electrical power. Sparks ran through her arm.

Not nearly enough to stun the creature. But it stopped to figure out the foreign sensation.

Fangtooth's head flipped around. Its piercing eyes focused on her again like twin lasers.

She needed more electricity. This raptor was only a little bigger than the one she'd electrocuted before. She could do this. She tightened her grip on its tail.

Fangtooth jumped into the air and swung in a violent arc to pull its tail from her grasp. It landed, then leaned toward her, mouth opened in what looked like a grin. Its dagger-sharp teeth shone bright in the fading light.

"Hey!" Cane tried to get the raptor's attention.

It ignored him and sniffed the air. Apparently, it preferred her scent.

Desperation swirled in her gut. She'd had her chance to shock it and get out of this unscathed. Her next touch, even if she electrocuted the raptor, could cost her a hand.

The nervous flow of electrons built inside her like a wave about to break. Whatever part of her the raptor took, she'd make it pay.

Behind Fangtooth, Cane leaped toward the raptor's back, intent on saving her.

"No!" she screamed and thrust her hands out.

The dinosaur turned to address Cane's threat.

She seized its short arm. The palms of her hands exploded with heat. The tips of her fingers flared with pain.

Fangtooth seized up as if she'd hit the creature with a Taser.

Cane had let go of Fangtooth and now rubbed his hands. Had she shocked him too? She tried to look at him but couldn't make her head turn. Her body wouldn't obey. She was as frozen as the raptor, like they were tethered somehow.

Cane came to her side and put his arms around her, gently peeling her fingers off the raptor and bringing her outstretched arm down. She relaxed as her flow of electricity eased. The tether was broken.

Fangtooth dropped to the floor of the boat.

For several seconds, all was silent and motionless. Then, Fangtooth's arms began to twitch.

Her mouth was heavy, but she pushed out the words. "It's not dead."

Fangtooth shook its head as if shaking off a hypnotist's spell. It focused on the two of them, mere feet away, and let out a horrendous growl. From its prone position, it jumped at her, leading with its claws.

Her stomach dipped as her body was lifted off the ground.

Cane hauled them both backward over the side of the boat just as Fangtooth reached the spot where she'd been standing.

Hitting the surface of the water jolted her, and then the water swallowed her in a smothering cocoon, or was that Cane's arms still around her? No, gravity had pulled them apart.

She kicked to the surface and quickly located him a few feet away. They were about fifteen feet offshore from the beach. No dinosaur swam nearby. Fangtooth must have stayed on the boat, which was now beaching itself on the brown sand.

"Are you okay?" Cane asked.

She swam over to him. "Fine."

"Can you tread water for a while?"

She waved a hand toward the beach. "Oh, yeah. I'm not swimming there until that thing leaves."

She flipped to her back and floated in the current to conserve her energy. The current naturally pushed them slowly toward the shore.

About five minutes later, Fangtooth left the boat,

bobbing and weaving up the sand. It hopped onto some rocks near the top of the slope, then looked around.

It scanned the shore and the open water, briefly focusing on them. With a parting shriek, it darted off and disappeared into the jungle.

She breathed a sigh of relief. Hopefully, something else out there would kill it.

CHAPTER TWENTY

AFTER A LONG TREK through the jungle, Cane stood outside the cave, staring blankly at the dangling zip line wire. No harness anywhere. Maybe it had slipped off when the wire broke? He reached down and pulled up the cable hand over hand. The end wasn't frayed as if snapped in a storm. Instead, it had distinct cut marks. Someone had chopped at it several times.

He looked at the yawning mouth of the cave. The setting sun shone from behind, leaving the area shaded. The more he focused, the more the different levels of shadow stood out. A silhouette moved around inside.

"Hey, y'all okay in there?" he called.

Rather than Neve's high voice, a gruff baritone replied, "The cave is mine now. Go find another one."

Oakley let out a gasp. "That's Chubs's voice."

How had Chubs gotten into the cave? He frowned. That didn't matter right now. Obviously, Chubs had taken over and cut the wire. Had anyone gotten hurt? "Who else is with you?"

"Do you mean alive or dead?" Chubs replied.

His hopes were dashed. "All of them."

"Two women alive."

A tight knot twisted in his chest. Two women? Neve was the only woman there when he had left. Who was the other one? Were they okay?

"One dead man. Three men tied up. They're all accounted for in *my* place. Take your freaky girlfriend and find somewhere else to go."

"What's the dead man's name?"

"Henry, I think."

A short silence passed while he tried to come up with some way to talk Chubs out of there. Those people were his responsibility. He never should have left them. Under his breath, he let out a frustrated grunt. But when he yelled back, he kept his voice even. "You know you have to come out of there sometime."

"Not for a while. Lots of storage. Dried meat and fruits, plenty of water. I'm set."

He was right. Once the cave was conquered, it was the perfect place to hole up. That was why Cane had chosen it.

Oakley tugged on his sleeve and said in a low voice, "The other entrance."

He nodded to her. That could work as long as Chubs didn't know about it. To Chubs, he yelled, "Don't hurt anyone else!"

No reply came. As they walked away, he stared into the mouth of the cave for as long as possible. A shadow passed back and forth, probably Chubs. No one else was visible.

The trip to the back entrance took twenty long minutes because they had to skirt the chasm while traveling through the dense tree cover. Once they hit the familiar open clearing, he picked up the pace until they stood over the skylight deep inside the cave. The regular members of the cave knew about this entrance, but Chubs likely didn't.

He held a finger to his lips to tell Oakley to be quiet. Even though the skylight was situated fifty yards into the cave, sound echoed dramatically off the hard rock chambers. Just opening the grate would create a considerable amount of noise.

Gently, he flipped open the latches holding the metal grate in place, resulting in two small clicks. Not bad.

The grate itself was covered in rust. Kaleo had used it a few weeks ago, so at least he'd broken through most of the rust between the grate and the opening. Cane bent over and gripped it with both hands, then whispered to Oakley, "I'm going in first."

She puckered her brow, though she didn't argue.

He yanked hard. The grate came free with a soft metallic screech, no louder than a cat's meow. He prayed that it hadn't echoed and alerted Chubs.

After gently placing it to the side, he dropped through

the skylight to the cave floor. His landing was punctuated by a hard thud. But no one came running.

He motioned for Oakley to drop down their backpacks and the duffel bag they had been able to retrieve from the boat. Then, it was her turn.

As she dropped in, he grabbed her waist to support her. When she regained her balance, they crept down the long tunnel together.

After a short distance, they heard Chubs talking to someone. Himself? Or the other inhabitants of the cave? Not Henry, God rest his soul.

"This dried *Hadrosaur* is tasty." Chubs's voice grew louder the closer they crept. "But I prefer compy meat. Something about those little guys tastes wild and untamed."

Holding Oakley back with one arm, Cane peeked around the archway into the living area. Chubs sat near the open curtain to the men's quarters, his feet up, sampling from a glass container. No weapons in sight.

Several bodies leaned against the wall of the men's quarters. He had to stretch to get a look at them. Justin, Dave, and Ted sat uncomfortably with their hands tied behind their backs. No sign of Henry. Perhaps Chubs was lying about killing him.

Justin glanced in Cane's direction. Their gazes locked for a second, then Justin quickly looked away. Dave and Ted hung their heads as if they'd given up searching for a way out.

Anger burned through his chest. Chubs had brought

violence to this peaceful place—to the people Cane had vowed to protect. He took a deep breath to calm his racing pulse.

A perusal of the room yielded no weapons, except a kitchen knife. He wouldn't be able to use his poison to stop Chubs for fear of killing the others. A knife would have to do.

When Chubs tossed a look over his shoulder into the men's quarters, Cane went for the blade. He grabbed it and advanced on Chubs. "Stay where you are."

Chubs almost fell over, then managed to jump to his feet. The glass container shattered on the cave floor.

Cane held the knife in front, the blade reflecting shards of the light coming from the cave entrance. Even though he'd vowed not to kill anyone ever again, he'd make an exception to save Neve and the others.

Chubs reached behind his back.

For what? Cane hesitated a second too long.

Chubs brought out a familiar weapon. An icy cold pulse rushed through his blood. Chubs had found the gun buried deep in the boxes in his room.

Chubs held it steady, not pointed at Cane, but at the tied-up men. Both Dave and Ted raised their heads, staring in alarm at the weapon. Justin gave Cane a subtle nod as if he accepted whatever was about to happen.

"Drop the knife," Chubs said.

He had no other option. The knife clanked as it fell to the stone floor.

"I'm sure you're not alone." Chubs walked sideways

toward the archway. His voice took on a high singsong tone. "Come out, come out, little Oakley."

Cane waved her away, trying to send her deeper down the tunnel.

At the movement, Chubs approached faster. He shifted the gun and pointed it at Cane.

She didn't move from the stone archway.

He scanned the area, looking for another weapon. If only he hadn't left his bow and arrow in the original boat. His backup set usually sat in the corner of the kitchen area. But it wasn't there now.

Chubs had angled his body to peer at Oakley. Her eyes were pressed tightly together, seemingly unaffected, but her plan was obvious. She was waiting for him to touch her.

He stayed five feet away, his shoulders hunched and his mouth tight. He pointed the gun at her midsection. "You started all of this." His tone held the venom of a pit viper. "*You* got me kicked out of my home. *You* came between me and Kaleo." He shuffled his feet, still not daring to come closer.

Oakley's eyes flew open. Anger boiled in her stormy blue orbs. The air around her shimmered as if the individual molecules rolled off her in near-invisible waves. She rubbed her fingertips together.

Chubs took a step back. The gun in his hand vibrated. He was afraid of her.

She flipped the duffel bag off her shoulder and heaved it at him.

It struck his left forearm. He grunted and fired the gun from his right hand.

The bullet missed her, ricocheting off the rock and down the length of the tunnel. Chubs covered the distance to her in two large steps. She reached for him, but he kept his body angled away. With his long reach, he raised the gun high in the air and brought it down on her temple. She crumpled to the ground, smacking the other side of her head as she hit the stone.

White hot fury surged through Cane. The webbing in his fingers tingled, the first sign of the pores opening. He fought to keep control. It was still too dangerous to let his poison loose in the cave.

He lunged at Chubs, grabbing the gun hand first and swinging it up to the ceiling.

The gun went off again, raining rock chips down on them.

He shoved Chubs around in a circle. He had to keep the man away from Oakley in case the gun went off again. The move spun them until Chubs had his back to both the kitchen and the cave opening.

Cane kept pushing with one hand on the gun arm and one hand on Chubs's chest. Maybe in the kitchen, he could grab another knife without letting go of the gun.

Chubs planted his feet and began to fight back. He swung an elbow and knocked Cane's hand from his chest. The change in momentum spun them around again. This time, Cane had his back directly to the cave opening.

Chubs smiled and dug his heels in. He was a few

inches shorter, but stockier, giving him more leverage. Unless Cane released the gun hand, he had no chance at fighting back. This stalemate only benefited his opponent.

He pushed with all his strength. It wasn't enough. Slowly, they moved toward the entrance and the open air.

Justin flopped to his side, arms still tied behind his back, and tried to inchworm toward them. But he wouldn't be any help.

The tropical breeze blew against Cane's neck. Inch by inch, his feet moved over the rough rock. He lowered his stance, shoving his shoulder into Chubs's chest.

Their motion halted.

Chubs twisted his gun arm free.

Cane was forced to lean back to grab his arm again. Then, Chubs resumed the deadly push toward the cliff.

He could only stave off the inevitable for so long. In seconds, he would slip over the drop-off. *Lord, help me.*

Just as the heels of his boots hit open air, something barreled into them from the side. They fell in a heap on the edge of the cliff.

The gun skittered away toward the kitchen. An unfamiliar woman stood over them with something long and metal in her hands. Translucent curls surrounded her head like a halo. Was she holding a baseball bat?

Chubs pressed a hand to his head as if this woman had hit him when she'd run at them. He rose to one elbow, then, ignoring her, attempted to climb on top of Cane.

He shoved Chubs in the chest to keep him off. Chubs pushed back, and they shifted closer to the edge. Cane's back bent over the last shred of rock before the drop-off. The breeze rifled through his hair. Adrenaline shot through his veins. He wouldn't go out like this. But he didn't have time to poison Chubs. Didn't dare hurt the woman.

With one massive shove, he pushed Chubs off to the side.

He moved away and struggled to his feet. At the same time, the woman hit Chubs in the head again with the baseball bat.

Cane raced to search for the gun, finding it near the kitchen sink. His hand closed over the handle.

A scream ripped through the air.

He kept his grip on the gun, staying in a crouch as he turned around.

Chubs held the woman in a choke hold, precariously near the edge. "I'll throw her over."

"Take it easy." He let go of the gun and stood slowly.

The woman's eyes were wide with fear, and if he wasn't mistaken, determination. Hopefully, she wouldn't do anything stupid.

Panic coiled in his belly as she slid her arm under Chubs's right arm. She was preparing to fight.

He took a step forward, trying to distract both Chubs and the woman. "You can't do this." His words were for the two of them. He took another step, turning on his soothing pastoral voice. "Why don't you come away from the edge? We can talk about why you're doing this. Let's discuss—"

The woman grabbed Chubs's wrist, flipped it at an awkward angle, then pushed away from him.

Chubs grabbed for her.

Cane ran forward, yelling at the woman, "Get back to the safe room!"

Instead, she planted her feet firmly. Then, in one fluid movement, she pivoted, lifted her leg to stomach height, and kicked Chubs in the side. This woman had training.

Her blow caught him just below the ribs and knocked him off balance.

She jumped forward, brought her leg back again, almost as if reloading, and kicked him in the solar plexus.

Chubs staggered backward. One foot slipped off the edge. His body tilted, holding still in midair for less than a second before gravity dragged him over. His hands shot out, grappling for anything.

He latched on to the woman's ankle.

Her mass slowed his fall but not enough. They both went over. No scream, no plea, just there one moment and gone the next.

Cane leaped forward, diving on the ground to grab on to her arms before she disappeared into the chasm.

She continued to kick at Chubs as gravity tugged on them both. Cane fought to keep his grip on her wrists. He had to be leaving bruises, but he couldn't let her go.

Chubs grabbed at the woman's knees, trying to climb up her body.

Another fast kick hit him in the face. He grunted and

blood poured from his nose. He let go with one hand to stem the flow.

The woman wiggled her body like a mermaid out of water. Cane struggled to hold on to her. "Stop."

She wrapped her hands around Cane's elbows, meeting his gaze with light-green stubbornness. She tightened her grasp, took a deep breath, then shimmied once more.

Chubs lost his grip with the other hand.

A surprised scream escaped from his mouth. His body dropped like a stone, free-falling hundreds of feet until he disappeared into the treetops covering the ravine.

Cane dragged the woman up the rough rocks and into his arms. They fell back together, exhausted, both of them trembling. He took several raspy breaths as the weight of her body on his and the soft sound of her breathless pants confirmed that they had both survived.

CHAPTER TWENTY-ONE

"WHERE ARE YOU?" Lumas asked into his headset.

Adler's voice came across tinny, as if he was halfway around the world instead of a thousand miles south. "In the bunker. Just stashed the kid in a secure room."

"Have you got eyes on Oakley?"

"She should have landed earlier today. I'll get the program loaded and double check her location."

Auburn came into the security room, her shoulders stiff with disapproval. It grated on Lumas's nerves how she seemed to judge his every action when it came to Adler. Her feelings for him complicated things.

"What if they find Penna?" Adler asked.

The hopeful tone in his voice made Lumas wary. "What are you asking?"

"Can I dispose of them? I mean if they lead you to Mom, then you have no need for them."

Lumas bristled at Adler referring to Penna as mom. In

fact, she was his biological mother and the only mother he'd ever known, but she had chosen her first son over Adler when she left them. It had branded him in an unusual way. Often, he would rant against her leaving; other times, he would speak of her with longing.

Good thing Lumas had insisted on an eye implant for him this time, otherwise the man might be tempted to disobey if they actually did find Penna.

"No," Lumas answered. "You can't kill them. They're more valuable alive."

A low grumble, followed by an even deeper reply. "Okay."

He glanced at Auburn again. How did Adler speak about him to her? Lumas had raised him like a son, but his natural defiance and lack of empathy sometimes muddled their relationship. Still, he was the strongest genetically enhanced asset that Lumas had at his disposal.

As Adler disconnected the satellite phone call, Lumas pulled up the video footage from the implant. True to his words, Adler sat at a computer console in the secure part of the bunker.

Auburn approached the screen and put two fingers on the image seen through his right eye. "Will he get to stay at home after this mission?"

Lumas almost laughed at her naïveté. There would always be another mission. Not to mention that Adler didn't want to settle down at the lab with Auburn. He only used her as a distraction when forced to stay there.

But telling her so wouldn't do any good. She needed to focus on her work instead.

When he didn't answer, she moved on to her next question. "Do you think they'll find Penna?"

"I wouldn't have let them go if there wasn't a chance."

A small smile broke across her face. "I could learn so much from her."

"Yes, you would, my dear." He wrapped his arms around her. She'd only been ten when Penna left. He'd become her whole world in an instant. In that sense, Penna leaving had been for the best. He'd molded and shaped Auburn's personality until his ambitions were hers. But when Penna left, his true goals had suffered. A tiny blossom of hope grew in his soul. If they found her, he could finally finish his plans for the company.

OAKLEY RESISTED the pull toward consciousness. Sleep. She needed sleep.

All the energy had been sucked out of her. In that blissful, immobile state, she didn't have to fight, didn't have to hide, didn't have to battle what might lurk deep inside, underneath her layers of control. If she couldn't move, she couldn't hurt anyone.

Sharp pain in the back of her head blasted through her contemplation. She groaned and rolled away from it but still didn't open her eyes.

"Could be a concussion." It was Neve's soft voice.

Had to be her probing fingers that sent another jolt of pain through Oakley's head.

"It hurts," she rasped.

"Sorry. Let's get you on a cot."

Her eyes flew open. Chubs had come at her with a gun. She'd thrown something at him.

Neve touched her shoulder gently. "Chubs is gone." She pointed at Cane and a blond woman who stood next to him. "Thanks to those two."

The woman gave a small wave. "I'm Dr. Wells Anderson."

"Doctor?" Funny how the doctor was letting Neve assess Oakley's head wound. But then again, if Dr. Anderson's shaking hands and bloodshot eyes were any indication, she didn't look up to giving a professional opinion anyway.

They helped her to a cot in the women's quarters. She lay back and rested her head. "What happened?"

Cane told her about Chubs hitting her over the head, then described his struggle for the gun. "Wells came out from the safe room to help me." He placed a hand on the doctor's forearm. "Very brave."

Wells flushed a deep pink. Neve quickly concealed a look of regret before she turned an admiring gaze to Wells. Did Neve feel like she should have come to help as well?

Cane finished the account with the terrifying plunge of both Wells and Chubs over the edge, and his rescue of Wells by pulling her up.

"I'm sorry I slept through it all." Oakley rubbed the

back of her head. "But I'm glad everyone's okay." She immediately regretted her words. If what Chubs had said was true, then Henry wasn't okay at all. She hadn't known him long, but he'd seemed like a nice enough guy. Chubs, however, got what he deserved.

She sat up and twisted her neck around. In the corner by the men's quarters, a human-shaped outline rested under a gray sheet. *Henry.* Another person dead, and it could have been Cane, Neve, or Wells. All because they had given Chubs a chance at life. Kaleo shouldn't have shown mercy.

"Henry loved the ocean," Neve said. "I think he would like to be buried at sea."

Cane cleared his throat. "As Henry's pastor, I'd like to preside over the service, but it may have to wait." He took an awkward step away from Wells, directing his words to Neve. "We have a lead on the whereabouts of the geneticist we've been looking for."

Wells looked confused, but to her credit, she didn't ask for an explanation.

Neve studied him for a moment, gleaning information in her quiet way. "You could say a prayer for Henry now, and then I'll get Taye to help me transport his body."

"Thank you." He took a step closer. "Also, can we talk in private?"

"Of course." She pulled a blanket over Oakley's legs. "You need to rest."

Just before Neve reached the curtain separating the rooms, Oakley stopped her. "Wait, where's Cody?"

"He's running around out there somewhere. When Kaleo and Taye trapped us in the cave, I made them set Cody free."

Hopefully, Cody would be okay out there. But she could use a little scaly comfort from her pet right now.

After Neve left, she drifted into sleep until the swishing of the curtain woke her. She blinked to focus on the tall figure holding the drape back with one hand.

"Sorry, didn't mean to wake you," Wells said. "I wanted to see if you needed anything."

Just some answers, but Wells wouldn't have the right ones. Instead, she asked, "Who are you?"

Before she could answer, Neve came sweeping into the room, followed by Cane.

"Good, you're up." He sat down on a nearby cot, gave a quick glance to Wells, then focused on her. "Do you remember the last communication I received from my mother?"

The firm set of his eyes hinted that she shouldn't say it out loud. She simply nodded and repeated it in her head. *Search for the fire along the coast that's rich. Brave the disease lurking in the ghost cliffs.*

"Neve knows of an old sanatorium located near Irazu Volcano."

Sanatorium. Disease. She started to nod, then stopped due to the headache. "A perfect place to hide."

"And rumored to be haunted," Cane added.

That would explain the ghost reference. Oakley sat up. "Let's go."

He put a calm hand on her shoulder. "It would be better to travel at night."

"What are you talking about? It's never a good idea to travel at night in the jungle."

He scowled. "It is when the FBI is hunting you."

Her heart skipped a beat. "The FBI is here looking for me?"

Neve pointed at Wells. "She was sent here to replace your government tracker."

Wells shrugged. "We could do it now. If you get the tracker implanted again, they'll stop looking for you."

"But I can't."

Wells raised an eyebrow, a request for an explanation, but that would mean revealing a lot of details. Oakley gave her an apologetic look. "I can't because someone else is looking for this scientist as well. If I get tagged, he might be able to use the system to track me straight to the geneticist."

"That may be the risk we have to take," Cane said. "If you don't get the tracker soon, Raptor will be on the hook for your disappearance."

He was right. She had to do it. She couldn't let Raptor be blamed for this.

Neve drummed her fingernails on the metal bar supporting the cot. "There's another way."

"What?" Oakley asked.

Neve only shook her head. "Leave it to me. I have an idea that might satisfy the FBI." She motioned for Wells to follow her out of the room.

CHAPTER TWENTY-TWO

THE SOUNDS of the jungle deepened to lower tones at night. A rumbling roar in the distance. The drawn-out croak of a frog. The ghostly hoot of an owl. Oakley shivered and tugged on the sleeves of her borrowed sweatshirt. They weren't supposed to be out at night. Dinosaurs had the advantage at night.

But Cane was right. It would be too easy for the FBI to find her during the day.

After Neve and Wells left her alone, neither of them had come back. Oakley had slept several more hours before Cane woke her and said it was time to go. When they left the cave at dusk, he said only that Neve assured him she would handle the situation. Perhaps she had a plan to distract the FBI until Cane and Oakley could return.

A new tracker would have to wait until after they completed the search for Penna Gallardo. Up to this point, the evidence indicated she'd left the lab to get away from the research and to get away from Lumas. If Oakley led him right back to her, he'd probably force her to continue her work.

But there was another possibility. What if Penna had never stopped her genetic tinkering? Maybe she'd continued it here, away from prying eyes? She might be as ruthless as Lumas. If so, they could be walking into a dangerous situation.

She shifted the weight of her backpack as they navigated a rocky hill. After they climbed out of the cave, Cane had led her to a cache of long spears, one of which she now used as a walking stick. The only other weapon they possessed was the tranquilizer gun she'd transferred to her backpack, and that wouldn't do them much good with empty darts. Cane had left his small gun at the cave with Neve for protection. It wouldn't be much defense against a dinosaur anyway.

A slight tap on the back of Cane's sweatshirt brought him to a halt. She stood on her tiptoes to whisper in his ear. "Do you know where we're going?"

"Yes. Stop at the tree house. Talk there."

He was right. There was immediate danger around them. She could worry about Penna later.

Briefly, Cody came to mind, but she pushed the longing away. Her pet was probably somewhere safe, sleeping for the night.

As they approached the tree house, Cane put his hand on her arm to stop her. The soft glow coming out of the slats in the windows wasn't unusual. Kaleo and Cane had pots with luminescent plants inside for natural light. However, the light was shifting in random patterns, creating drifting shadows. Someone was inside.

By virtue of the pheromones they both emitted, Cane's hesitancy came through loud and clear. Should they go see who was inside or skip the stop entirely?

A few seconds later, they were spared the decision when the trap door flapped open. Cane held his spear ready to attack whoever came down.

A pair of jean-clad legs descended the first two rungs on the ladder, then a dark face peered out. She smiled in recognition. *Taye.*

His gaze darted around the shrouded jungle. "Quick, come up."

Taye dashed back up the ladder, followed by Cane. She passed her spear up to Taye like Cane had done and then began to climb. One rung from the top, a pair of tanned hands grabbed her wrists and hauled her into the loft like a stuffed animal being swung around by a child.

She gasped and grunted as she smacked against someone's hard chest. The scent of coconut, lime, and hyacinth enveloped her. *Kaleo!*

He dropped kisses on the top of her head until she looked up fast and managed to catch one on the lips. They froze there for a second, lips barely touching, before he reached a hand behind to cup her head and kissed her deeply. She was still suspended off the floor with his hand supporting her waist and her body pressed to his massive chest. She threw her arms around his neck and let the sweet tingles sweep her away.

When their lips parted, he lowered her to the ground and brought his forehead to hers. "You shouldn't have come back."

She broke into a grin. "You missed me, huh?"

He bit his lower lip in an uncharacteristic display of self-doubt. "More than I would miss my own heartbeat."

His words left her speechless, so she sought out his lips again, kissing him until her pulse pounded in her ears and the subconscious hum of electricity tried to surface. She broke away abruptly. She couldn't lose control or she might hurt him.

Fear and desire weren't a good mix. The combination left her shaky and queasy. Besides, they were making a spectacle of their affection. She tugged on the bottom of her sweatshirt and looked around at the tree house to reorient herself. Cane and Taye talked quietly in the corner, holding a bow and arrow set between them.

"It's no problem," Taye was saying. "Take it. My other set is at the compound."

"Thank you," Cane replied before turning to Kaleo and Oakley. She searched his face for a reaction to her reunion with Kaleo, but it was a placid expression of resignation. "What are you guys doing here?"

Kaleo turned to Cane as if registering the question, but then swiveled back to her. This time, his golden-brown eyes held no smolder. He was all business. "Have you seen Raptor since you got back?"

"No, we went straight to the cave where we had to confront Chubs."

"Confront? What do you mean?"

She filled them in on Chubs's takeover of the cave and his ultimate fate.

Kaleo smoothed the hair back from her face. "Never a dull moment with you."

"I told Neve we needed to kick Chubs out," Taye grumbled.

Cane spoke up. "She said you guys went off to hunt a dinosaur and left them alone?"

"We've been helping Raptor handle the FBI and keeping track of Demon Dragon," Taye answered.

At her raised eyebrows, Kaleo explained. "It's a carno that doubles as a flamethrower."

"Just what we need, more deadly dinosaurs." Oakley tilted her head. "Now that you say that, we had a brush with him before we left."

"It picked up my scent." Kaleo pointed to her. "And probably yours from the blanket we used when we faked your death." A moment of silence passed before he spoke again. "The good news is that since we've seen Demon Dragon, we're seeing less of Red Grizzly."

She made an effort to relax her shoulders. The constant danger of this place never ceased to overwhelm her.

"Are you going to tell him?" Cane asked.

She shifted her attention back to Kaleo and stood mute for several seconds, captured by the essence of him.

The upward quirk of his full mouth. His wavy hair hanging to the top of his rough jawline. The amused slant of his eyebrows. When she found her voice, she told him and Taye about the trip to the research lab, their breakout, and the dinosaur on the boat. She left out the procreation and kissing parts.

"We're going to check the sanatorium on the volcano," she said, "to see if Penna might be there."

"You're going off information delivered to your adoptive mother"—Kaleo pointed at Cane—"in a phone call from your birth mother over fifteen years ago?"

She scowled. "When you say it like that, it sounds stupid."

Kaleo raised both eyebrows. "What am I missing?"

"Penna was brilliant. If she found a safe place to hide from Lumas, why would she take the risk of leaving it?"

He threw up his hands. "Maybe because dinosaurs took over the country five years ago?"

At least he was embracing his sarcastic side. That growth probably had a lot to do with her. "Once they created the island, this would have been an even better place to hide. No tourists. No government. Grow your own food, find shelter from the dinosaurs, and you're set." At his skeptical look, she tried again. "You're right. She could have left. But from what I saw, she knew the dinosaurs were in Costa Rica already. Maybe she saw them as an extra layer of protection against Lumas finding her. Plus, Lumas framed me in order to send me here to find her. He has to have some reason to think she's still here."

"So, you believe two women scientists survived in this abandoned, supposedly haunted, sanatorium alone?"

She blew out a frustrated breath. "We have to find out."

The sarcastic expression melted off his face. "Then I'll go with you."

"I'm sorry." She took his hand between hers. "I'd love to have you come, but if they are there, too many people could spook them. If they go into hiding again, we'll never find them."

Kaleo glanced at Cane, and a look of understanding passed between them. Penna was Cane's creator as well, plus his mother had left him the message to help him find her. He had as much right to this quest as she did, even though he probably cared less about finding Penna than about finding his birth mother.

"Take care of her," Kaleo said.

"Always," Cane replied.

She put her hands on her hips. "I'm fairly good at taking care of myself, thank you."

Kaleo narrowed his eyes. She couldn't blame him. She *had* just told him about being hit on the head and incapacitated for the fight with Chubs. Probably not the time to be bragging about her abilities.

Kaleo sighed. "I'll go tell Raptor you're back. We'll try to stall the FBI a while longer."

"And I'll go check on Neve," Taye said.

Cane patted Taye on the shoulder. "She'd appreciate that. And if you wouldn't mind setting up the zip line again?"

"Sure."

They gathered their things. Cane gave his spear to Taye in exchange for the bow and arrow set. All three men went down the ladder first before letting her come down. By the time she reached Kaleo to say goodbye, he was tensely watching the trees in front of them.

She stood on tiptoe to brush a kiss on his cheek. Just as her lips touched his skin, the source of his anxiety became clear. A barely discernible thump, followed by a slight vibration. Then, a quiet puff of air as faint as a breeze.

He put a hand on her arm and gently pushed, motioning for her and Cane to slowly walk away. They took two steps, and Kaleo and Taye did the same in the opposite direction. Perhaps they could slip sideways into the jungle while the predator came straight at them.

Another silent step, almost in unison.

The huff of breath again, stronger this time.

Leaves shook and rustled, obscuring all other noises. If only she could see it coming. The tree house and the tree canopy blocked the moonlight, reducing everything else to shifting outlines.

More than likely, the dinosaur could see much more of them than they could see of it. Taye and Kaleo had an advantage due to their darker skin. Even without the reflecting moonlight, her pale skin and Cane's light hair served as twin beacons in the dark.

Kaleo gestured with his hand for them to keep moving. They took another step.

Massive footsteps crashed in front of them. The dinosaur had taken the most visible targets.

"Jump!" Kaleo yelled.

Instinct had already propelled her out of the way as a huge head lunged down. It hit the ground where she'd been standing. Flames leaked from between its teeth and singed the carpet of leaves. In the brief illumination, she gaped at the immense head of a *Carnotaurus*. With the stubby protruding horns, Demon Dragon seemed like an appropriate name.

"Over here!" Kaleo yelled at the dinosaur.

Cane grabbed her arm and pulled her downslope while Kaleo continued to yell. Heat washed over her, surrounding her as if she'd stepped into an oven.

She dodged over a downed tree, struggling to keep up with Cane's long legs since he still had a grip on her. Demon Dragon thrashed through the forest. Was it advancing on them or heading in the other direction? Cane mumbled under his breath. He was praying for them. Hopefully, he was including Taye and Kaleo in those prayers as well.

AFTER HALF A MILE, the sparser tree canopy in this area allowed some moonlight to filter down. Oakley slowed her pace and chanced a look behind. The forest was clear. She tugged Cane's hand to slow him down.

"We lost it," she whispered hoarsely.

He stopped to listen before nodding. "Probably thanks to Kaleo."

She put her hands on her knees and tried to catch her breath. In between huffs, she asked, "Do you think they're okay?"

"Yeah. Of course."

His lack of conviction was chilling.

"Kaleo always makes it through," he said, more forcefully.

Was he trying to convince himself or her? It didn't matter. She'd believe Kaleo was fine until proven wrong. "How much farther?"

"Two hours, maybe three. Before sunrise, for sure. I just don't know if we should approach in the dark or wait."

She straightened to her full height. "Let's decide when we get there."

For the rest of the trip, they kept silent. No other animals bothered them with the exception of a stealthy puma that was easily frightened by a swipe of her spear.

Finally, they came to a clearing that allowed them to check out the landscape ahead. The volcano rose before them, its silhouette cutting out a coal-black portion of the night sky. An old road sliced across the face of the mountain like a curving scar.

"Neve said it's a mile down that road."

She stared at it dubiously. They still had half a mile to go before reaching it, and traveling on it could be akin to offering themselves up as a dinosaur buffet. On the other hand, maybe they would be safer in the open where they could see predators coming.

They ducked back into the forest for the ten-minute walk to the edge of the crumbling pavement. What had looked like a solid road from a distance turned out to be a rutted, pitted mess. She shrugged and began to walk down the center. After their close-up encounter in the jungle with Demon Dragon, this way was probably safer.

The road wound in and out of the trees, alternating between darkly shadowed and moonlit. Approximately a mile later, Cane stopped at a rusted iron gate. Beyond it was the outline of an expansive structure. With missing front steps and a set of dormer windows that resembled eyes, the building seemed to sneer at them. Jagged glints of moonlight reflected off broken windowpanes. The entire facade belonged in a horror film. No wonder the locals claimed it was haunted.

"Decision time. I say we wait until daylight."

Cane nodded. "I agree. If they're here and we sneak up at night, they might bolt."

Unless Penna's a mad scientist and this is a trap. But she said nothing as he led her to a copse of trees near the gate where they hunkered down to wait.

"You can sleep if you want," he said. "I'll keep watch."

"But I slept most of the day." Though she couldn't deny the appeal of sleep.

"Yes, but you also probably have a concussion."

Maybe that was why her head had ached the entire trip. "Okay, but first, a question. Do you regret not telling Wells what is really going on?"

"We barely know her."

"Apparently Raptor trusts her, and from what you said, she did save our lives."

Several more seconds ticked by before he answered. "Maybe I should regret it, but I don't. No matter how understanding a person is, knowing something like what we are ... Well, it changes things. It changes how people look at you." He glanced over at her. "It even changed how you look at me."

She opened her mouth to protest.

He put a hand up to cut her off. "You of all people should get it. When the person next to you can kill you with the flick of a wrist, it destabilizes the relationship."

She would've just said it scares people, but she did get it. For the first time, she tried to purposefully send a pheromone his way, one that would speak calm to him. Except it might have worked only on her because she fell asleep against his arm before she had the chance to ask him if he felt anything.

CHAPTER TWENTY-THREE

OAKLEY WOKE to the hum of insects and the twitter of birds. Her arm was wrapped around a warm object, and her head lay on something firm. She opened her eyelids and got an eyeful of Cane's purple sweatshirt. Tilting her head up, she met his somewhat embarrassed gaze.

"Sorry." She pulled away from him.

At this elevation, the morning had risen cool yet humid, similar to the cloud forest where the resort and the cave were situated. She pulled her sweatshirt sleeves over her hands and peered outside of the circle of trees that had kept them dry and protected last night.

The sanatorium rose from the clearing, looking more like a dilapidated, abandoned estate in the light of day. A large main house was framed on two sides by additional square wings. Misty clouds hung at treetop level, giving the structure an eerie atmosphere. Most of the windows were made up of foot-square glass panels, but half of the panels were missing or broken. The rusted gate looked even more decrepit, with the two sides held together by a rotting length of wood wedged between the bars. Not a place anyone would go on purpose, unless they were trying to hide.

They ate a breakfast of dried meat and fruit before approaching the gate. Through the bars, Oakley allowed her gaze to sweep over the building again. Who would want to live here for fifteen years? Kaleo might be right. Perhaps Penna and Cane's mother had moved on long ago.

A dull crack drew her attention back to Cane.

"Look at this." He held out two halves of the rotting board which had broken when he'd tried to open the gate.

Attached to the back of each piece was a copper wire held in place by small tie rods. It didn't look new, but someone had placed it there for a purpose. She followed the wire as it coiled around the bars and into the surrounding trees where it met a newer-looking wooden fence.

"An early warning system?" she asked.

"That's my guess."

Her heart rate soared. "Let's get up there, then."

He agreed with a nod but didn't seem as eager as her. With cautious movements, he squeezed through the gate. They had to be careful. If someone was up there, they now had a chance to run or arm themselves.

She squeezed through and joined him on a cracked sidewalk. A sign partly buried in the wild yard read *Keep*

Off the Grass. This place must have been a tourist destination before the evacuation. Probably as part of the World's Most Haunted Places.

Rather than try to enter at the main entrance, since the steps had long ago rotted away to leave the door three feet off the ground, they headed for the wing farther up the volcano. That door sat level with the ground. As they passed the gaping, broken windows, she searched for activity. Everything was quiet.

At the decaying wooden door, Cane pushed, but it wouldn't budge. It didn't have a handle, so it wasn't locked. Something was reinforcing it from the inside.

"Let me try." Her small arm fit through the hole where the handle had been.

Mindful of the rusty edges, she pushed her arm through up to her biceps. She twisted it around, searching along the door frame. Where the door met the wall a few feet up, her fingers brushed metal. Some sort of metal bar. It moved in only one direction. She flipped it up and almost fell when the door swung inward.

They entered a large, empty room with several pillars running down the center. The remains of a sink sat along the far wall. An old kitchen perhaps?

No sound greeted them. Not even the rustle of animals living in the walls.

Then, a quiet meow made her spin around. A plump, hairy cat with tortoise shell fur stepped delicately down the stairs to their right. Well, that explained the lack of rodents. The cat showed no fear as it stalked toward them.

"Is it just you, sweetie?" She bent low to rub its head.

As if in answer, the cat began to walk back toward the deeper parts of the sanatorium.

She looked at Cane. "Might as well follow the furry tour guide."

It led them up a dark, curving staircase. Paint in various colors chipped from the wooden slat walls. The stairs ended at a narrow hallway, along which were several doors running down both sides, most of them open. As she followed the animal past the rooms, she peered inside each of them. Several held the remains of rotting furniture and old rusted bed frames. Graffiti marked the walls.

One clean room caught her eye. It was furnished with two cots, complete with bedding, and a wooden dresser. The windows in the room were intact and appeared to be the dormer windows she'd seen from outside.

The cat breezed by them all, leading them to a closed door at the end of the hall. It sat outside the door and mewed softly.

She tried the doorknob. Locked.

Obviously, someone had been here recently. But had they gone? Or were they hiding in the locked room?

She turned to Cane. "What do we—" Her breath caught in her throat as she looked over his shoulder. A person stood in the center of the hallway, silhouetted in shadow. The outline of a long-barreled gun pointed at the ground.

Cane spun around.

They had only their primitive weapons. No match for a rifle or shotgun.

She stood still as the person approached. It was a woman with long, wispy dark hair. Oakley's heart pounded in her chest. Not just any woman. This was Penna Gallardo, many years older than the pictures she'd seen in the office, but her, nevertheless.

"What do you want?" Penna asked.

Cane moved in front of Oakley, but she grabbed his arm. "It's her, Cane."

"What did you call him?" the woman asked.

Oakley pushed past Cane and took two slow steps toward her. "You're Penna."

She tilted her head but didn't answer. Instead, she raised her rifle up. A grim expression crossed her face. "Lumas sent you."

"No. He tried to persuade us to find you so we would tell him where you are, but he doesn't know that we're here. And we don't plan on telling him."

Penna gave a sharp laugh. "Sure."

This wasn't going well. She tried a different approach. "My name is Oakley, and this is Cane."

The gun lowered a fraction. The woman moved forward a step and pointed one finger at Cane. "Come into the light."

He obeyed, stepping in front of Oakley again as he walked toward Penna. Oakley peeked around his shoulder.

Penna peered at Cane for several seconds before her

hands started to shake. "Yes, I see it. It's in the tilt of your nose and the slant of your lips. Not to mention the strawberry-blond hair."

"What?"

"You look just like your mother, Eloisa."

Cane gasped. Oakley put a comforting hand on his shoulder.

"She told me that she and your adoptive mother had named you Cane for the sugarcane fields surrounding your adoptive mother's house. Eloisa said it was the perfect place to hide you, out in the middle of nowhere."

"Is she here?" He breathed out the question like a prayer.

Penna lowered the gun to point at the worn floorboards again. "No. She never came. I don't know what happened to her."

A garbled moan came from him. Oakley hung her head out of respect for his distress.

As her chin hit her chest, a sharp pain pierced her right eye. Like someone had stuck a needle into it and was trying to rotate it out of the socket. She grunted as she rubbed it with a knuckle.

Penna shuffled closer. Cane turned around to look at her, but she couldn't stop focusing on her eye. Tears rushed down her cheek, coating her eye but not relieving the pain.

A firm hand gripped her chin and raised her head level. She opened her eyes. Penna stared at her with a furrowed brow. The pain immediately evaporated.

"Is the pain gone?" Penna asked.

She nodded while wiping the tears away.

"Do you wear contacts?"

She shook her head. Penna came even closer, examining her eye with concern. She pulled the lower lid out, frowning as if dissecting a repulsive bug. A few seconds later, she swore and began pacing across the hallway.

"What is it?" Cane asked.

"On my doorstep," she muttered as if talking to herself, one hand buried in her pocket. Abruptly, she stopped and looked straight at Oakley.

Before Oakley could ask what she'd meant, the woman advanced on her, whipping her hand from her pocket. Her fist held a syringe. In one swift motion, she stabbed Oakley in the arm and depressed the plunger.

Oakley jerked away but it was too late. The dim light filtering into the hallway quickly faded to a haze. Cane's arms surrounded her as she slipped into darkness.

CHAPTER TWENTY-FOUR

CANE LEANED against what was left of the doorjamb in the clean room of the sanatorium, staring at Oakley's sleeping form. The anesthesia had knocked her out for over two hours.

While she slept, he couldn't sense any thoughts or feelings from her, and it unnerved him. She was the first and only woman he could understand. Communicating with her was effortless. Maybe that was why he'd wanted to pursue her, even though he'd known of her attraction to Kaleo.

Penna spoke from over his shoulder. "Packed and ready to go. She will wake soon, then we should leave."

He nodded. "While we wait, can I ask you about my mother?"

She looked at the worn floorboards for a brief time before she moved to sit on the other cot in the room. She motioned for him to sit as well.

As he did so, he studied her. Fine lines creased her forehead and the corners of her dark eyes, but her hair was almost black with very little gray. What would his mother have looked like at this age? "So, she was supposed to join you here."

"Yes. We were to meet in Cartago first before traveling here. She never showed up." Penna pressed her lips together. "I held out hope for a long time. Maybe Lumas followed her, or maybe she was being cautious. Maybe she went to see you and just needed a little more time. After six months, I realized he had gotten to her somehow. For all that time, I stayed in Cartago and lived off cash. Prior to coming out here, I'd convinced the owner to lease us one of the outbuildings at the sanatorium. When Eloisa didn't show and Lumas didn't come snooping around, I moved in."

"By yourself?"

"At first." She reached out a hand as if she might touch him again, but she stopped inches from his knee. "Your mother gave me the greatest gift you can ever give someone—the truth. I was blinded by the challenge of scientific discovery. I wanted so badly to have a breakthrough that I didn't stop to consider where my research might go. I thought I had control of it." She clasped her hands together. "Turns out, I was the one being controlled."

Next to them, Oakley stirred and rolled to her side. Her eyes fluttered open, and her gaze locked on to Penna. "What did you do?"

Cane leaned toward her. "She took a camera implant out of your eye."

In the dank, creepy operating room, Penna had conducted the operation on Oakley as if she were an accomplished surgeon at Mayo Clinic. Geneticist, surgeon, survivor in hiding. Penna was talented at many things.

"I designed it to keep tabs on some of our specimens," Penna said. "The pain came when you tried to look down because whoever was controlling the mechanism wanted you to keep looking at me."

When Penna had explained it to him, a cold dread had frozen his heart. If Lumas and Adler had seen everywhere that Oakley had been, they had seen the people in the cave. And that was how they'd known about his abilities. Oakley hadn't told Lumas; he'd seen it firsthand through her implant. The violation left Cane raw inside.

Oakley touched the bandage over her right eye. Her mouth dropped open. "My eye has been bothering me for weeks. That's what it was?"

Penna nodded slowly. "Do you know when he might have installed it? You would've had a small operation."

She placed a hand on her forehead. "Of course. There was confusion at the hospital when they installed the government tracker before I came to the island. They lost me for a while, and then when I woke, my eye was swollen."

"I suppose he could have had someone do it then."

Now that Lumas knew where Penna was, he would

likely send Adler—the man who'd tried to kill Oakley already—to kidnap her. *Adler.* The truth hit Cane anew. Oakley said Adler tried to kill her when she was blindfolded, but he'd run off when her blindfold slipped down. It made sense now. Adler had known of the eye implant all along, had known Lumas didn't want Oakley dead, but he was willing to kill her anyway.

Oakley's eyebrows furrowed. "But I shorted out the tracker on my arm. Why didn't I short out the camera?"

"You were designed with a fatty layer surrounding your spinal cord at the base of your neck. It won't block all of the electrical pulse, but it blocks enough to protect your brain tissues and keep you alive. The eye camera would have to be hit by a direct shot of electricity to short out, especially since it runs on your own low-level biological current."

Oakley's voice held a tinge of shock. "He's been watching everything?"

He put a comforting hand on her arm. She had to feel violated as well. But now it made sense how Adler and Lumas always seemed to be one step ahead of them.

Oakley peered at Penna. "Adler told me I was sent here to look for you. How did they know you were on Extinction Island?"

"My stubborn streak. In the last few years, I'd seen an increase in different types of dinosaurs. It became clear that someone was trying to continue my work by copying what I'd done. I knew Lumas had something to do with it. I began removing the trackers from those dinosaurs so they couldn't find them again to replicate them. It wasn't much, but it was the only way I could hinder his progress."

Cane asked, "Why is he so obsessed with you?"

"We lived together for years and I raised Auburn for ten of those years. I'm the one who escaped from him. I know all his secrets. But that's not why. He's obsessed with me because I'm the only one who can continue his work."

"What work do you mean?"

She blew out a breath. "It started with Adler. He was my first genetically manipulated person." She dropped her gaze to the floor for a few seconds before returning to gaze out the window. "I had an autistic son, Elliot, whom I was desperate to help. I could see he longed to communicate but didn't know how. I started researching nonverbal communication in animals."

Cane nodded. "The pheromones."

"Yes. Lumas gave me a place to make my ideas happen. Elliot was five when Adler was born. We raised them together while I went on with my research." She pointed at him. "Your mother was with me during those early years. Eloisa was brilliant. We used her DNA along with modifications inspired by the pink dragon millipede, which can release hydrogen cyanide for protection."

To hear her talk so matter-of-factly about the genetic manipulation of his DNA disturbed him. Even so, he spread the webbing of his fingers apart, exposing the pores.

She smiled a little too eagerly. "When your mother got pregnant, I had no idea. She kept it a secret. She'd heard Lumas talking about how any child born through the program would become property of the company. She wanted to give you a normal life, so she quit before we knew about you or your twin—"

His heart quickened. "I have a twin?"

"You *had* a twin. We implanted two embryos, one male and one female. Only you survived. Your sister must have miscarried in the womb early on. After you were born, Eloisa gave you to your adopted mom to protect you."

A sharp pang jolted through his chest. He'd always wanted a sibling. To have one as close as a fraternal twin and to have lost her before he even knew her ...

Penna took in a deep breath and blew it out, obviously determined to get through this quickly so they could leave. "After she quit, I didn't see Eloisa again for ten years. Not until Elliot's funeral. When Adler was fifteen, he killed Elliot by pushing him down the stairs." She took a moment to clasp her trembling hands before continuing. "Of course, Adler couldn't go to jail for what he'd done. They would take a DNA sample and possibly find out how he'd been altered. There could be no justice for Elliot."

"I'm sorry," Cane said, fidgeting on the cot. This conversation had taken longer than expected. Now that Oakley was awake, they should get going. "Perhaps we should finish this at a later time."

"Just give me a minute. Trust me, you'll understand shortly. Eloisa came to Elliot's funeral. She told me Lumas wasn't who I thought he was. She convinced me to leave, but I had to do it right. I escaped with the only thing of importance that I had—a single embryo created from part of my DNA. I couldn't leave it behind."

Where was Penna going with this? That was fifteen years ago.

She directed her voice toward the door. "Teagan, will you please come in here?" She stood and faced the door. "I had the embryo implanted just after I arrived in Costa Rica."

A girl came to the doorway, about fifteen years old, with long, stringy brown hair and muted green eyes. Something about her eyes struck a chord in him. She glanced nervously between the three of them.

Penna swept a hand at the girl. "Cane, I'd like you to meet your half sister, Teagan."

His mouth went dry. If Penna was Teagan's mother, then for them to be half siblings ... "Who is Teagan's father?"

He held his breath, waiting for the truth. From the look on Penna's face, the answer was apparent, but he needed to hear her say it.

She drew back her shoulders. "Lumas Verret."

His head and heart swam with chaotic emotions. Two minutes ago, he'd mourned a lost sister, only to now be introduced to his half sister. But beyond that, to find out he was related to the man who'd kidnapped them. What was he supposed to do with all of it?

As a long moment ticked away, he wrestled with the longings and fears inside him. Teagan stood quietly, surveying them. He glanced at Oakley. Her wide eyes and furrowed brow reflected the same swell of confusion.

Finally, with great effort, he pushed the tangled mass of feelings away and got up from the cot. Bottom line was, he suddenly had two women and a girl to protect. Lumas had wanted Penna all along, which meant Adler was surely on his way. It was well past time for all of them to get out of here.

CHAPTER TWENTY-FIVE

"I DON'T KNOW where Oakley Laveau is." Raptor put his hands out in mock surrender.

But Special Agent Gabe Glaser wasn't looking at his hands. The long vein in Raptor's neck pulsed. This man routinely faced down convicts and dinosaurs. What was making him so nervous right now? Perhaps he was nervous because he was lying.

Gabe planted his feet and stared the man down. "Oakley is nowhere to be found. And I've seen no evidence of Dr. Anderson's death."

"What more do you need to see? A *Carnotaurus* attacked them both."

"At some point, the dinosaur did attack," Gabe agreed. "But it didn't get both of them. For that matter, why hasn't the mainland heard about dinosaurs that can breathe fire?"

Raptor shrugged his shoulders, almost comically. "You

know how it works. Certain parts of the government have been keeping it quiet."

Gabe crossed his arms near his waist, subtly drawing attention to his holstered sidearm. "Dr. Wells Anderson is still alive until proven dead. The same goes for Oakley Laveau. I won't stop until I find them. You might as well help me."

Raptor's features relaxed as he shook his head. "I wish I could."

This appeared to be the truth at least. Raptor wanted to help but couldn't for some reason. Gabe perked up at an odd expression that briefly crossed Raptor's face as he glanced at the tree line outside camp. Gabe twisted his head fast enough to catch a glimpse of a brown-haired man disappearing into the foliage.

"I'll be back," Raptor said.

He let Raptor go with a nod. Of course Raptor had informants on the island, but Gabe wouldn't be kept in the dark.

He waited until Raptor left, then slipped into the trees after him. Quietly, Gabe came toward the men in a wide circle. Getting close enough to hear without them being aware was tricky. He placed every footfall carefully, avoiding sticks and leaves as much as possible. They were being cautious because they spent several minutes looking around, not speaking.

When he could barely see them through the foliage about five yards away, he settled into the nook of a nearby tree. Glimpses of the other man revealed tanned skin and long brown hair. His features appeared to be of Hawaiian descent.

He spoke in a gruff voice. "The cargo has returned."

"Good," Raptor replied.

Obviously, they thought they might be overheard and were trying to speak in code. They weren't very good at it. The "cargo" had to be Oakley. She must have left the area and come back. Maybe she'd been hiding in another part of the island. That would explain why Gabe hadn't seen any sign of her.

"Plans?" Raptor asked.

"Just a little more time to find the creator."

Raptor nodded like he knew what in the world that meant. He clapped the Hawaiian man on the back. "Thanks for the update."

As Raptor headed toward camp, Gabe didn't follow. He'd find out much more about Oakley by following the Hawaiian man.

The Hawaiian slipped through the trees, fast and nearly silent. Gabe tried to do the same, but his leg muscles were twenty years older than his prey. More than likely, the man knew Gabe was there and wouldn't lead him to Oakley, but maybe she would come to visit. At the moment, it was the only lead he had.

Gabe checked his pistol to make sure the safety was off. This man had a large bulge in the back of his jeans. No need to take any chances.

A hundred yards from the camp, the Hawaiian went to put his foot down, but instead held it several inches above the ground. He listened hard with his head turned in the opposite direction.

The hair on Gabe's arms and neck stood at attention, and his heart rate picked up. Other than two young *Velociraptors*, which he'd killed with a bullet between the eyes, the only serious attack he'd faced since arriving was the *Carnotaurus*. He'd lost Jack and Sykes to that ugly dinosaur's fire-breathing appetite. Was this predator something just as lethal?

A flash of red and green leathery hide whizzed by in front of him. Before he had time to react, another dinosaur, this one with gray striated skin, streaked through the trees, following the first.

The dinosaurs ran a full circle around both men before coming to a stop between them. The redheaded one faced off with the Hawaiian guy. The gray one faced Gabe. Both were raptors, but the red one posed the biggest threat. It was a large *Utahraptor*, probably the one Raptor had warned him about, called Red Grizzly.

The two predators had separated them. Divide and conquer, just as Gabe would have done.

The Hawaiian man pulled something out from the back of his pants. Red Grizzly darted backward to avoid a strike from a homemade whip.

Gabe squared off with the gray dinosaur. It was quite a bit smaller, more human-sized, so it had to be some sort of a *Deinonychus*, with the addition of two long fangs on both sides of its mouth. Every direction he moved, it mimicked him, except it seemed to move at the same time as he did. The exact same time. So precise that it seemed off, somehow wrong.

He moved his hand toward his back. The dinosaur did too. He twisted to the left. So did the dinosaur, the same way that monkeys mimic humans at the zoo. The only indication that it meant him harm was the snarling grin on its face. But that was enough.

Gabe grabbed the hilt of his weapon. The dinosaur leaped at him.

He fired at its head.

It bobbed at the last second, catching the bullet as a glancing blow to the side of its neck.

The dinosaur screeched, drawing the attention of Red Grizzly, who left its prey to come help. These reptiles had some kind of strong bond.

As the dinosaurs came together, both men circled away, ending up back-to-back. Glancing over his shoulder, he locked eyes with the Hawaiian for a second before they both decided to take advantage of Red Grizzly's concern over its injured hunting partner. They ran back toward the safety of the campsite.

He looked back once. Red Grizzly glared at him but made no move to pursue.

Along the way, the Hawaiian veered off into the jungle and disappeared, leaving Gabe with more questions than answers. Who was he? How was he connected to Oakley? And the most crucial question to address, how often did Red Grizzly and his gray friend hunt this close to their campsite?

"WE AREN'T TAKING them back to the cave, right?" Oakley asked Cane, who had taken the lead on their trek through the trees. Lumas would have seen every place she'd been.

A welcome numbness had invaded her chest. She was pushing down issues that would inevitably resurface, but she couldn't deal with the recent revelations at the moment. Cane was Lumas's son? Did Lumas know? He had to at least suspect. And the eye implant. That was how he had known about the people she'd killed. And how he'd known about Cane's abilities.

Penna's story fit all the facts and filled in most of the blanks. She had done everything possible to escape from Lumas. The only thing that mattered now was keeping her and Teagan away from him.

"I know a place that Neve told me about," Cane said. "Near where she grew up."

Behind them, Penna walked easily, casually carrying her rifle as if her life was uprooted every day. Teagan, however, trudged in front of her mother with heavy steps. What would it be like to grow up in the midst of criminals and dinosaurs, to know nothing besides death surrounding you? At least she would have felt safe inside the sanatorium's walls. Now, she had to be terrified.

Despite the reluctant steps, when she looked up to meet Oakley's gaze, her expression was clear and bright. Their eyes locked on to one another for several seconds.

Teagan's penetrating green eyes were staring deeper into Oakley than even Cane's could. It took her breath away.

She broke off the eye contact, focusing instead on her feet. No one spoke. Listening to the rhythm of their steps made her sleepy again. She must still be dealing with the hangover from the concussion or maybe the anesthesia. Whatever Penna had given her was probably obtained long ago, before the evacuation.

In front of her, Cane stiffened. Then, her own skin began to tingle, marking the presence of a predator. Next came a familiar prickle at the back of her brain—the pheromones. Adler had to be close.

Teagan shuddered. Of course, she would feel it as well.

Picking up on the tension, Penna raised her rifle and scanned the encroaching foliage.

From their right, Adler strode boldly out of the jungle, holding a rifle directed at Penna. "Toss it over here."

Penna had been caught looking the other way. She glowered at him and let her rifle fall to the ground by her feet.

He shook his head. "Over here."

She complied with a grunt.

"I stumbled upon a walking buffet. Lucky me. I get to pick and choose who to kill first." He directed his gaze at Penna. "Good to see you, *Mom*." He laughed and moved on to Teagan. "You, I'm at a loss. Some kind of affair Mom had after she came here?" He took a step toward the girl. "No, that's not it. There's something about your smell. Did she tell you we can sense each other?"

Lightning fast, he reached out to grab Teagan's arm, but she'd already pulled it away. He tried again with the same result. As if she'd known what he was going to do before he did it.

"Interesting," he said.

Oakley squeezed between Adler and Teagan. Adler backed up rather than let Oakley get her hands on him. Good, he should be scared of her.

Then, the hypocrisy hit her afresh. What was Adler except a manipulated human like herself? Shouldn't she have some compassion on him? Half his DNA was Penna's after all.

She could at least try to talk to him. "Why are you doing this?"

"You really are the curious type, aren't you?" He raised his eyebrows. "It's annoying. All you need to know is that all four of you are coming back to the research lab with me." He leveled the gun at Oakley. "I'd rather kill you immediately, but ..." He tapped his temple next to his right eye. "Father is watching."

Lumas had given him an eye implant as well? Not too much trust going around at Asperten.

A determined glint shone in Adler's eyes. The same one she'd seen in Daric toward the end. So much for trying to understand him. He would find a way to kill her, and probably Cane, at the first opportunity. If it would have been just the two of them at stake, she would consider obeying Adler until they could turn the tables on him. But if Lumas got Penna under his control again, he'd make more deadly mutated people. And then Teagan would be at Lumas's mercy as well.

Adler twisted his body to speak to Penna again. Beside Oakley, Teagan shifted, blocking Oakley from Adler's sight. The girl appeared somehow afraid and peaceful at the same time. Oakley handed Teagan her spear, then focused inward. She let the desire to defend Teagan build inside her chest. The electrical potential bubbled through her blood. She closed her eyes and pictured it as a river of pure energy that she could direct. With her mind, she pulled it from her core, congregated it in her chest, then pushed it through her arms. It simmered white-hot and boiling in her fingertips.

Cane had captured Adler's attention and was distracting him with a discussion about peacekeeping.

Adler tapped his rifle. "I've been on missions for him. Peacekeeping is a joke."

She angled her body so she could grab Adler without touching Cane. *Keep him talking.*

"So, tell me who this little morsel is." Adler's head swiveled toward Teagan again, and he caught a glimpse of Oakley.

She had to strike now.

She pivoted and dropped to one knee to catch him on his lower thigh. His leg muscles seized up, followed by the muscles in his core and extremities, including his trigger finger.

"Duck!" she yelled.

The rifle blast tore through a tree just over Cane's shoulder.

Adler fell to the ground. She let go of him. He was still breathing but appeared unconscious.

"Should we kill him?" The quiet question came from Teagan. "He wanted to kill us. Mom, tell her to shock him some more."

Penna put a hand on her daughter's arm. Her tone was soft, but her words were the clipped cadence of a scientist. "That won't kill him. We'd have to shoot him."

Did any part of her still consider Adler as a son? Would she grieve for him if they killed him?

Penna fixed a glare on Teagan. "And despite the grim suggestion, we are not shooting anyone in front of an impressionable fifteen-year-old." She stood in front of Cane. "Take us to your safe house."

CHAPTER TWENTY-SIX

AN HOUR LATER, Penna and Teagan sat on two torn sofas that they would use as beds inside the main lounge of the old Lankester Botanical Gardens. Oakley toured the room, pulling out vines that had pushed through the weathered boards from the outside. The floor was relatively clean, and the dark wooden walls steeply sloped to the peak of the intact roof. For Extinction Island, the place was almost homey. Despite the cobwebs, the one missing window, and no cots, this should be a step-up from fifteen years in a spooky sanatorium.

She helped unpack Penna's limited medical equipment. If they ever got Lumas off their backs, they could make a return trip for more supplies—Penna had an entire surgical room—but for now they'd taken only what they could carry.

Penna appeared to be adjusting with the ease of someone who'd been on the run for a decade and a half.

But Teagan sat on a couch with her hands folded, barely looking at anyone.

"I'm fine," she said without raising her head.

How did she seem to answer questions that hadn't been asked? She was fairly intuitive for such a young girl. Oakley lifted a blanket and draped it around Teagan's shoulders. "In case it gets cold tonight."

"Thanks." Teagan nodded toward Penna as if prodding Oakley.

Come to think of it, she did have an important question. "Penna, why did you say we had to shoot Adler?"

"Because your powers won't kill him." She looked over at Cane. "Neither will yours."

"Why not?" he asked.

"Adler was my first generation. I couldn't work on your powers until I worked out how to protect you from yourselves. The safeguards had to come first. Adler doesn't have your abilities, but he is protected from them."

"Help me wrap my head around the family tree here." Cane's voice was filled with frustration. "Is Adler my half sibling as well?"

"It's complicated." Penna glanced at Teagan, who suddenly stood to her feet and fixed her mother with a glare. Penna shifted her eyes down in a defeated expression. "Cane, he's not your half brother, but he is Teagan's."

"Explain it, Mother," Teagan ordered.

A heavy sigh escaped Penna's lips. "When Eloisa came to Elliot's funeral, she told me she had suspicions regarding Adler. Lumas had provided the sperm sample for Adler's embryo, claiming it was his. I had no reason to question him. But after talking to Eloisa, I ran a DNA comparison. Adler's real father was listed in the criminal database. Michael Calais was a sociopathic killer, who was serving out a sentence on death row for killing five people. I imagine they executed him before this place was even built."

"Why would Lumas do such a thing?" Oakley asked.

"For the genetics. He hoped I'd create a sociopath."

"There's more," Teagan insisted.

Penna shifted on the couch. "I couldn't stay with him any longer, but I had to know the why behind it. I had to find out the extent of what I'd done. We tested every modification on the dinosaurs before we tried them on human embryos. I scoured every document on the computers. Buried in the line items for the dinosaurs, I found some expenditures from human testing that were allocated to the cost center DBT. It took more digging, but I discovered DBT is an acronym for the Division of Biological Termination."

"Doesn't sound like a peacekeeping force," Oakley mumbled.

"DBT is exactly what it sounds like—a division of assassins for hire. And not just any kind, but those who can perform undetectable assassinations." She focused on Oakley. "Like sudden cardiac arrest from a burst of electricity." Her eyes shifted to Cane. "Or suffocation from a deadly gas that's hard to find in an autopsy."

Her revelation hit Oakley like a punch to the gut. They had been bred to be assassins. She searched out Cane. Fear and horror pulsed between them in dreadful waves.

"I understand now," she whispered. "What Lumas told me at the lab. He said he switched to creating females because they were less intimidating. But in a peace-keeping situation, you'd want an intimidating, strong force to influence people to keep the peace. On the other hand, a petite woman is perfect if you're trying to lull your target into complacency. Present them with a seemingly defenseless woman who is actually deadly." She paused for a moment to wipe a cold sweat off her forehead. "My sister and I were made small for a deadly purpose."

The implications were staggering. Instead of the defenseless gazelle hoping to outrun a predator, she *was* the predator. She was the stalking lion. No wonder her own mother had been afraid of what she could become.

She captured those appalling thoughts before they hijacked her mind completely. She needed to focus on the issue at hand. Even though all of them had been bred for the same purpose, the most dangerous one among them was Adler. Unlike the rest of them, he wanted to be an assassin. To protect Penna and Teagan, they had to eliminate him. But to kill him, she might have to get her hands dirtier than ever before. She faced Penna. "How can we kill Adler?"

From across the room, Cane gave her a disapproving glare.

"I mean, how *could* we kill him," she amended, "if we have to, that is?"

Her words hung in the air for a moment. This had to be difficult for Penna.

Oakley softened her voice. "How would you feel about Adler dying?"

A dark shadow passed over Penna's face. "Adler has made his choices." Her expression cleared, and she spoke in a factual tone. "Guns would do it. Dinosaurs even. Pretty much any mode of death other than electrocution or poisoning."

Maybe they could use one of the traps on the island. Kaleo knew the location of each one. But they'd have to rule out all of the traps that use poison. Unless ... "What about another type of poison besides hydrogen cyanide?"

"That could work. Adler has LTNF, lethal toxin neutralizing factor, the same protein that you and Cane have, that protects him from hydrogen cyanide. It's a peptide that neutralizes venom in opossums. Such a beautiful example of how to break down the poison so you aren't poisoning yourself when you release the toxin." She snapped her fingers. "Oh, and tetrodotoxin, from the puffer fish, wouldn't affect any of you either. I modified your sodium ion channels to give you immunity." She crossed her arms over her chest. "To answer your question firmly, yes, any other poison besides hydrogen cyanide and tetrodotoxin would kill him."

"As theoretically fascinating as this is ..." Cane stood up. "Now that you're situated, I need to get back to the cave. If Lumas and Adler have seen everywhere Oakley has been, then the cave isn't safe. Adler will look for us there."

"What about Kaleo?" Oakley asked.

Cane picked up his bow and quiver. "The compound has better security. We can warn them tomorrow."

"I'll go tonight."

He narrowed his eyes at her. Her reasoning was two-fold, though Cane would probably only guess at the one. She did want to see Kaleo, but there was someone else she needed to visit as well.

"What about night predators?" he asked.

"Night is safer for me anyway, remember? The FBI issue. Besides, we can walk halfway there together." She turned to Penna. "That reminds me. Did you create a *Carnotaurus* that can breathe fire?"

An uncharacteristically sheepish look passed over Penna's face. "Not exactly. But I may have left the plans for *Carnotaurus ignis* in my office. It's loosely based on the bombardier beetle."

"The what?"

"A beetle that combines hydrogen peroxide, hydro-quinone, and several catalysts to cause an explosion that protects it from predators. I know why you're asking. I've seen that dinosaur too. Someone is trying to continue my work."

"Auburn," Oakley said.

"That's what I figured." Penna held up a rifle. "If you both need to go, she can have Adler's rifle as protection."

Cane glared at her. "Thanks for helping."

Penna shook her head as if men were completely frustrating. At the moment, Oakley agreed. She could choose to risk her life to do the right thing, the same as Cane.

He stayed silent for a while. But she didn't need his permission to go. Either that showed on her face or he felt her pheromones because his scowl deepened.

Finally, he handed the bow and quiver to her. "Then you'll need these to get Kaleo to come meet you."

CHAPTER TWENTY-SEVEN

FOR SHELTER, Taye Turner chose the only shack with a mostly intact door. He swept Neve inside and closed the tattered door behind them. When Cane had come to the cave to warn them to evacuate, he probably wondered why Taye was there. But after what the women had gone through, he couldn't leave them to fend for themselves. The gang at the resort compound probably thought he was on an extended hunt.

Cane had suggested taking everyone from the cave to an old janitor's cabin at a nearby abandoned school, but Neve thought it made sense to split up. Adler would have less chance of tracking them if they left different trails. Taye had agreed and offered to join her. Besides, it wasn't just Adler they had to worry about. That crazed FBI agent was almost as unpredictable.

A quick glance around the one-room shack revealed a single bed constructed of wooden planks with an old blanket on top. Neve tentatively sat on it, testing its strength. "It will hold."

"I'll sleep on the floor," he said.

"You will not. The floor is disgusting."

He looked down at the detritus of animal droppings and moldy leaves and couldn't argue with her.

"Sleeping is a biological function that two people can do next to each other without other motives."

She was right. Trouble was that his heart had other motives.

She patted the side of the cot, so he walked over and sat down nearest the wall. Normally, sitting this close to her would only happen in his amorous dreams. Unfortunately, he couldn't enjoy it. The dirty, cramped quarters of the shack came too close to the conditions of the hovel he'd lived in during his last days at Acadia Paragon in Mississippi. Danny, the leader of that group, used to lock him in a dirty wooden shed for days at a time without food. Water came solely when it rained through holes in the roof. If only Taye could have withstood the isolation better. If only he'd just run away when they eventually let him out.

"You okay?" Neve asked.

"Sure. I'm just ... Nothing." Putting his pain into words was too hard. "Let's get more comfortable."

The cot's frame was too narrow for them to lay side by side. The best way for both of them to sleep was if he put his back against the wall and she lay between his legs. He swung his leg behind and over the cot to situate his back on the wall, then he motioned for her to lay against him. She hesitated, but not for long. She wouldn't refute her earlier words. Neve was nothing if not consistent.

Her slender body rested perfectly along his. Her head fell right at the center of his chest. He wrapped his arms around her and resisted the temptation to kiss the top of her head.

Maybe this would help him relax. Maybe it would even help her relax more around him. With Cane, she was self-assured, putting her opinions out there. With Kaleo, she mothered his myriad of bruises. But with him, she was hesitant, tentative, even shy.

"Why did you choose to come with me?" she asked.

"To protect you."

"I see." It was a reasonable answer, and yet, her tone rang with disappointment. "Just so you know, I can take care of myself. I've lived here my whole life."

"And you'll die here if you're reckless."

She shrugged. "I am going to die here."

Stupid phrasing on his part. They would all die here. "Yes, but I don't want you to die before you really live."

As the words left his mouth, the spark of truth shot through him. She deserved so much—love, marriage, children—even if it wasn't with him. But she asked for so little in her life.

"How are you dealing with what happened to Chubs?" he asked.

She stiffened in his arms. He ran his fingers along the

side of her arm, trying to coax her into opening up. Her voice was shaky when she spoke. "I was a coward."

"How so?"

"Wells left the safe room to help, but I didn't. I was afraid of what Chubs would do to me." Her breath hitched. "To my body."

He held her tighter. "From what I heard, Wells has some martial arts training. She had more of a chance to defeat him than you."

Neve sank into a sulky silence. Had he said something wrong? She risked her life constantly to help others. This woman was no coward. If anything, the true coward here was him. Oddly, she'd never asked what he did to end up on Extinction Island, and he'd never had the courage to tell her. She simply accepted him for what he was now.

"Am I a coward, Neve?"

She pushed off his chest to turn around and face him. "What? Of course not."

"I've done cowardly things." He swiped a dreadlock from his face. "I grew up in a cult where I hurt people."

"You must have been forced to."

"I was coerced, yes. But I could have done more to stop it." He opened his mouth to tell her about Sympathy —he still called her that, even though her real name had been Kelly—but his throat only let out a garbled rasp.

"You don't have to," she said.

"I want you to know." He meant it. Though it might end any possible future between them, she needed to hear about his past. "They called me Flint because I was good at doing the hard things. Danny, our leader, gave me many types of duties. He called them burdens. Sometimes, my burden was to threaten people. Most often, the burden was to hurt them. Broken fingers. Bruised ribs. Fractured legs. Some of them were innocent people who didn't do anything except threaten our activities."

Neve bit at her lower lip but didn't speak.

"Once, he even had me poison the food at a local restaurant to take revenge on some people who had spread rumors about his operation."

She touched her throat.

"Two people died, but that's not why I ended up here." He sat straighter on the cot. Pushing the words out was the real burden. "At the time, I believed Danny wanted what God wanted. As Flint, I was a righteous soldier. When Danny told me to kill, I did. And I got away with it."

Neve took his hand, and he grasped hers tight like a lifeline.

"One day, he told me that a girl from our group had spoken to the police. We called her Sympathy, probably because she was the weakest of us. She was quiet and mousy. I couldn't imagine her having the courage to go to the cops. But Danny convinced me that she betrayed us."

Unbidden images of blood and matted hair turned his stomach. No going back. He'd done it, so he needed to own it.

With a shaky voice, he continued, "I shot her three times in the head—three for the holy trinity—and buried her in the woods on our property." He swallowed through his dry throat. "Two months later, I learned from one of the other men that it was a lie. Sympathy hadn't spoken to the police. Danny wanted her gone because ..." His voice cracked as he shoved out the final words of his confession. "She was pregnant."

Neve threw herself around his chest and hugged him fiercely. Her compassion broke the dam of pain inside him. He gripped her back almost as tight while his eyes misted with tears. Thanks to Cane, or more accurately, thanks to God, he was a different person now. Flint seemed like a stranger.

He clung to her for several minutes before he could speak again. "Neither of us are cowards. It takes courage to face up to our human failings." He pulled back to force her to look at him. "And it takes courage to see those failings and love anyway. In that sense, you are the bravest person I know."

She gave him a sweet smile that made him want to kiss her. Perhaps she wanted that too. Instead, he merely stared into her lovely almond-colored eyes. The timing wasn't right. In the light of day, his horrific story might hit her harder. He would give her the chance to change her mind about who she thought he was.

After a few more minutes, she settled her head back on his chest. "Do you think the others are okay? Did Cane take them all, even Wells?"

"I don't think Wells would allow herself to be left behind." In fact, the way he'd seen her look at Cane, she wasn't walking away from the man who'd saved her life anytime soon.

"Should we go find them tomorrow?"

"I need to check in with Raptor first. Don't worry. Cane will take care of them." Of that, he had no doubt. He might not always agree with Cane's decisions, but he was as different from Danny as night was from day. Danny had taught Taye to sacrifice to please Danny. Cane taught by example, sacrificing his own needs to take care of others. The same as Neve. "Do you ever wonder if you sacrifice too much for your friends?"

She gave a little chuckle. "Unless it's too much, it's not a sacrifice."

They lapsed into peaceful silence. After fifteen minutes, he suspected she'd fallen asleep, but then she spoke. "Thank you for coming with me."

His heart swelled, and he smiled. "It wasn't a sacrifice."

He smoothed her hair back from her face in a rhythmic motion until he heard her soft, shallow breaths. She was finally asleep.

CHAPTER TWENTY-EIGHT

THE ARROW with the yellow fletching flew across the canyon toward Kaleo's balcony. Even though lights shone brightly in his room, the night was too dark to be sure she'd hit the potted lime tree near the pool. Hopefully, he'd get the message to meet her and come soon.

She hunkered down near the ravine where Kaleo had deposited her after they'd faked her death last week. Appropriate for a nighttime meeting, if not a little noir.

Within a few minutes, she heard rustling in the bushes nearby. It was probably too soon to be Kaleo, plus he wouldn't make so much noise. Then again, neither would a true predator. She nocked an arrow to be safe.

Near the bottom of a bush, a downy green head poked out. *Cody!* She lowered the arrow. "Hey, little guy. So glad you found me. Didn't think you'd want to be out in the dark."

"He's been bedding down near the compound."

Kaleo's deep voice sparked surprise and warmth inside her. "You've been moving around so much he can't keep track of you."

The sad inflection and the furrowed brow meant he wasn't referring just to Cody.

"I'm sorry."

He held up the arrow. "I was hoping it was you and not Cane."

She grabbed it. He held on, using her grip to draw her closer. His gaze fell to her lips. Even in the cool night, heat pooled low in her gut. He could start a chain reaction inside her with one look.

Her cheeks had to be blazing red. Thank goodness it was dark. But it wasn't dark enough to mask his chiseled jaw, the bold tilt to his lips, or his smoldering eyes. Without thinking, she leaned into him.

He trapped her chin between two fingers and raised her head. She gave in to the pull, dropping the arrow and putting both hands on his chest. His hard muscles tensed under her touch.

When his lips met hers, sparks ignited from head to toe. She wrapped her arms around his neck. His hands gently tugged out her ponytail holder, then he buried his fingers in her hair.

The sparks continued to build, spilling over inside her, creating a cascade of tingles that rolled over her skin. Not soft tingles of desire, but pulses of spiraling shocks that melded the two of them together. This heat was quickly growing out of control. But as Kaleo kissed her over and over, she couldn't find the strength to pull away.

A shock burst from her lips, not unpleasant, but it stunned her for a few seconds.

Kaleo grunted but didn't let her go. She should stop this. It could be dangerous for him. Still, she couldn't summon the willpower to stop.

His hands cradled her face. The heat swelled until she was at a boiling point. Another spark shot through her lips.

He absorbed this one as well with a lower, almost satisfied grunt. When he finally pulled back, she bit her lower lip, trying to regain her breath.

He lowered his forehead to hers. "I've missed you."

"I've missed you too." Cody nuzzled her leg as if chiming in himself. "And you, little guy."

"What happened at the sanatorium?"

She filled him in on finding Penna and Teagan, including the confrontation with Adler.

"Why didn't you just shoot him?" Kaleo's voice had a frustrated edge to it. .

She opened her mouth, but no words came out. He had a point, but as Penna said, shooting Adler in front of Teagan sounded like child abuse. Not to mention Penna was his mother. Even if she knew he was dangerous, she wouldn't want to watch him die.

Kaleo picked up her hair tie and handed it to her. "It will be hard to catch him off guard again. We only have two guns here at the compound. If he has more ammunition, he can probably outshoot all of us."

She scooped her hair up and secured it in a bun. "I think I know how to even the odds. I need to talk to Misty. Will she come out to see me?"

"No, she doesn't go out at night. But I can get you in."

"Isn't that risky?"

He captured her hand and pulled her along. "Only if we get caught."

They made a wide circle around the ravine and the resort compound until they came to the southernmost wing. She trailed behind him as he stayed in the shadows of the concrete retaining wall.

The wall ended on the opposite side of the same ravine. Kaleo reached around behind the wall, unhooked something with his arm, and swung it back. A free-hanging ladder unfolded in front of her. "This is how I come and go when I don't want anyone to know I've left." He hooked his foot in. "Let me go first to make sure the area is deserted. I'll tug on the ladder when it's safe."

The ladder pulled away from the wall as he climbed. She averted her eyes to keep from staring at his backside. It was too easy to ogle him.

A few seconds later, the ladder leaped out of her hand. All clear. She climbed on, and it swung back under her weight. The dark chasm of the ravine stretched below her feet. If she lost her grip ... Well, she couldn't go there.

She focused her gaze on the balcony above. When she

crossed over the railing, she stepped onto a patio outside of an unused room of the resort.

"Misty sleeps in a room not far from here," he whispered. "But let's see if she's still in her playroom."

He led her to where the hall ended in a rough wood-plank wall with a wooden door, both of which looked like they'd been added long after the resort was abandoned. After a quick knock, he opened the door and stepped inside.

"Don't touch anything," he said.

She followed him over the threshold. The area had once been a three-seasons room that Misty must use as a greenhouse and laboratory. Long tables holding plants covered the eastern wall where they would catch the morning sun. Along the southern wall sat desks with several pestle and mortar combinations, plus implements of all kinds, from hammers to knives to meat tenderizers.

Misty hunched over one of the desks, her curly gray hair splayed out on the desktop. She was asleep, hopefully.

"Misty." Kaleo touched her shoulder.

She jerked awake. The frown lines around her light gray eyes relaxed as she focused on him. Then, her eyes lit up when they found Oakley. "My dear. I thought you were gone."

"She has gone," he said. "She's only here because she needs your help."

"Of course." Misty stood to her full height, at least six

inches shorter than Oakley, and looked her over. "You look well."

"It's not for me." She hesitated for a moment. Misty had killed two husbands, but maybe she'd renounced that part of herself. Maybe she wouldn't want to help if she knew her assistance could kill someone. On the other hand, Misty would try to make Kaleo happy. Years ago, he'd saved her from the abuse of a former gang leader. "I need poison."

She didn't even blink. "There are lots of poisons available. What does it need to do?"

"It needs to be fast-acting and deadly. Most of all, not tetrodotoxin or hydrogen cyanide."

"I see." Misty's voice was businesslike, but her eyebrows lifted in excitement. If nothing else, she would enjoy the challenge of this. "Any other requirements?"

Oakley shook her head. "I don't think so."

"How do you plan to deliver it?"

"Probably on the tip of a knife."

Misty shook her head, the fluffy curls bouncing like white cotton candy. "Too obvious and too much potential for accidental poisoning of the wrong person."

"What about the tip of an arrow?"

"Same."

Oakley sighed. "What do you suggest, then?"

"Everyone instinctively avoids the tip of a knife. You need something that no one would expect to be poisoned." She laughed. "Then, you need to make sure everyone you care about knows not to touch it." Another rueful laugh. "I lost a dog that way once."

Oakley stayed silent. How was she supposed to respond to that?

"Let's work on the poisonous compound first. I have a concentrated derivative of yellow-bellied sea snake venom. It's a cousin to the cobra, you know."

No, she didn't know.

"I sent Taye all the way to the Pacific side of the island hunting for the animal. What a trip he had trying to find them." She let out a low whistle. "It's the same stuff I tell Kaleo to put on the poisonous spears of the traps, so watch out for those setups." She looked up at Oakley. "You know, the ones with the arrow pointing to the right—"

"Yes, I know."

Misty put a hand on one hip. "But do you know where all of them are located?" Without waiting for an answer, she began hunting through the papers on her desk. "You should really have one of my maps."

"A map?" Oakley had never seen a map of the traps on the island. She'd just run into them at all the wrong—and sometimes right—times.

Misty waved a hand at Kaleo. "He doesn't use one. Says he has their locations in his head."

"I do," he confirmed.

Misty narrowed her eyes. "But what if you forget?"

He shook his head at her ranting.

"Here it is." She held up a folded six-by-six-inch square of paper.

Oakley set her backpack on the ground before taking the paper and unfolding it. The map was small, yet somehow it covered all of northern Costa Rica. With a tiny pen, Misty had marked numbers in certain locations. Those numbers were classified into columns in the margin, indicating which type of trap. This was invaluable. "Are you sure you can you spare this?"

Misty nodded. "I have another one."

"Thank you." Oakley kneeled down to place the map in her backpack. Wait, she also had a weapon in there. She dug out the tranquilizer gun and darts. "What about these?"

A smile graced Misty's face, making her look years younger. "Not inconspicuous, but that will work even better." She grabbed two of the darts, leaving the gun in Oakley's palm, then moved to the other side of the row of desks. "And let's try this as well." She picked up an innocent looking tube that could have been toothpaste. "It's got quite a kick."

This time, it was Oakley's turn to smile. Misty was a deadly kind of eccentric—exactly what she needed.

CHAPTER TWENTY-NINE

GABE STARED hard at his phone. Could he trust what it told him? The tracking app had just refreshed from the satellite and now indicated an active location for one of the trackers that Dr. Anderson had brought to the island—one of the trackers earmarked for Oakley Laveau.

He stepped out of the tent and around the electrified perimeter wire. Raptor sat at a picnic table they had carried over from an old campground nearby. He was sharing some fresh fruit he'd apparently brought for the other men, now only two of them, plus the doctor.

Just the guy he needed to see. He sat across from Raptor and tossed his phone on the table with the screen face up. "Oakley's tracker is suddenly active. Did you know?"

Raptor blinked before glancing at the phone. "Really?"

Either he was an excellent actor, or he hadn't known.

Dr. Anderson must have survived to complete her work. It didn't make sense for anyone else to implant the tracker. If Oakley had gotten her hands on them, it would have been in her best interest to destroy all the trackers.

"Great!" Raptor exclaimed. "All is well. You guys can go home now."

"Not just yet." The signal came from too far away, and it was too late in the day to head that direction. First thing tomorrow, he'd check it out.

"Why not?"

"We still have to find Dr. Anderson and bring her back. Plus, I'm not convinced Oakley is an innocent bystander in all this. I think the kidnapping was conceived to avoid tagging her. If that's the case, then Oakley might be responsible for killing my partner."

Raptor's face fell. Not a big surprise, given the history between him and the inmate.

Gabe folded his arms across his chest. There were too many odd coincidences here. Oakley was Raptor's former employee. Dr. Anderson knew Raptor's girlfriend. Dr. Anderson was a member of CADRE. No matter how innocent Raptor's countenance, Gabe couldn't ignore the coincidences piling up.

This whole intrigue revolved around Oakley. He wouldn't stop until he found her. Whatever part she had in the plot, he would make sure she paid for it.

OAKLEY SPENT the night at the resort compound helping Misty prepare the poison. When she became so tired she couldn't keep her eyes open, she crawled into a bed in a room next to Misty's. In the morning, she and Kaleo met Cane at the tree house. Then they began their hunt for Adler. Kaleo took the lead, she was second, and Cane followed behind her, holding the loaded tranquilizer gun. He'd insisted on being the one to shoot Adler in order to protect the people from the cave. More than likely, he was trying to keep her from having to kill again.

Despite Misty's claims, the poison might not be strong enough to kill Adler quickly with all of his adaptations, so once Cane shot him with the dart, Oakley would be ready with their backup weapon—a tube filled with plastic explosives.

Kaleo advanced their little hunting party, holding his whip and a rifle in opposite hands. They crept quietly toward the bunker owned by Asperten International, which was embedded in a hillside. According to Raptor, Adler stayed there the last time he came to the island.

Previously, whenever she'd needed to find Adler, he would almost magically appear. But now that the eye implant had been removed, he would have no idea where she was. That freedom gave them the advantage of surprise, if only they could find him first.

Not wanting to get too close because the facility likely had cameras, they circled around the metal door. Kaleo settled them down to watch and wait in a large group of bushes sheltered by a few trees. Kaleo and Cane were closest to the door, while she had to peer over their shoulders to see it.

An hour later, she shifted to stretch her legs. Cane reorganized his bag, laying the extra dart on top within easy reach for reloading. Maybe this was a waste of time. Adler could have found somewhere else to sleep. Perhaps he'd guessed she would come for him here.

After another hour, something in the air changed. She looked over at Cane, whose eyes were wide. He felt it too. Adler was here, but where?

Kaleo must have sensed their alarm because he raised his gun and scanned the foliage along with them. Cane aimed the tranquilizer gun to their right. She unscrewed the lid from the small tube, then pulled from her pocket a flexible metal wire she'd gotten from Misty.

"Surprise." The deep voice came from above them. "I'm impressed. This is exactly where I would stake out the bunker."

Oakley's gaze darted up. Adler sat high in the V-shaped notch of a tree to their right, nearly invisible in the thick foliage. The dark barrel of a rifle pointed down at them. He had to have been there the whole time, otherwise they'd have heard him climb up. Why had she only sensed him just now? The implications draped over her like a cold, wet blanket. Adler must have mastered control over his pheromones. He'd purposely let them get settled, then watched them for hours, maybe hoping they'd do something stupid, like separate.

From his perch, Adler had the better angle, but both

Kaleo and Cane held weapons on him. As he shifted in the tree, more of his head became visible. He had some sort of gauze tape, the kind that sticks to itself, wrapped around his head and over his right eye.

Her mouth went dry. It was the same eye as the implant. Adler had made sure Lumas couldn't watch.

With his left eye, Adler looked disdainfully at Cane. "We both know you aren't going to use that. You pose about as much danger as your mother." He angled his weapon toward Kaleo. "He's the only real threat out here."

Cane's hand shook on the tranquilizer gun. Good thing they had a backup plan in case he couldn't pull the trigger to end Adler's life. But she'd have to get a lot closer to use the explosives.

With the gun trained on Kaleo, Adler kept his gaze on Cane. "Lumas knew how to pick his employees. No family. No friends. No one to miss her after she died. Wish I could tell you she passed easily, but there was a lot of blood." He grinned. "I'll never forget her, though. Killing her was my first mission."

Cane's jaw pulsed. Corded tendons bulged on his neck. Waves of anger flowed from him like lava pouring out of a volcano. Her muscles went rigid under the onslaught of his pheromones.

He swallowed hard as if to gain control of his emotions. Just when it seemed he'd succeeded, his hand began to shake again. He gritted his teeth and grunted.

Then, his finger twitched. He narrowed his eyes and pulled the trigger.

Adler responded at the same moment, squeezing off a shot as they all ducked for cover.

She dove onto the ground and rolled under a bush.

Had Adler been hit? Cane's hand had been vibrating so much, no one could guess where the dart went. If it didn't hit Adler in a muscle somewhere, then she'd need to use the other dart.

And what about Kaleo? Did Adler's shot miss?

A heavy weight landed across her back. She rolled over. It was Kaleo's arm, and he appeared uninjured. His gun had landed several yards away. Through the low foliage, Cane's blond hair stood out. He'd taken cover opposite them.

She lifted her head a few inches. The contents of the bag had been strewn about when they'd scrambled apart. No dart in sight. It was likely lost in the undergrowth.

Another shot blasted past them. Too close. Adler apparently couldn't see them, but he had enough of an idea of where they were.

She had to do something or all three of them would die. But they were pinned down. What could she do?

A flicker of possibility came to her. If Adler could control his pheromones enough to mask them, she could probably increase hers to call forth a small distraction. For once, maybe the attraction the dinosaurs had for her could work in her favor. It was a desperate move, but she had to overcome Adler's high-ground advantage.

She closed her eyes and probed the back side of her mind—the spot that prickled whenever Adler was around and whenever Cane felt a strong emotion. She directed a pulse of electricity to that area.

Her eyes flew open as another shot rang out and a spray of dirt hit her jeans. Adler's aim was improving. He had them cornered, and it wouldn't be long before one of his bullets hit the mark.

A menacing roar drove ice through her veins. Huge feet stomped not ten feet from her head. This was a distraction all right, but not exactly a small one.

She and Kaleo rolled away from the dinosaur, which put them right back into Adler's sightline. He leveled the gun at her head, a gleeful grin on his face. Before he could pull the trigger, a stream of flames lit up the tree.

Demon Dragon had found them again. And it was her fault.

Adler leaped from the tree, dropping his gun as he fell. He landed on Cane's back. Both men rolled on the ground, a jumble of flying fists. Now was not the time for hand-to-hand combat. She crawled in their direction, the toothpaste-sized tube still clutched in her fist.

"Run!" she yelled at Cane.

Adler grabbed Cane's shirt, refusing to let him go.

Demon Dragon pushed its head through the trees to investigate the noise. Its feet remained near her lower body. Kaleo grabbed her under the arms and pulled her backward.

It drew in a huge breath through its nostrils and let

out another long stream of flame. Adler and Cane rolled to the side just in time to avoid being barbecued.

Demon Dragon started to suck in air again. She couldn't let it shoot another fireball at them. She looked at the tube in her hand. But she couldn't use up her only weapon either.

Then, she saw the bag with the last tranquilizer dart lying near the leftmost toe of Demon Dragon's foot. The tranquilizer gun was nowhere in sight, but she might still be able to use the dart. As long as the creature stayed put long enough for her to reach the bag.

She shoved the cap on the tube, put it in her pocket, and shrugged off Kaleo's hands. She darted forward, only to jump back quickly.

Demon Dragon shifted its stance. One of its huge feet stepped on the bag. The crunch of glass vials made her cringe. They had filled two vials with poison, leaving the others empty. Her only hope was that the one with the poison hadn't been damaged. She crept forward this time to reach for a feathered dart that poked out from the open bag.

In a quick motion, she swiped it free. The glass remained intact, the milky white poison sloshing inside. From her crouch near the dinosaur's foot, she glanced up. Demon Dragon's head towered ten feet above her, its jaw muscles rippling underneath layers of scaly skin.

Its mouth opened.

Adler had twisted Cane's arm around behind his back and now held Cane in front of him like a shield.

She had only seconds to save Cane from being charred. With a closed fist, she slammed the needle into the thick skin of its foot. The reverse pressure discharged the poison.

Demon Dragon roared, and its massive head swung toward her, knocking her to the ground. It twisted its head farther to inspect its foot.

A tense few seconds passed as the animal glared alternately at her and at its foot.

Then, Demon Dragon picked up its afflicted leg and shook it. The poison must have already started to paralyze the muscles.

As it put the leg down, it swayed. Its hips rocked back and forth.

She crawled backward through the leaves.

Demon Dragon leaned toward her, found its leg would no longer support it, and crashed forward.

She scrambled out of the way just as it came down between her and Cane and Adler.

Strong hands grabbed her below the armpits again and hauled her up. Kaleo wrapped his arms around her briefly, then propelled her away from Demon Dragon. "We have to go."

Why? What they had to do was help Cane kill Adler. She still had the tube and the wire in her pocket.

But Kaleo tugged her insistently. She glanced over his shoulder, and her stomach quaked.

Her pheromone call had worked too well. Behind them stood Red Grizzly and a familiar smaller raptor with green-gray skin and two large teeth sticking out on either side of its jaw. Fangtooth nodded in their direction with a high squawk.

The blood ran out of her face. Clearly, they both remembered her. If she didn't get out of here soon, she'd be dead within minutes. Probably seconds. She pumped her arms, running as fast as she could behind Kaleo. And for the first time, she prayed. *Please, God, help us survive.*

CHAPTER THIRTY

CANE'S RIBS burned from Adler's continual blows. If only he had the tranquilizer gun or Adler's gun, both of which probably lay under Demon Dragon's massive body.

When the beast fell, Cane had slipped his arm out of Adler's grip. But then, Adler stepped up his attack, landing several hits to Cane's face. His right eye was starting to swell shut, but it was the ache in his ribs every time he breathed that signaled a broken bone.

Adler attempted to climb on top of him again. Cane punched him in the side of the head.

The man grunted and rolled away.

Slowly, Cane got to his feet while Adler did the same. They stood staring at each other.

Kaleo and Oakley hadn't come to help, which meant they were dealing with their own issues. It was up to him to handle Adler. But despite his earlier bravado, he hadn't killed anyone since Sam and might not be able to.

The pores in his hands flared open, then closed. His poison wouldn't help him with Adler. This had to be decided using their fists. Would beating a man to death, even in self-defense, be acceptable to God?

Oh, Lord, what do I do? Our lives have been touched by such evil.

Next to them, Demon Dragon thrashed and moaned. The huge jaws snapped open and closed not five feet behind him.

Adler shifted his body to peer over top of the dinosaur's prone form. Looking for Oakley. She'd been his highest priority target.

"Why do you hate her?" Cane asked.

Uncertainty crossed his face, the first human emotion he'd ever displayed. Just as quickly as it came, the uncertainty passed, replaced by bitter hatred. He picked up a thick stick and held it like a baseball bat. "Because she was the one who got to grow up with her parents."

This was about Penna leaving him. Who knew he was capable of caring about having a parental figure in his life?

"You're being used. You're no different than us," Cane said. "Are we really your enemy?"

Adler swung the stick at his head. Apparently so.

He ducked and the blow missed, but the follow up hit came too quickly to avoid.

Adler slammed a fist-sized rock into his temple.

Pain exploded through his head. His vision closed in, then darkness overtook him.

"HOLD THIS." Kaleo swiped his gun from the ground and thrust it at Oakley.

She hefted the rifle as he unfurled his whip, the tip making a *thwack* on the leaf cover. Red Grizzly recoiled and dipped its head toward the scar on its chest, as if it remembered that encounter.

Intelligence radiated from behind Fangtooth's piercing gaze, surpassing even Red Grizzly. Together, these two made a formidable team, and she'd brought them together. But what were they doing here specifically? Most predators stayed away from other predators, especially the big ones. Were they smart enough to follow in Demon Dragon's shadow to eat its leftovers?

Kaleo slammed the whip into the ground at Fangtooth's feet. It jumped back, glanced at Red Grizzly, then took another step back.

Red Grizzly stomped its feet, looking as if it would attack despite the risk.

Fangtooth honked while taking another step back.

Red Grizzly flipped between staring at its companion and the humans several times in succession before it snorted its acquiescence. As the two dinosaurs trotted off into the jungle, she tried to relax but couldn't. They had to get back to help Cane.

She grabbed Kaleo's arm. He stayed put and shook his head. With the whip, he gestured to the jungle around them. What did he hear?

Anchoring her feet, she tuned in to all of her senses. Rustling continued throughout the jungle, though none of it indicated something large. Then, a ripple of tension ran down her back. A low-level version of the warning that shot through her whenever Adler was around. It was so faint she could have ignored it completely. But now that she focused on the sensation, she pinpointed the location.

It came from behind Kaleo.

The raptors had left to regroup and try a different tactic.

She opened her mouth to tell him, but he put up a cautioning hand. She shifted her head to indicate behind him. He began to turn just as the attack started.

This time, it didn't start with Fangtooth's loud honk. It was a soft snort.

Then, Red Grizzly erupted from the trees behind them. It slammed its body linebacker-style into Kaleo's side.

Fangtooth lunged at her from the front.

She was too late to hit Red Grizzly. But she fired the rifle at Fangtooth. It jumped out of the way. The bullet grazed its backside. A wound near its tail spilled blood onto the leaves.

The dinosaur spun in a circle, attempting to see the injury, but it couldn't.

She lined up the weapon. She'd get a good shot off this time.

Fangtooth stared at her from only ten feet away, assessing her threat level.

She fired.

It darted to the side. The shot whizzed past the right side of its head. How had she missed from this close?

With an angry honk, Fangtooth disappeared into the trees. At least she'd made her point.

Quickly, she searched for Kaleo. She couldn't find him. Red Grizzly must have shoved him farther into the trees.

She took a step in that direction but was pulled back by a strong arm wrapped around her throat.

Adler.

His other hand reached for the gun. She tried to yank it away, but he twisted her arm around and jerked the rifle from her grasp.

She reached out to shock him. He deftly shoved her forward and stepped out of range.

"Where's Cane?" she demanded.

"Sleeping for now. Though I imagine one of the dinosaurs around here will consider him a free meal before he wakes up." Standing five feet away, he motioned with the gun for her to move deeper into the forest. "Don't even think about lunging at me with your electricity. I'll shoot you before you make it over here."

She hesitated. It might be worth her life to get rid of him. But then who would help Kaleo and Cane?

He sighted the weapon on her chest. Going after either one of them now would only get her shot and lead Adler straight to them. Though it killed her inside, she had no choice except to obey, leaving two of the men she cared about most alone in the jungle.

321

RED GRIZZLY'S attack had thrown Kaleo sideways into the trunk of a large tree, wedging him between two thick branches. He was pinned by eight hundred pounds of pure dinosaur muscle. Fortunately, Red Grizzly appeared just as stunned.

A shot had rung out several seconds ago, but the bullet obviously hadn't hit RG. The dinosaur came out of its stupor and snapped its jaws at Kaleo's face. He put a forearm in the creature's neck to block it. But that wouldn't be enough for long.

He twisted his other arm around and grabbed Red Grizzly by the larynx. Circling his fingers around the thick skin and cartilage, he squeezed with all his force.

Red Grizzly's tongue came out as it tried to swallow, but Kaleo held tight.

It thrashed its head back to escape his grip. His fingers slipped from the creature's neck.

It lunged at him again. He ducked and swiveled to the left, hiding behind one of the thick tree branches.

Mouth open, RG hit the branch with a crunch.

Kaleo closed his eyes as wood splintered into his face. What was happening with Oakley? Had the other dinosaur gone after her?

His eyes shot open again because of thrashing near his feet. One of the dinosaur's legs was tangled up in the whip, immobilizing the wicked claw.

But the other claw was free. RG reared back and struck out with its foot. Kaleo tried to twist away. The claw slashed into the back of his thighs, almost yanking him from his feet.

Pain didn't come, but it would soon. Was this how he went out? Death from the claws of a dinosaur wouldn't be a surprise. One of them was bound to kill him eventually. But hopefully not today.

With both hands, he grabbed the whip and yanked.

RG swayed backward. It tried to balance on its tail but failed and fell to the ground on its spine. *Thump*.

With a flick of his wrist, Kaleo uncoiled the whip from its leg.

RG jumped up.

He sent the whip sailing toward its neck. It dipped its neck at the last second. The strike hit its muzzle with a snap.

A gash appeared between its nostrils. Blood oozed from the cut.

RG snarled and bared its two-inch-long, serrated teeth.

Kaleo had a flash of those teeth tearing into Daric's stomach two weeks ago. At least Daric had already been dead.

He tried to step back but couldn't support himself without the tree. His left leg burned in sharp agony like needles were stabbing his thigh. His right leg had fared only a little better.

This might be the one battle he lost, but he wouldn't give up. He hadn't lost it yet. Before RG could attack again, he struck out with the whip a second time. The tapered end wrapped around its neck.

He yanked the whip to the ground, plunging the creature's face into the leaves and dirt.

RG swung its head. The whip held firm. Maybe he could strangle it.

He slipped the whip over a tree branch. Even with this leverage, he likely couldn't lift the creature. But he didn't have to. Just tightening the noose might be enough.

With all his body weight, he heaved the whip downward. The force stretched out RG's body.

It fought, swinging its head again more violently. Its teeth snapped at his arms. Its claws swung wide, coming perilously close to Kaleo's stomach. Would he feel it if one of those claws ripped through his flesh? Or would adrenaline block the pain long enough for him to die?

The creature's thrashing motion dislodged the whip completely. RG was free.

Kaleo swiped the whip through the tree to release it, then snapped it at RG again. The creature jumped back, barely avoiding a strike to its belly.

Staring hard at Kaleo, it twitched its head back and forth. Its leg muscles tensed. It was eager to run at him but held off solely because of the whip.

For his next strike, he flicked his wrist and snapped the whip sideways. It brought a bloody stripe across RG's neck.

The creature yelped and pressed its front leg to the wound.

Thrashing came from the jungle beyond RG. The green-gray dinosaur with the fearsome teeth appeared. The one from the boat that Oakley had called Fangtooth. It ran past them both, screeching and bleeding from its tail. RG's gaze trailed it with uncertainty.

Since it looked like it wanted to follow its companion, Kaleo gave it some incentive. He snapped the whip at its legs. It leaped back and turned away, saving its legs, but taking the strike near the end of its tail.

It gave a high-pitched bark of anger and glared at him for several seconds. Then, it darted away, tracing Fang-tooth's path.

Kaleo relaxed, though briefly. The injured green-gray dinosaur meant Oakley had fought back. Was she okay?

He pushed off the tree and made it two steps before he pitched forward and hit the ground. Pain seared through the back of his legs as warm blood trickled over his exposed skin. He cursed under his breath. He dragged himself across the leaves while pulling the whip along. Somehow, he had to get to Oakley.

———

TWENTY YARDS away from the bunker, Adler motioned for her to stop. He held the gun on her, his face a mask of grim determination. He stood just two arm's lengths away from her. Too far to shock, but close enough that she couldn't run without getting shot. Maybe she could get him talking and find a way out of this.

"Did you know?" she asked.

"Know what?"

"The reason we were created."

He shook his head, not as if saying no, but as if saying she was the dumbest person on the planet. "Most people come into this world by accident with nothing to help them. We were created for a purpose." He winked at her. "A lucrative purpose. Too bad you won't embrace it."

That wasn't entirely true. She'd used her power to kill, just not for money. What was the point in hiding the truth from herself any longer? She was different from Cane. When she deemed it justified, killing was an option. Did it matter why she did what she did any more than it mattered why a leopard would take down a gazelle?

You are not the sum of your choices. Cane's words from the research lab taunted her. Most of the time, she didn't *have* a choice.

"Is that why you hate me so much? Because you were the prototype?"

He shrugged. "Even with all the advantages you've been given, you won't use them to the full potential."

"So, the bottom line is that you're jealous."

He laughed. "Your power is wasted on you, which makes you a liability." He ran his gaze down her body. "Even if you could have had a dozen gifted babies with tall, blond, and handsome back there." A triumphant blast of pheromones came from him. He patted the gauze loosely draped over his right eye. "What Lumas doesn't know won't hurt him ... or me. Right now, he probably thinks I'm sleeping in."

As he withdrew his hand, a piece of gauze stuck to one of his fingers. It pulled away from just the corner of his eye. He frantically worked to replace it.

She wouldn't get a better chance than this. She spun to her left while yanking the plastic tube out of her pocket and thumbing the top off.

Adler turned with her, trying to keep her in sight of the eye he wasn't messing with.

But she was faster. She squeezed the explosives out of the tube in a four-inch-long cylinder and tucked it into his left jeans hip pocket, leaving an inch sticking out.

She continued to run in a circle while tugging the long flexible wire from her other pocket. More than likely he had no idea what she'd done. By the time she completed her circle, he had composed himself and again pointed the gun directly at her.

He glanced down at the three feet of wire trailing from her fist. "Planning to whip me to death with that puny thing?"

Then, his visible eye widened.

"If you shock me, I'll shoot you."

He was right. If she tried to shock him with just this, his muscles would seize up, and he'd involuntarily pull the trigger. She waved the wire around, letting it weave and curl at her command. "You're right, this could never hurt a strong man like you."

His mouth twisted at her sarcasm. He backed up a step.

Oh, no you don't. You're not getting away from me this time. She took a step closer.

This unnerved him even more. He glanced around squinty-eyed, looking for ambushers. But they were alone.

"Don't you want to know where Penna and the girl are?" she baited.

"I'm supposed to believe you would tell me?"

Another step forward. "Why not? I'm all about reuniting mothers and sons."

"Liar." This time, he held his ground. "But no worries. I'm not nearly as interested as Lumas in finding them. I don't want more apex predators. Kind of dilutes my unique skill set. Besides, if I want to know where they are, I'll torture it out of your friend back there. Assuming he isn't dinosaur kibble already."

The distance between them was just a few feet. Perfect.

"I suppose, your sister might miss the chance to know you, but I'll be there to comfort her."

"Such a great guy," she sneered. From within, she tapped into her reservoir of anger, starting with the first time she'd met Adler—when he'd pushed an innocent boy into the water with an alligator. As the emotions roiled inside, she quickly funneled them through her right hand and to the wire. "You know, there's one key difference between my sister and me."

"What's that?"

"She's got bad taste in men." Oakley swung the electrified wire in a wide arc, gratified by the fear darkening his features.

As if tossing out a Hail Mary, he shouted, "Eric is here!"

Time stopped, and her pulse stopped with it. What did he know about her brother?

She flicked her wrist back to recall the wire.

The wall of foliage beside them split down the center. With a horrendous roar, Demon Dragon shoved its massive head into their little clearing. Its teeth were bared and dripping.

The poison hadn't killed it!

It barreled into her side, shoving her and the wire into the same arc she'd just tried to avoid.

The wire sailed toward Adler's hip pocket.

"No!" She opened her hand to let go but too late. The electrified tip landed on the very top of the small, pasty cylinder.

A ground-shuddering explosion engulfed Adler and threw her and Demon Dragon in opposite directions.

Her ears rang with the blast. A piercing pain throbbed in her head. She opened her eyes to the gaping maw of Demon Dragon lying flat on the ground next to her. Its razor-sharp teeth were as long as her head.

Beyond the dinosaur, Adler's body lay on his side. He'd been thrown back twenty feet. His features were blackened and barely recognizable. A sooty hole caved in half of his chest. His left hip area was gone, leaving a stump of bone sticking out from his leg. There would be no helping him.

No asking what he meant about Eric.

Movement near her head sent her heart racing again. Demon Dragon shifted and focused its black pupils on her.

She rolled over and moaned, her entire body aching.

The creature shifted its weight backward onto its haunches, preparing to stand.

She scrambled away. It lunged for her but could only reach so far while still on the ground. She had to get away before it could chase her. She clambered to her feet and ran.

CHAPTER THIRTY-TWO

THUMP. Slide. The gigantic beast crashed through the jungle after Oakley, hindered only by its necrotic leg. *Thump. Slide.*

With fear pheromones pumping from her pores, she had to be leaving a lingering scent trail along the way. Where could she go, then?

Her underlying sense of direction kicked in. At least she was leading the creature away from Cane and Kaleo. But how would she kill it?

A trap? The same way she'd killed Camocroc. While still rushing headlong through the branches and over fallen logs, she brought up her mental image of Misty's map. She'd tried to memorize the locations of the traps as Kaleo had, but she hadn't gotten as far as memorizing what type of trap was located where.

She burst through the foliage and slid to a halt just before plunging over a fifteen-foot-deep ravine. Now she could pinpoint exactly where she was. A trap lay north of here near the confluence of the river that created the ravine.

"Over here!" she yelled, on the off chance that Demon Dragon would come charging out and plunge over the edge.

The creature emerged on a run from the trees but saw the drop-off at the last second. It dug its one good leg into the thick dirt.

Too bad. It had been worth a try. She spun around toward the mouth of the ravine, ready to run again, but her path was blocked.

Red Grizzly stalked toward her.

Her heart hammered hard against her chest.

On her other side, Demon Dragon gave a mighty roar.

Her gaze darted between them. No way would she be a plaything, torn apart by two dinosaurs.

Instinct drove her flat to the ground.

Demon Dragon let out a stream of fire intended to cook both her and Red Grizzly. The flames sailed just over her body and caused Red Grizzly to leap out of the way.

She rolled as Demon Dragon's jaws came down for her. Its nose hit the dirt, and the ground shook.

She jumped back to her feet. Red Grizzly was running in the opposite direction from where she needed to go. A small wave of relief flowed through her. One down, one to go.

Setting her course for the head of the ravine, she

dashed through the foliage. The ominous *thump, slide* continued behind her. Demon Dragon wasn't giving up, and even injured it was faster than her.

Finally, she spied the tree indicating the trap. Three arrows pointing up. Something sharp at least. Possibly the one listed as "barbed wire" on the key? She hadn't gotten a chance to ask what that meant.

She sprinted past the tree while searching the area. Ahead, a barbed wire had been strung between two thick kapok trees. Now how to avoid it while getting Demon Dragon to run into it?

There. At the bottom. An eighteen-inch gap.

She slid feet first under the metal curtain like coming in for a home run. At three inches long, the barbs were impressively wicked.

Demon Dragon was focused on her, seemingly oblivious to the danger ahead. Perhaps the wire was too thin for it to see.

It smacked into the barbed wire and stuck like a gnat on flypaper.

It bellowed while it thrashed, something between a roar and a groan. The wire appeared to be all one piece, looped around the tree trunks, and held in place by ropes anchored nearby. Even so, this wouldn't hold Demon Dragon for long.

It arched its back, stretching the wire to the limit, then pressed forward, straining the anchoring ropes. Its fire defense came out at random intervals. The wire would melt soon under the heat.

She searched around. No weapons. No means to get far enough away before it freed itself. She had only one option, if she could summon the strength.

Circling around to the opposite side, the one farthest from its lethal mouth, she squatted on the ground. Between the barbs, the wire fit her hand perfectly. She grabbed it and dug deep inside. It would take everything she had to kill a dinosaur this big.

She dove into the pain of her mother trying to kill her. The bathtub water closed over her head. She gasped for air as her mother held her under. The pain of betrayal pierced her soul again. No mother should try to kill their child.

Demon Dragon's muscles froze.

She moved on to her wrongful conviction, bringing up the dead sightless eyes of her best friend. Monica had done nothing to deserve death.

Demon Dragon twitched, causing the curtain to sway. The smell of sizzling skin met her nostrils.

She revisited Daric trying to strangle her. Her neck twitched as she remembered his fingers tightening and choking off her air supply. His eyes had lit with pleasure from her struggles.

Fire leaked from Demon Dragon's mouth in a slow trickle.

Finally, she channeled all her fears about Adler's last words. *Eric.* Had Adler taken her brother? Was Eric somewhere scared and hoping for rescue? Had Adler hurt him?

The unending pain and anger flowed from her soul, through her chest, and out her fingertips.

She tightened her grip on the wire as the vibrations of the metal curtain turned violent. The last minute was the worst. Maybe it was the brain fighting and refusing to give up.

She held on. She needed one more surge of electricity. She delved into her fears about what might have happened to Kaleo and Cane. Whatever their fate, it was her fault. She'd insisted on pursuing Adler, and she'd summoned the dinosaurs to their location with her push of pheromones. Guilt and pain rolled through her in pulsing waves.

Demon Dragon's head flopped back.

Her breath caught in her throat. Had it worked?

The creature let out a long, strangled breath before it stopped moving.

She released her sore and stiff fingers, then slumped against a nearby tree, exhausted. The beast was dead.

CHAPTER THIRTY-THREE

GABE HAD TRIED to leave camp earlier in the morning but was delayed by an impromptu field report to Agent Noah Brooks. When the boss called, it was wise to answer.

As soon as he'd hung up the phone, a hungry dinosaur —Raptor called it a *Therizinosaur*—had breached their perimeter. The electrified wires hadn't provided as much protection as expected. The animal was an herbivore and not dangerous, but damage had been done, mostly to his agents' psyches. Once they'd chased it off, they needed to rebuild the fence, and Gabe had to reassure his skittish agents that they were safe.

Now that he had finally begun the hunt for Oakley, Raptor had decided to tag along. That was a problem. Not only was Raptor likely to keep him from exacting justice on Oakley, but as they walked, he kept talking. The normally stoic man couldn't seem to keep his mouth shut.

Every creature for a hundred yards would hear them approach.

Gabe glanced down at his phone. Oakley's location flashed two hundred yards to the west.

Time to fix the problem. He halted and put a hand up for Raptor to do the same. Keeping his back to him, Gabe slid his backpack to the front and opened it. He had to surprise the bigger man, otherwise one of them could get hurt.

In a quick motion, derived from hundreds of arrests, Gabe whipped around with an open handcuff and snapped it on Raptor's closest wrist.

His eyes grew wide. "What are you doing?"

"Keeping you out of jail." Gabe tugged him toward a large tree trunk.

Raptor shook his head and pulled back.

"You've interfered in this investigation long enough." Gabe held tight to the handcuff. "If you don't let me do this, I'll have to tell Agent Brooks that you've obstructed justice and recommend you be charged with treason for aiding and abetting prisoners."

"You can't prove any of that."

"I don't need to. All I have to do is tell Agent Brooks about how you couldn't find your ex-employee and how you brought your girlfriend's friend down here to tag her. He can do his own surmising."

Raptor's arms went slack.

Gabe pulled him over to the tree and handcuffed him

around it. "I'll come back to release you as soon as I've captured her."

As he left Raptor, he took quiet pleasure in the anger written across the man's face. It reflected the same level of frustration Gabe had experienced since he'd arrived. It was good to finally give some of it back.

He dropped his gaze to his phone. The dot representing Oakley had moved on, leaving him a total of three hundred yards behind. He ran to catch up, leaping over fallen trees, pushing through branches, and wading creeks like a man twenty years younger. The thrill of the hunt—the exact reason he'd become an FBI agent in the first place—brought out the best in him. It was why both he and Jack hadn't completely given up field work even after twenty years with the Bureau.

When her location registered at a hundred yards away, he slowed his pace, taking more time for stealth. No other trackers showed up on his screen. She was out here alone.

Her path moved in a southwesterly direction through an area of the jungle he hadn't yet explored. Where could she be heading?

He crept along, making a steady gain on her. She hadn't lived in the jungle for long, a mere few weeks, so she probably hadn't developed an instinct for jungle noises. He could afford to move faster.

The distance shrank to fifty yards between them. He still couldn't see her because the forest grew denser the farther south they went.

Within ten yards, he caught sight of a lithe form moving swiftly through the foliage.

His pulse quickened. *Finally.*

His next step was careless. A stick broke with a sharp crack. Had she heard him?

The woman looked around, her dark hair swishing, but the leaves were too thick to see her face from this distance. At least that meant she couldn't fully see him either.

Suddenly, she broke into a run.

"Stop, FBI!" he yelled while unhooking his pistol from its holster.

The woman turned to look at him as she darted around trees. Her face was blocked first by a tree trunk, then a large branch. He couldn't get a good look at her. When she passed the tree and came into a more open spot, she'd already returned to facing front.

He sprinted to keep up with her. "Stop, or I'll shoot!"

Her steps faltered, but she didn't look back again. Dark hair streamed behind her, whipping in different directions as she dodged trees. Somehow, the woman knew this area better than he did. She wasn't stopping because she thought she could escape him. And she might be right.

He clenched his jaw. He couldn't let her get away.

She was almost to the other end of the small clearing. If she reached the trees, she'd disappear and he'd lose her.

He planted his feet and took aim, gauging the rhythm of her strides. A tiny pinch squeezed his gut. He hadn't seen her face, but the tracker matched. It had to be her.

At the edge of the trees, she'd probably dodge to the right. Most people did because most people were right-handed. He aimed a little to the right and pulled the trigger.

The shot hit her in the shoulder, bringing her down in a forceful forward dive.

A smile spread across his face. Now he'd get some answers and at last find out what happened to Jack.

He crossed the clearing cautiously, searching for a weapon or signs of aggression. The woman lay on her stomach, her arms folded under her body, her dark hair covering her face.

She groaned, but otherwise didn't move.

At her side, he knelt. He kept his gun out, pointed at the ground, just in case. With one hand, he brushed the hair from her face.

"No." He stood and staggered back. "How?"

He scanned her features. The too-high cheekbones. The slope of the arching eyebrows. The darker skin tone. None of it matched the mugshot. This wasn't Oakley Laveau.

CHAPTER THIRTY-FOUR

JUST AS TAYE fractured the chain joining the handcuffs with his spear, a shot rang out. Raptor took off in the direction of the sound with Taye following behind. It was the same direction in which Glaser had disappeared. That couldn't be a coincidence, and it couldn't be good.

They ran for fifteen minutes before the jungle broke into a clearing. Raptor's fear was confirmed. On the far side, near the tree line, the body of a woman lay as still as death.

But it wasn't Oakley. It was Neve.

Taye took two slow steps into the clearing before apparently realizing it was her. "No!" He ran to her side and dropped to his knees. "She said she wanted to check on her friends, but she was supposed to wait for me. I went hunting for our lunch."

Raptor crouched on her other side and put his fingers to her neck. "She's alive, but barely."

Taye smoothed the hair from her face, then pressed his cheek to hers.

A porous medical cloth had been pressed to the wound, probably government issued. Raptor carefully peered underneath. The shot had gone into Neve's shoulder from the back, perilously close to her heart. She needed immediate medical attention.

"Don't leave me, *corazon*," Taye whispered in her ear.

Raptor tapped him on the arm to break him out of his grief. "We have to get her to Wells."

Taye slipped his arms under her and picked her up, gently cradling her against his chest. She moaned. Her eyelids fluttered, but she never fully regained consciousness.

Raptor went before them, brushing branches out of the way and cutting through vine curtains. He stopped intermittently to check the direction with Taye, then returned to making a clear path.

"Who did this?" Taye asked, his voice mournful.

Raptor didn't answer. The question was rhetorical since he had to know it was the same man who hand-cuffed Raptor.

"Why?" Taye pressed, but it was impossible to know whether he was asking again why Neve had left without him or asking why she was shot.

Raptor answered as if he meant the latter. "Glaser must have thought she was Oakley."

A plaintive groan came from Taye. His voice was

pinched with sorrow. "She must have had Wells implant Oakley's tracker in her."

That explained why the tracker suddenly became active, but not why Glaser would shoot Oakley in the back. The man hadn't seemed like a loose cannon. Glaser did all things with calculation and precision.

What would happen now? Surely, he'd discovered that he shot the wrong person. So, why had he left her to die? And what action would he take after discovering that Neve ended up with the tracker?

OAKLEY BROKE through the foliage to find Kaleo's immobile body. She sucked in a horrified breath and held it. Blood spattered the ground, his clothes, the nearby leaves, even most of his whip. His eyes were closed, and his body lay still.

Had Red Grizzly killed him?

She took a step closer and kneeled, ignoring the blood staining her boots and jeans. She reached out to feel his chest. Tiny movement up and down. He was alive! Thank God! She let her captive breath out in a whoosh.

A nearby squeak had her jumping to her feet. Cody hopped into view. "Hey, buddy."

She patted him on the head as she kneeled down again. "Kaleo," she whispered.

He groaned. His head shifted restlessly, but he didn't wake. Cody nuzzled his cheek. Still, he didn't wake.

She checked him over. No injuries on the front of his body.

Using both hands and with a huge effort, she rolled his body a quarter turn. Blood seeped from the back of his thigh, probably his other one too, if the pool of blood underneath him was any indication.

When she let him go, he flopped back down. She needed to get a better look at those wounds. She grabbed beneath his knee and raised the dead weight of one of his legs. Gently, she probed the skin around a large slash mark.

His eyes flew open. He sucked in a pained breath. "Ouch."

"That's a bit of an understatement. It looks like RG shredded your leg back here. You need someone to sew you up."

He let out a long sigh. "Neve is with Taye. I don't know where they are."

"What about Wells? Cane said he took the people from the cave to the alternate backup location last night. Would that include her?"

The mention of Cane brought another spike of fear to her heart. Had Adler killed him before he'd come to get her? She didn't have time to find out. She couldn't run back through the jungle to look for him, she needed to get Kaleo help. He would die if the bleeding didn't stop.

"Probably. The alternate location is part of an abandoned school to the west."

"Is it far?"

"Far enough."

She pushed down the unexpected flush of guilt. The reason they couldn't use the first choice of safe house—the tree house—was because of her. But she hadn't caused this chain of chaos. Adler and Lumas had. "Let's hope they stayed with the backup plan."

Kaleo gingerly sat up. The blood pooled faster under his now bent legs. She ripped several strips off the bottom of his shirt to staunch the flow, then thought better of it. She tied them around his upper thighs to use as tourniquets.

Between him leaning against a tree and her supporting his other arm, he got to his feet.

He waved a hand at the ground. "Don't forget."

"Of course." She left him against the tree while she coiled the whip and stuffed it in her waistband.

They hobbled along, managing only a few feet every couple of minutes because of the size difference between them. Cody bobbed behind them.

Several minutes later, she heard a shuffling in the jungle.

They both froze. Now would be the worst time for a dinosaur attack, though it was certainly possible with the smell of blood drifting all around them.

"Oakley?" The loud whisper was Cane.

For the second time in an hour, she thanked God for saving someone she cared about. "Over here," she whispered back.

He came through the foliage.

Her eyes widened at the goose-egg bump near his temple. "Are you okay?"

He waved her away and put his shoulder under Kaleo's other arm. "Fine. Just a headache. I had to use a little poison on a few curious predators when I awoke, but I'm all good."

"As usual, you have perfect timing."

He leaned forward and gave her a half-hearted wink. "Don't you mean God's timing?"

She almost laughed at the irony of Cane with his bruised head holding up his friend with the torn-up legs while praising God's timing. His faith was deeper than she could comprehend. She pushed down the urge to simultaneously kick him and hug him for it.

They trekked through the jungle with Kaleo barely walking on his toes but made much better progress together.

"I had no idea you weighed so much," she said.

Kaleo grunted out his reply. "Pure muscle, baby."

"Yeah, shredded muscle," Cane mumbled.

It seemed like an insensitive comment, unusual for Cane, but Kaleo laughed as if it had been a joke on a late-night talk show monologue. At least they had all made it through alive. But her gratitude began to wane every time Adler's last words ran through her mind.

Where was Eric? Her brother should be safe on the mainland with her dad and stepmother. But was he here? Had Adler done something to him?

By the time they reached the school where the rest of

the cave people were hiding, all three of them were soaked in sweat, despite the cool temperature of the cloud forest.

Cane knocked at an old janitor's residence. The door cracked open and an eye peeked out. Then, Wells hurried them and Cody inside. She quickly assessed the situation and gestured to one of several cots near the far wall. "Bring him over here."

They laid him down on his front where he let out a pained sigh. Wells glanced at him before turning her attention to Cane. She lifted her hand to touch his lump but stopped short. "What happened to both of you?"

"I'm fine," Cane said. "Help him."

Oakley stepped up. "A big raptor sliced his legs."

Wells nodded. "Take off the tourniquets and remove his pants while I get some water."

Oakley untied the cloths. Cane grabbed a knife and cut the material off by the seams. A full view of the damage had her holding in a gasp. The claws had ripped through large sections of his muscle, in one area almost to the bone. Blood began to seep again from the deepest wound.

Wells came over, holding a bowl of water, some thread, and a clean cloth. "Hey, I'm not going to lie. It's bad." She placed the water on the floor and glanced back at Oakley. "But I'm good at what I do. He'll be fine."

Turning to Kaleo, she said, "The downside is I don't have any pain meds for you."

She went to work stitching and bandaging. Kaleo groaned and bit into the small pillow under his head.

Unable to listen to his pain, Oakley took a seat on a cot near Cane, absently scratching the smattering of feathers on Cody's head. Cane lay with his arm covering his eyes.

"Thank you," she said.

He lifted his arm for a second, then returned to his previous position. "For what? My hesitation almost killed us all." He gave a disgusted snort. "I've never been so angry. If my hands had been around his throat, I could have strangled him easily."

"And yet, you kept enough control to keep your poison from escaping."

He sighed. "I guess there is that. It would have only killed Kaleo, and I couldn't let that happen." His voice dropped an octave. "I just can't get over how much I hated Adler in that moment. I didn't try to kill him to keep everyone safe. I *wanted* to kill him. I wanted him to suffer, to hurt as much as he'd hurt my mother." He shifted his arm to stare at the ceiling. "Lord, forgive me."

She placed a comforting hand on his knee. "Hey, you might be a pastor, but you're still just a man."

His gaze darted to her, and he looked like he might argue. Finally, he gave a curt nod. "Amen."

Oakley rose to check on Wells's progress. She'd just finished Kaleo's most damaged leg and was applying a bandage.

The door flew open and banged against the wall. Apparently, no one had thought to bar it after they had entered. Oakley spun around.

Taye swept in, carrying Neve and followed by Raptor.

"She's been shot." Taye's voice held panic.

Exclamations of outrage and shock exploded from the cave people, all of whom knew and loved Neve. Wells took charge in the midst of it. "Where?"

"Entrance wound in the back," Raptor said. "No exit wound."

"Lay her face down over here," Wells directed.

Someone brought her a fresh bowl of water as Wells cut Neve's shirt up the back. The bullet wound stood out as an angry circle of blood and torn flesh. Oakley turned away when Wells began digging around in the hole with tweezers.

Oakley grabbed Raptor by the shirtsleeve and dragged him to the other side of the shack. "What happened?"

"Apparently Neve instructed Wells to implant your tracker in her."

His words drowned her in a sea of regret. When she had refused to have the tracker implanted in order to protect Penna, Neve had only said she'd take care of it. This was what she'd meant? "Why?"

"I imagine she never planned to leave the island and did it to protect both of us." The same sadness in his voice pulsed through her heart. "Taye went out hunting. Neve was supposed to wait for him, but she went out on her own to check on the people here. Agent Glaser tracked the signal, obviously thinking it was you."

Her knees went weak. Others continued to get hurt because of her. "And he shot her in the back?"

"He was gone by the time we got there, but it had to be him."

"Why would he do that?"

"Guess he's not too happy about what happened to his partner," Raptor said. "He blames you."

Of course. And why shouldn't he? The craziness of the last week all started with her desire for answers.

Soothing pheromones came from Cane's side of the room. Again, his words floated through her head. *You are not the sum of your choices.* But her choices continued to make matters worse for everyone. She'd left the island, only to have the FBI show up. She found Penna and Teagan, only to endanger them. She eliminated Adler and may have put her brother in jeopardy. The sum of her choices didn't add up to much good. But could Cane be right? Did her life matter in some way that went beyond the mistakes she'd made?

Raptor held her by the shoulders. "He will come after you again."

She blew out a breath and focused her thoughts. "I may have a bigger problem than the FBI agent. Just before Adler died, he said Eric is here. Do you think Adler could have kidnapped my brother?"

He stared at his feet while considering her question. "The long game wasn't Adler's strength. But he might have done it on Lumas's orders."

She nodded and stared at her own feet. It did sound like something Lumas would do. With Adler dead, Lumas might be the only one who would know if Eric was being held and where. She would have to track him down.

Then again, maybe not. Lumas now knew about Penna. Oakley had found the one thing he'd wanted for fifteen years. She wouldn't have to go anywhere. Lumas would come to her.

CHAPTER THIRTY-FIVE

A COOL BREEZE woke Eric Laveau. His muscles were stiff, and his head was foggy like that time he'd eaten a whole jar of salsa before bed and spent the night tossing and turning with gas pain. He squinted at the brightness of the white walls in the unfamiliar room. Had they moved him? Had he slept through his dad's visit?

He searched for memories of what had happened, but they were foggy. A dark-haired man had taken him from home using plastic ties to bind his hands and a handkerchief to keep him from screaming. It was the most scared he'd ever been.

Then, he'd woken on a bed at the lab where his dad worked. No plastic ties and no handkerchief. The same man promised Dad would come to visit the next day. He shouldn't have believed the man anyway because he was a bad man.

The last memory came into focus. His dad never

came. It was the dark-haired man who returned the next day and gave Eric a shot that put him to sleep.

Where was the man now? Would he come back with another shot?

Eric swung his feet off the small bed, letting them dangle a few inches above the tile floor. He'd always been short for his age, but that didn't bother him none. Smart and funny were more important than tall, especially in fifth grade.

He should go find Dad before the man returned.

He looked down. The cool breeze came from a vent underneath the bed. He scooted away before dropping his bare feet to the chilly tile. His shoes had gone missing, but he was still dressed in the sweatpants and T-shirt he'd worn to bed the night the dark-haired man had come. Was that two days ago? Three?

In the corner sat a table with a box on top. He ignored it and went straight for the door. He pushed down on the lever handle. It didn't move at all.

He shoved at it, trying to wiggle it. Nothing.

He pounded on the door. "Hello? Anyone out there?"

No answer.

He pounded harder. "Let me out!"

No sounds except the hum of the air coming from the vent.

He continued to pound on the door and scream until his throat and his fists ached. Exhausted, he slumped against the cold metal. A tingle of panic zipped down his spine. He might really be alone here.

Just him, a bed, and a box. Might as well see what was in it.

It was heavy, but he transferred it to the bed before looking inside. He pulled the stuff out and laid it in a row on the white bedding. Three bags of chips. A dozen granola bars. Six bottles of water. Some sort of flat, flexible meat covered in plastic.

Not exactly donuts and pizza, but he could eat this for a while. His stomach let out a low rumble of agreement as he ripped open a granola bar.

After his crunching stopped, silence took over again. With nothing else to do, he lay down on the bed and stared at the white ceiling. His foggy mind started to clear after the granola bar. He probably wasn't at the lab anymore because he couldn't hear the ocean.

Where was he? Did his dad know where to find him?

He let out a long shaky breath. He was trying to be brave, but it was hard. His dad had better come get him soon.

AUBURN VERRET SAT on the floor of the control room with her knees pressed to her chest and her arms wrapped around them. Tears leaked from her swollen eyes, down her red cheeks, and fell in pools on her bare kneecaps. Her mind refused to believe what was surely true.

It was almost ritual now: Watch the footage showing

the brief glimpse of Oakley's face. Check the tracker for vital signs. Break down and cry for twenty minutes. Repeat.

Oddly, every time she checked the tracker, she expected a different outcome. Adler had been so alive, so in control of his life, and even her life. How could he be gone in the blink of an eye?

Dad had watched the replay with her once, then he'd stormed out without a word. It was better, actually, to be left alone in her grief. Another wave of disbelief washed through her. She rode the wave, pouring out her pain in salty tears until she was a dried husk.

She glanced at the blank screen. He had been facing off with Oakley. He'd closed his eyes, and they'd never opened again. If only she had audio to help her figure out what happened, but the eye implants didn't have microphones.

Her own eyes ached. For the moment, though, they were clear. Time to watch again. Maybe this time she'd believe it.

When the scene was over and the screen went black, the tears formed again, staying just under her eyelids. As if the raw pain inside, instead of springing forth, was now coalescing into a hard, tight ball. A knot of hot, dense matter that would suck her in and crush her with the gravity of grief until she was a black hole of heartache. And she would allow it.

Her fingertips brushed the mouse, bringing her screen to life again. Rather than rewatch the recording, she pulled up the computer code for her secret program. To keep it secret, especially from her father, the program had no user interface, it contained solely operational code. Her cursor hovered over the list of identifying numbers— her sister's number.

Her stomach cramped, and her palms began to sweat. All she had to do was type in the number along with the kill switch code, and justice would be done.

But that would mean disobeying her father. He still wanted Oakley alive. He might not know of her program, but he would suspect her if Oakley suddenly dropped dead.

Plus, it would be too easy a death. Not real justice.

Auburn closed the program. Her jaw clenched so tight that it ached.

Soon, Lumas would leave for Extinction Island because he'd found his prize. She would go with him for her own reasons. It was time to teach her sister a thing or two about pain.

MORE BLOODY RED GRIZZLY, manipulative Lumas, courageous Kaleo, electrifying Oakley, and enigmatic Auburn to come in book 3 ...

Dear Reader,

I hope you enjoyed this tooth-and-claw-filled adventure with Oakley. Every time I sit down to write, I feel like a little kid playing with her dinosaur toys. Writing these books is the closest I'll ever get to petting a dinosaur (Oakley's pet Coelophysis, Cody is modeled after my dog named—you guessed it—Cody!).

If you enjoyed *Deception Island*, I would appreciate it if you would consider leaving a review on Amazon or Goodreads. Your opinion matters! Even just a few sentences can help more people to enjoy the same adventure and it is the kindest thing you can do for an author.

To explore more of the Jurassic Judgment world, including dossiers on characters, a special author interview, exclusive bookmark/postcard files, and how all the special abilities are based on real animals, visit the **secret** Jurassic Judgment Junkie page (link: https://

janiceboekhoff.com/jurassic-judgment-junkie). Note: you cannot access this page from the menu on my website, only from the back of this book or by typing the above link into your browser.

If you're interested in learning about my new releases and book recommendations, sign up for the quarterly newsletter on my website (https://janiceboekhoff.com). I'd love to connect with you.

Blessings,
Janice

FUN FACTS ABOUT EXTINCTION ISLAND

- Oakley's name is a nod to our time living near Baton Rouge, Louisiana. We lived in Oak Alley Estates subdivision for two years.
- On a family trip to Maui, we went to a luau where one of the performers (a fire dancer) was named Kaleo. I knew immediately it was the perfect name for the gang leader.
- Cane got his name from the sugar cane harvesters that my husband worked to build while we lived in Louisiana.
- Auburn (Oakley's twin) was originally named Autumn. I was watching the NCAA basketball tournament with my husband (2019) and I needed Auburn to win over Kentucky for my bracket. I made a deal with God (wink, wink) that I would name Oakley's sister Auburn if he would let them win. So I

had to hold up my end of the deal. P.S. I topped the bracket for our family that year!

- I gave Oakley the job of Reptile Expert because of a swamp tour we took when living in Louisiana where I was able to hold a baby alligator!
- Cody, the *Coelophysis*, was named after Cody, our Vizsla (that's a dog in case you weren't sure). Both of them are great pets and stick to their people like glue.

For more plus pictures, visit the secret Jurassic Judgment Junkie page.

ACKNOWLEDGMENTS

My writing journey has been an amazing ride—one that would have crashed and burned without all of these wonderful people. Thank you for being you and for all you do!

Todd, Zach, Jenna, and Riley—your support means more than I can ever say. Not to mention your willingness to answer every time I ask, "What's the most gruesome way to kill a dinosaur?" I love the brainstorming help and how proud you are of the work I do. And I'm so proud of all of you!

Crystal Joy and Amelia Judd—every writer should have such talented critique partners. I couldn't have done this without your brainstorming help and the help with the emotional arcs.

Carol Brandon, Donna Feld, Lisa Lee, Mary Johnson —your comments have enriched this novel and are a blessing to me. Thank you for spending your precious time reading the first draft.

Kim Mesman (Mesman Designs)—as always, I love this cover! Thanks for being so flexible and easy to work with.

Linda Yezak—you are a gifted editor and have a way of bringing out the best in a manuscript. I'm grateful for your insights and corrections (all further mistakes are mine).

Amazing readers—you are my reason for writing. Thank you for each adventure that we take together. I am blessed to have you here and hope to see you again at the end of Book 3.

Happy Reading!
Janice

ABOUT THE AUTHOR

Blessed with an insatiable curiosity and a low tolerance for boredom, award-winning author Janice Boekhoff (pronounced Beau-cough) has worked more than twenty jobs ranging from Loan Consultant (important, but mortgage paperwork makes her sleepy) to Landfill Environmentalist (literally her smelliest job) to Research Geologist (the job that gave her the best suntan and the most adventures). She began writing as a way to express all the unique ideas colliding in her head. A Midwest native, she writes from Eastern Iowa where she lives with her hubby, three basketball-loving kids, and one adorable Vizsla.

www.ingramcontent.com/pod-product-compliance
Lightning Source LLC
Chambersburg PA
CBHW070822190726
48292CB00006B/2081